I'm a big fan of religious-themed  ılay's approach. With plenty of haunted hc , and a flawed but likable crew of demon ı fine debut and a quick read to get the ch

~ The Horror Fiction Review

I adored this horror novel, in every sense. Author Tony Tremblay knows how to terrorize his characters and his readers. I read this over two evenings/nights, which was really brave of me, since THE MOORE HOUSE is super scary. I won't be forgetting this novel for quite a long time. I especially won't forget the explosively terrifying opening scenes involving a homeless, feckless, drifter--and THE MOORE HOUSE.

~ The Haunted Reading Room

THE MOORE HOUSE is an unrelenting tale of possession, distantly echoing themes of The Amityville Horror, The Exorcist, and Poltergeist. From the opening page the reader is pulled into the fictional hell of Tony's mind, and it doesn't stop until the final pages. There is no fat on this book - it is lean and muscled, at times brutally graphic. Typically it takes me roughly a week to finish a novel these days, but this treasure was devoured within two days. Not because it's an easy read, but rather the almost seamless and unpretentious style in which Tony writes.

~ Michael Upstills Reviews

Tony's writing will fill any horror reader's appetite ~ rest assured.

~ Buttonholed Book Reviews

THE MOORE HOUSE

TONY TREMBLAY

An imprint of Haverhill House Publishing

The Moore House © 2018 by Tony Tremblay

Cover design © 2018 Dyer Wilk

978-1-949140-99-6 (Hardcover)
978-1-949140-98-9 (Trade Paperback)

For more information, address:

First Edition

Twisted Publishing
An imprint of
Haverhill House Publishing LLC
643 E Broadway
Haverhill MA 01830-2420

Visit us on the web at **www.HaverhillHouse.com**

Dedicated to John McIlveen

Acknowledgments

I would like to acknowledge those who have inspired or help shape this novel into its published form. This includes my family, especially my Christian wife who has not read this novel and has no desire to. Though she believes I stand a good chance of divine punishment because of my writing, she still loves me. I love her, too.

A heartfelt thanks to my classmates of the 2016 edition of The River City Writers – Write Better Fiction seminar, my fellow writers in The Blank Page writers group who meet at the Goffstown, N.H. public library, and to my Necon family.

I owe a huge smile and a sigh of gratitude to Sandi Bixler, Robert Perreault, Holly Zaldivar, Stacey Longo, Rob Smales, Linda Nagle, Bracken MacLeod, Catherine Grant, Dyer Wilk, and Kevin Lewis.

In some cases, a thank you seems inadequate. I want to express much more gratitude to the following three people but I'm not sure I have the words to convey how much their support meant to me during and after the writing process. The Moore House exists because of these men: Christopher Golden, the great James A. Moore, and John McIlveen. All of them good men, and even better brothers.

RUINING TONY TREMBLAY

An Introduction by
Bracken MacLeod

I'm here to ruin Tony Tremblay for you. I'm going to talk about *him* as much as I discuss his work here because I want you to see this guy for who he really is.

You see, the writing community is small. It may seem large on the outside, but trust me, once you start publishing and going to professional conventions, the world shrinks. You see the same people, you meet friends who are also friends of people you had no idea were connected, and you hear stories. Oh, the stories you sometimes hear. This world gets smaller when you're a genre writer. And even smaller still, depending on the genre itself. The community of professional horror writers is a pretty tight group. We can all fit in a phone booth. Okay, maybe it's not *that* small. Still, my point is, word travels, and reputations are easy to make and hard to shake once they've gotten ahold of you. And boy does Tony Tremblay have a reputation.

See, he's widely known in horror circles. We've all had frequent encounters with Tony, and we all have a very strong opinion of him as a result. In fact, he's even earned a nickname; and try as he might, he can't slip it. See, no matter what Tony says now or how hard he fights to saddle someone else with this sobriquet (and I've *seen* him try to pawn it off on another writer), it's his. Earned and paid for. We all know really well who he is.

Tony Tremblay is...

The Nicest Guy in Horror

You wouldn't know it to read his work though. If you've read him without ever having met him, you wouldn't be blamed for pondering what core of darkness sits at the heart of the kind of a man who could write what he does. Don't misunderstand me. He's not a one-trick pony. Read his story collection, *The Seeds of Nightmares*, and you'll know what I'm talking about. His short work has breadth, slipping easily from quirky, oddly humorous folk horror, like his story "Chiyoung and Dongsun's Song," to sentimental magical realism like in (one of my favorites), "Stardust." But both those stories are still dark at their core. What Tony does really well is explore darkness. Read "Something New" or "The Visitors" in *Seeds...* and tell me he doesn't know how to sell a shadow. Better yet, read his story "The Reverend's Wife" in the anthology, *Into Painfreak*, and tell me this guy doesn't have a mean streak that'd make you think twice about ever wanting to meet him, even in a brightly lit place. But like I said, I'm here to *ruin* Tony Tremblay for you. The guy is damn nice. That's the nature he's known for, and he has to live in it.

Like Oscar Wilde says, "One can... live down everything except a good reputation."

Now, unkind people *can* be nice—those qualities, kindness and niceness, *are* different, by the way. A real monster can even fake being kind for a bit, but after a while, they always slip and you see through the act. I've known Tony for almost eight years, and I'll tell you, he doesn't slip. He's as kind and caring a person as you'll ever meet. That's his *character*, reputations be damned.

And then, knowing I'm a firm atheist, he Tuckerized me in *The Moore House* as a hard-drinking, hard-screwing, sinner of a bitter priest.

Think that's the mean streak I was talking about coming out? The crack in the reputation revealing his true character beneath? Nope.

The fact that he thought to name that character after me makes me laugh hard, and he knew it would. Because it wasn't done out of malice or mocking, but with affection. Even when he tries to go low, he ends up on high ground.

So, whatever you think about him after reading stories like "The Pawnshop" or "The Reverend's Wife" (and I strongly recommend you read *both* of those either before or after this book—since they're all connected), know that you're probably wrong about Tony if you haven't been fortunate enough to meet him. The man who could think of those things, and the rest of what is about to follow in *The Moore House*—let me assure you, it's not cute little Bambis and Thumpers frolicking in a sunny dell—is indeed The Nicest Guy in Horror. Though, truth be told, there *is* a core of darkness in there. And he goes to that core to write stories like the one you're holding in your hands. So turn up the lights.

The Nicest Guy in Horror is about to do some pretty terrible things.

God bless.

Bracken MacLeod
Massachusetts
15 May 2018

THE MOORE HOUSE

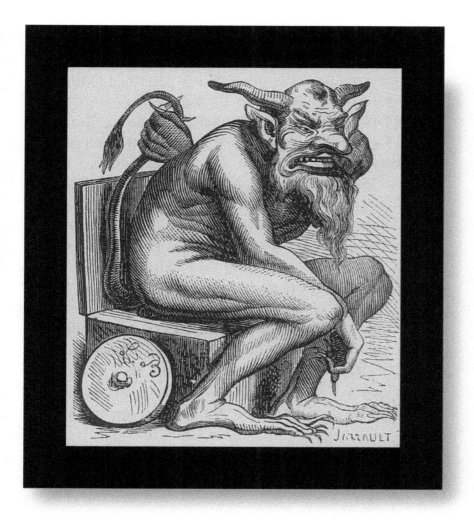

PROLOGUE

It was said the Moore house had a black soul; many Goffstown residents would agree. Then again, there were those who considered it irrational that a man-made structure could possess or influence moral character. But if you were to ask the joggers, dog walkers, and kids on bicycles who had come within its vicinity, they would not deny that the Moore house intrigued them.

While it may have stimulated a specific *appetite* in a victim, its initial assault on each of its targets was similar—the Moore house excelled at *enticement*.

It tempted the uncertain who yearned for conformity. It called to the disaffected with assurances of acceptance. It welcomed the indigent with promises of sanctuary—the structure exuded a dominance the weak could not ignore. The strong may have felt a stab of guilt, a tug of regret, or an urge toward hostility when they crossed paths with the house. But those feelings were temporary—forgotten almost as quickly as they had appeared, once the building was out of sight.

The Moore house's soul had an appetite that it usually held at bay, but when the hunger rose, it became voracious. That afternoon it would feed again.

Behind the house, a man squatted in a drainage ditch, stagnant water seeping into his boots. He rubbed his eyes with liver-spotted hands that hadn't held a bar of soap in months. He inhaled deeply, the fluid in his lungs gurgling, choking off some of the incoming air. After regulating his breathing, he dropped his hands to his chin, ragged fingers combing through his steel wool beard, the nails catching on gray bristles. Yanking them free, lice in their dozens tumbled from their feeding grounds. He raked his mop of grease-hardened hair, not flinching at the legion of small insects that scampered across his scalp.

The rains had moved on two days earlier, yet standing water surrounded him. He wondered why everything around the house was so damp when temperatures had been warm enough to evaporate a child's swimming pool.

The ditch traversed the property line behind the house. He peered through a neat row of red maples, so different from the thick, wild woods behind him, all pine and oak and dark silence. The maples were mature, the lowest of their branches hanging four feet off the ground, high enough for an unobstructed view of the structure.

He scanned left and right in rapid motion. He'd been around long enough to know that patience was not only a virtue, but it could stave off a good ass-beating. He'd learned the hard way. Life on the streets was what it was, but he was damned if he'd be a victim of his own recklessness again.

He had first noticed the house three days earlier.

His scavenging didn't usually bring him that far out of town, but harassment from the police and business owners had forced him to look for food and shelter farther afield. Intrigued, he'd stopped to inspect the house, despite the pouring rain.

Now, he found himself revisiting it. He wanted more.

Unremarkable though it was, the house seemed to call to his sense of adventure. It was a brown three-storied Victorian with no garage, and needed a fresh coat of paint, but was otherwise in good shape. The curtains, dull red and sun-bleached in spots, were closed but for a small gap, just like the first time he had been there. He peeked through the gap, searching for the flicker of a television screen – or indeed any source of light. He saw nothing.

He turned his attention to the lawn, which was overgrown and speckled with weeds. There was an absence of dog shit or ugly urine-stains in the grass. He was relieved: he didn't like to mess with dogs.

As the man stepped out from the ditch, his boots made squishing sounds from the water that had seeped into them. He approached the rear entrance of the house, cautious, pausing along the way at a maple tree that caught his attention. He walked toward it and stopped. After a minute, he took hesitant steps to the rear entrance of the house.

He faced a padlocked, solid metal door. It looked impenetrable, which he considered a good omen. No one could be living in a house that was locked from the outside.

Moving on, he approached the nearest window. The bottom sill was chest-height, offering a limited view of the room within. He could see a bed—rather, two stacked mattresses, void of blankets and pillows. The bedroom seemed otherwise empty.

Searching the ground for a rock, he found one large enough to break the window.

"Try opening it first."

He dropped the rock. *Where the hell did that come from?*

He wasn't sure and wondered if it had come from inside his head—only the voice was so clear and so loud. He surveyed the backyard. Taking a deep, raspy breath, he struggled to control his nerves. He wasn't prone to hallucinations, even after he'd been fortunate enough to score some weed or a bottle, so he discounted the notion that his mind was playing tricks on him.

Maybe the house is trying to help me.

The thought was comforting. People had been screwing him over

3

since he was ten years old when his uncle had crawled into bed with him during a sleepover. If he couldn't trust his own kind, maybe it was time he put his faith elsewhere. Putting it into a house was messed up, but what did he have to lose? He stepped closer to the window, placed his hands on the bottom sash, and lifted. It opened without resistance.

He pushed the window up as far as it would go, and even with his many layers of clothing, there was plenty of room for him to shimmy through. He grabbed the bottom of the frame with both hands, jumped, and pulled himself up. He leaned forward through the opening, but his belt buckle caught on the sill. He'd found the thin belt in a dumpster months ago, the oversized buckle embossed with a lewd picture of a woman. He laughed at the notion that her tits were large enough to catch on the sill, then he backed out of the window a few inches. Teetering, he lowered himself onto his belly for balance as his lower half dangled outside. Taking a moment to catch his breath, holding the window frame tightly, he gazed around the room. There was a door, partially open, that led to a hallway. He tilted his head and listened. Except for his breathing, the house was silent.

He had found sanctuary.

Relaxing his arms, he leaned forward, extended his hands, and lowered them to the floor. As he touched down upon the worn floorboards, a tickle—not unlike a low-voltage current—ran through his palms. The sensation intensified, then transformed. Like a swarm of yellow jackets rising through the floorboards to attack, needles pressed into his palms. The pain traveled up his arms and he rocked his shoulders in a vain attempt to throw it off.

What the hell is this?

Despite the pain, he managed to raise himself up, using the wall for leverage. The needle jabs stopped as soon as his palms were off the boards, but his exertion had thrown him off-balance. He felt himself slipping towards the floor.

Screw this place! I'm out of here!

The window slammed down on his thighs with brutal force, breaking both femurs on impact.

His screams echoed off the bedroom walls. He fell forward, yet somehow found the presence of mind to keep his hands from touching the floor. His palms landed flat against the wall beneath him; his limp legs hung outside the window.

He fought through the pain, willing his lower limbs to move. He concentrated, willing them to spring to life and start crab-walking up the side of the house, but there was no response. Despite the agony below his hips, he struggled. His legs were useless, a dead, searing weight.

He shifted his bulk onto his left hand, trying to twist his body so he could get a view of the window. The best he could do was a quarter turn, and from that angle, all he could see was a portion of the frame out of the corner of his eye. Pinned down with no way to escape, he eased back into his previous position. A sound, like the sweep of a broom, froze him.

Is that sniffing? Oh, God, please don't let it be a—

A dog's muzzle poked through the open bedroom door.

Fear gathered his reserves and he marshaled them into action. The man's back stiffened as if iron; he lifted his upper body until he was parallel to the floor. Despite the pain, he rocked his ass back and forth in the hope it would dislodge the gravity of the window. Reaching back, he tried to grab onto the sash in an attempt to lever himself out of the opening. The distance was too great. His adrenaline-fueled strength petered out; he fell forward, and this time his palms rested on the floor. Moments passed as he stared at his hands. He waited for the stinging, but nothing happened. He was confused, but the feeling was short-lived. The sniffling was getting louder, closer. He raised his head.

Standing two feet in front of him was the biggest German shepherd he had ever seen. At least he *thought* it was a German shepherd. It had the colors of the breed, the pointed ears, and the snout, but that's where the resemblance ended. This dog was twice the size of any he'd run into on the street. Its eyes were missing, the sockets dark, without a glimmer of life, but what held his attention was the dog's mouth. It was open and filled with row upon row of teeth.

The agony in his legs made it difficult to focus on the dog. The pain, the fear, was too intense. His bladder let go. The beast leaned in, jaws open to their full extent. When it was within inches of the man, the dog stopped, extending its neck until their noses touched. The man's bowels let loose.

"You think you're in pain *now*?"

Oh shit, oh shit! It talked!

The dog nodded. "Oh yes, it talks, and oh, what conversations we will have after you die. You think you're tired now? You think you're hungry now? You have no idea how much more tired and hungry you are *going* to be. You have no idea how much pain awaits you."

The German shepherd lunged, ripping into the man's face, pulling skin and muscle from bone. Screaming, the man's hands flew to the beast's mouth. His fingers wrapped around the dog's lower jaw and he pulled. Rows of ragged teeth clamped down. Pulling his arms back, the homeless man fell to the floor. Without digits, his stumps slid on the pooling gore.

The odor of blood filled the man's nostrils, vanishing seconds after it appeared. The remnants of his nose, pushed along by the dog's tongue was the last thing he saw before everything went dark.

The gnashing of gristle between the beast's teeth and subsequent gulps filled the man's ears. Those sounds were the last he would hear.

The dog didn't stop tearing him apart until the window prevented it from doing so. Finished, the beast shook bits of flesh from its head and coat. It walked to the door but faded to nothing before reaching the hallway. The human carnage covering the room was sucked into holes that could not be seen. The floor was clean; the bed snow white once again, and the window was closed and clear enough to sparkle if the sun hit it. Outside the house, under the bedroom window, a pair of legs dripped blood onto the ground.

CHAPTER 1

Celeste sat at a dining room table in the Millman family home in Leominster, Massachusetts, silent, her hands folded in her lap. The 1960s-era ranch was about to play host to the investigation of a possible demonic presence.

This was Celeste's first assignment as an empath with Agnes and Nora, two older, more experienced women. Celeste studied the two women. She considered them attractive for their ages, if a little on the heavy side. With their similar builds, matronly hairstyles, and soft voices, the two could almost be sisters—If Nora weren't African-American or Agnes wasn't white. Aside from a simple greeting, Nora hadn't spoken much during their brief introduction before entering the home. Not that she wasn't talkative, just cautious; her snarky sense of humor hadn't always been well received. Agnes had been equally reluctant to share information but had instructed Celeste to concentrate on the father. Agnes would focus on the mother, and Nora the daughter. Their superior, Father MacLeod, had told Celeste to listen, learn, and take cues from her two partners. That's what she'd do.

The Millman family—the young daughter bookended by her mother and father, sat opposite Celeste and the two other women in her group. Although it was the Millmans' home, it was the family rather than their visitors who fidgeted in their seats. The parents couldn't have been much older than their late thirties, their daughter possibly crossing the mid-point of her teenage years.

The mother slouched in her chair, a posture Celeste initially took as a sign of despondency, but after a prolonged view, she caught what might have been indications of defiance. Though the woman's shoulders were sunken, she held her neck straight and her chin up. Her gaze was focused but unthreatening as she measured up her visitors one at a time. Whenever the woman shook her head, it was unclear whether she was silently critiquing them or chasing away errant thoughts.

Celeste switched her attention to the father and flinched. He stared at her with a neutral expression, his eyes hard and his glare unwavering. Something in his eyes made her uneasy: they were dilated, his irises dark except for two brilliant pinpoints—reflections from an overhead lamp. He might have assumed he was projecting stoicism, but his body betrayed him. The man squirmed in his chair as if trying—and failing—to get comfortable. His daughter leaned away from him.

The girl was in constant motion, as she had been since they'd sat down. Her upper body bobbed to a peculiar rhythm; if she was following a tempo, it was more chant-like than hip-hop. Her head was bent too low to see her face, so Celeste imagined the young girl's eyes were wide open, directed at a random spot in her lap.

Celeste next observed her partners. Agnes, the oldest and the one in charge of the meeting, sat in silence, patiently waiting for the right moment to begin.

Nora leaned forward, her elbows on the top of the table and her gaze fixed on the daughter. Nora's glasses rested on the tip of her nose, held secure by a beaded strap wrapped around the back of her head. Celeste grinned; Nora looked like a librarian!

Mrs. Millman kicked off the conversation. "Thank you for coming."

Agnes nodded politely. "Father MacLeod told us about your troubles, Mrs. Millman—"

"Please, call me Mary."

"Okay, Mary it is." Agnes gave a small smile and another nod before continuing. "We're very sorry you are all experiencing such tough times. As we understand it, you contacted Father MacLeod for assistance in dealing with supernatural occurrences in your home."

The daughter lifted her head. Ceasing her bobbing and weaving, her eyes locked on Agnes. Her mother reached a hand out to her.

"Yes," Mary replied.

Agnes continued. "While the Massachusetts Dioceses doesn't receive many requests to investigate such things, it is not unheard of. As infrequent as these occurrences are, the Church has neither the time nor the workforce to investigate every one of them. They call for outside help—third parties, like myself, Nora, and Celeste—to do the preliminary work. If we determine there's a reasonable explanation, either physiological or psychological, the Church will cease any further investigation. They will, of course, be happy to provide comfort and support however they can, but they'll go no further."

The girl's father spoke up. "Look, I know my wife asked for this, and I thank you for coming, but"—a tinkling sound stopped him short. It was off to Celeste's far right. They all turned toward it.

Against the wall, an oak china cabinet with glass doors shuddered. Dinnerware rattled, glasses clinked; the contents colliding with one another as the room filled with the sounds of plates breaking and glasses shattering.

The cabinet rose an inch, then fell back to the floor. It happened again—several more times, in quick succession. With each occurrence, the thumping resonated through Celeste's shoes.

The rattling of the dinnerware grew louder, each time the contents of the cabinet clattered against the doors. The panes fractured, then burst, spewing pieces of dinnerware and shards of glass onto the floor.

Celeste stiffened. She closed her eyes, made the sign of the cross and formed a protective X over her chest with both arms. After a short prayer, she opened her eyes.

The Millmans had enveloped their daughter in their arms. Both Mary and the young girl had their eyes closed, but their mouths were parted enough to display gritted teeth.

The father's eyes were open, focused on the cabinet.

Celeste gathered her courage and leaned back in her seat. As previously instructed, she blocked out the noise and concentrated on the father. She had expected to pick up signals of terror from the man, but this wasn't the case. Instead, an overwhelming feeling of guilt coursed through her. She bolted upright in her chair. Something else came to her before she broke contact.

She cut away too soon. It was fleeting, but she couldn't deny the sensation of pleasure that lingered in her groin. Confused, she studied the man's face. He was a far cry from Harrison Ford; definitely not groin tingling material.

An explosion made them both jump. She turned her head toward the sound to see the double doors at the bottom of the cabinet had blown open. Pots, pans, and appliances sailed out with enough force to dent the floorboards. The eruption lasted only seconds; when it was over, the utensils lay still on the hardwood. Then the rumbling started. On the floor, the remnants of the cabinet vibrated, and inching forward, they crawled toward the dining room table.

The eruption had been a shock, but the sight of cookware creeping toward them pushed Celeste close to the breaking point. She trembled, her teeth chattered. The skin on her hands turned red with the balling of her fists.

When Father MacLeod had asked her to join this investigation, she'd seen it as an opportunity to use her talent to further God's work. She was told that she'd only be sharing her impressions of the Millman family with Agnes and Nora, nothing more. The priest never told her about *this* shit.

Forks, spoons, and knives vomited forth from the ruined cabinet drawers.

Celeste, eyes wide, her shoulders shaking hard enough to induce pain, looked up at the ceiling, silently praying for this to end. God's answer was not the one she'd been hoping for. The cabinet lifted once more, higher this time—more than a foot off the floor—then slammed down hard enough to cause two of the legs to split. The cabinet rocked in place for a moment, then twisted a hundred and eighty degrees before toppling. The remaining fragments of dinnerware discharged through the newly created openings like a volcano.

Unable to contain herself any longer, Celeste jumped from her seat. "Agnes," she screamed, "What the hell is happening?"

Agnes stared at the daughter. With a sigh, she switched her gaze from the girl to Celeste. Shushing her, Agnes lifted her right index finger and pressed it to her lips. Turning to Nora, she opened the palm of her left hand. With the same index finger, she mimicked a scrawl on her palm. Nora nodded, producing a notepad and handing it over. Agnes jotted something down, and the two women reviewed it. Then, once more, both sat quietly and faced the family as more hell broke loose.

Celeste swallowed hard. *What the hell? A piece of furniture is doing a jig and all they do is tell me to shut up and write notes to each other?*

It was Mary who brought the episode to an end.

"Stop! *Please, God, make it stop!*" she pleaded.

The phenomenon ceased. Except for whimpers from the family, the dining room fell silent. Seconds passed. No one moved. Celeste's heartbeat hammered. She held her breath, eyes darting around the cabinet. It was still. Nothing inside the cabinet shattered. Nothing crawled toward them. She let the air rush out her nostrils.

She saw the relief on the family's faces. Agnes and Nora, their heads bowed, whispered and examined the notepad.

Mary stood. "You tell me this isn't a supernatural occurrence the Church should be investigating. Stuff like this has been happening at least once a week for the past two months. My family needs help!"

Agnes stared deep into Mary's eyes. The contact lingered until Mary looked away.

"Excuse me, Mary," Agnes replied. "I'd like to have a brief discussion with Nora and Celeste. Would you all mind leaving the room for a minute or so?"

Mary leaned back at the request, blinked, then nodded. Clearly, it wasn't the answer she had been expecting.

The mother gently tugged on her daughter's shoulders and motioned her up off the chair. They walked towards a neighboring room, the father close behind. Before he rounded the corner, he turned back, scowling at Agnes. She shooed him away with a head gesture, and he walked on.

Celeste sprang from her chair. "What the hell just happened? Are all your investigations like this?"

Agnes pushed her seat back and stood. "Come on, let's talk over there." She pointed to the wall where the china cabinet had stood. Nora and Celeste followed Agnes, accompanied by the sounds of crunching underfoot.

When she reached the wall, Agnes bent to pick up something leaning against the baseboard. She held it high for the other two to view. It was a belt buckle, embossed with an image of a woman with extremely large breasts.

"Strange thing to store in a china cabinet," muttered Nora.

Agnes turned the buckle around and, after a short inspection, frowned.

Considering what they had just experienced, why would Agnes pay so much attention to the buckle? The embossed pattern alone warranted a quick discard. Celeste had to admit it was an unusual find, though, and she was curious to know if Agnes was picking a vibe up from it. The woman passed it to Nora who studied it for a moment. Celeste refused to touch it. Agnes sighed and set it back against the baseboard.

"No," Agnes said, finally answering the second part of Celeste's question, "Not all our investigations are like this. Tell us, what did you sense from Mr. Millman?"

Celeste went into detail about the acute feeling of guilt she had picked up.

Agnes asked if there was anything else; even the smallest thing could be important.

Celeste turned red, lowering her head. "Well, there was one other thing. It only lasted maybe a second or two, and I'm not sure if it's connected to this."

"What was it?"

"I—I'm embarrassed to say."

"Look," Agnes pressed, "Get over it. We need all the information we can get."

Celeste whispered, "I was aroused for a moment. I can't explain it."

Agnes and Nora turned to each other, made eye contact, but did not speak.

"Okay, this is what we're going to do," Agnes went on. "We're going to call the mother and daughter back in here. The father stays out. You're not to say anything, Celeste. Nothing. No matter where this conversation goes with them, you must not react in any way. You will listen and learn. Do you understand?"

Celeste nodded. *It's as if Agnes already knows me.*

Agnes gestured towards their seats. Celeste and Nora returned to them while Agnes disappeared into the other room to talk with the family. It was obvious the talk didn't go well—the father was taking loud exception to having been left out of this phase of the investigation. Though Celeste couldn't make out everything that was said, Agnes' tone was evidence she wouldn't change her mind. The argument continued for several minutes, often with Mary's voice added to the mix. Celeste and Nora exchanged glances. Their attention turned to the dining room entrance when they heard Agnes come around the corner with the girl and Mary. The three of them sat back down in the same seats as before. Agnes spoke first.

"Now it's just us ladies—so, shall we begin?"

Mother and daughter nodded.

"I'm going to ask you a few questions first, Mary, then I'll turn to your daughter."

Mary leaned forward, putting an arm around her daughter. "Her name is Amanda."

"Yes, I know, but I was addressing you."

"Oh. I'm sorry." Mary blinked a few times, leaning back in her seat.

"Now, Mary, would you say you have a loving home?"

"Yes. Yes, I would."

"Do you love your daughter?"

"Why would you ask me that?"

"Please answer."

Mary pulled her daughter closer. "Yes, of course. With all my heart."

"Do you love your husband?"

Mary hesitated. "Yes."

"Are you and your husband having any marital problems?"

"What do you mean?"

15

Agnes smiled. "I mean things like, are the bills being paid? Are you comfortable in each other's presence? Do you have relations on a level that you're happy with?"

Mary lowered her head. She removed her arm from her daughter's shoulders and placed her hands on her lap.

"Yes, the bills are paid. He has a job and I work part-time, mostly nights, but not every day of the week. My working late has separated us more than we'd like, but we're putting money away for Amanda's college. Most of my earnings are earmarked for that."

"That's good," Agnes offered. "Saving now is a good start. Let me ask you one more question. Do you think your husband is having sexual relations with another woman?"

Celeste gaped. What could this possibly have to do with the odd occurrences in the family's home? *Was that the arousal I felt?*

Mary didn't answer right away. She froze, staring at Agnes. Celeste couldn't tell if Mary was mortified by the question or afraid to answer. The silence was long and uncomfortable.

"I don't understand the question," she said, her voice timid, "But no, I don't think he's cheating on me."

The ceramic and glass shards on the floor rattled. All heads swiveled toward the sound. Celeste's skin prickled. Would the ruined dinnerware resume its march toward the table? It didn't. The rattling stopped as abruptly as it had begun.

Agnes dismissed the incident with a rueful smile and resumed the conversation. "Thank you, Mary. Now, Amanda, I'd like to ask you a few questions."

The young girl nodded.

"Do you like living in this house?'

Amanda stared at Agnes. The young girl cocked her head to the left, but her gaze was unwavering. After a moment, Amanda straightened in her seat.

"Yes, I do like my house."

Agnes smiled. "That's nice. Do you love your mother?"

"Yes." There was no hesitation in her answer.

The corners of Mary's lips curled upwards and she reached over to hug her daughter. "I love you, too," she whispered.

"Do you love your father?"

There was a crash near the wall. Everybody jumped. The china cabinet had reanimated, smashing against the wall. It split into pieces from the impact. The sound grew loud enough to cause Celeste to bring her hands to her ears. In less than thirty seconds, the destruction was complete. Wooden fragments lay still on the floor.

Amanda's dad burst into the room.

"What the hell is happening in here?" he screamed at Agnes.

Agnes ignored him and focused on Amanda. "Did you do that?"

Amanda's eyes went wide. She shook her head. "N-no, I—I didn't. How could I?"

Mary leaned forward, face red. "How in the world can you think she could do something like this? What is wrong with you people? Can't you see there's an evil presence in this house?"

"Please, everyone, I'll explain," said Nora, her voice calm, steady. "Mr. Millman, take a seat."

He sat.

Nora continued, addressing Mary. "We do believe there is a presence in your home, but, in this case, Agnes and I don't think it's evil. In fact, we believe its origin is human."

Mary blinked. "What? Are you saying *we're* doing this? That we're putting on some kind of act?"

"No," Nora responded. "We don't think you're putting on a display. We believe what you have here is a poltergeist phenomenon."

"What?" Mr. Millman asked. "A poltergeist, like in that movie? Even if that were true, isn't that an evil presence?"

"That movie was Hollywood clap-trap," Agnes interjected. "Poltergeist is a German word meaning *knocking spirit. Knocking* because it uses sound to catch attention, *spirit* because the one doing the knocking can't be seen. The most prevalent causes appear to be from adolescents who have severe emotional or psychological issues. These young people feel trapped, unable to explain or share their problems with others. Their frustration manifests itself as psychokinesis, the ability to move objects by will."

"Wait ... just ... a ... minute." Mary's voice shook. "Are you saying our daughter caused this china cabinet to self-destruct? Are you saying it's been *Amanda* terrorizing us for the past two months? She—she couldn't—wouldn't do that!"

"Results from past poltergeist investigations also reveal the adolescents involved usually don't *realize* they're the cause."

Mary shook her head. "No, this can't be. Amanda would tell us if there was anything wrong. Wouldn't you, dear? There's nothing going on that you can't tell us about, is there?"

Before Amanda could answer, Agnes broke in. "Mrs. Millman. Now is not the time to address this. That can wait until after we leave. I will say, if your daughter is hiding something, she's not likely to reveal it any time soon under the current circumstances. However, when you do discuss this with her, ask her pointed questions: it may serve to speed the process along and end these occurrences."

"Pointed questions? Like what?" asked Mr. Millman.

Both Celeste and Nora turned to him.

Nora made eye contact with Amanda. The older woman's expression softened. After a few seconds, she sighed and then switched her gaze to Mary. "For one," Nora said answering the question while peering intently at Mary, "Ask Amanda if your husband has been taking sexual liberties with her."

Mr. Millman shot up from his chair. "How fucking dare you! Get your black ass out! All of you—get out now!"

Celeste's mind went numb at the accusation. She blinked, trying to refocus. Thoughts came back to her, one by one, each one worse than the other. How could Nora and Agnes be so sure of their accusation? Was this the proper way to confront the family? *If it's true, what'll happen after we leave?*

Images of Mr. Millman reacting violently and then further abusing Amanda flashed before Celeste's eyes. Her chest tightened, and she gagged. If the man *was* raping his daughter, what in the world must have been going through the poor girl's mind right now? How could Mary not have known this was happening? Celeste recalled Agnes' instructions not to interfere; to remain silent; to learn. She decided to follow those instructions—for the moment—and pay attention to the family's reactions. She'd fantasize about castrating him later.

She focused on Amanda first. The girl's head was lowered, her shoulders hunched. Celeste couldn't see her expression.

Mary's narrowed eyes were on her husband. Her chin was trembling. Tears flowed onto her cheeks.

Following Mr. Millman's outburst, outrage framed the man's face. His eyes were darting, his face red, his lips pursed. He scooted over to Amanda, bent down, and wrapped an arm around her shoulders. "Amanda, honey," he pleaded, "Please tell your mother it isn't true."

Celeste's skin crawled as the man held his daughter. *He's intimidating her!* Celeste leaned forward, waiting for Amanda's response.

Amanda's voice was low, reticent, and she didn't raise her head. "No. It's not true."

The debris on the floor rattled, then fell silent.

Agnes sighed, motioning for Celeste and Nora to rise. The three investigators stood. Agnes addressed Mary.

"A couple of things before we leave. I suggest you look up poltergeists. With enough digging, you should find some help in dealing with your daughter's emotional state.

"We'll be reporting our findings to the Church. Unless new information comes their way, or there's new evidence to the contrary of our findings, they'll consider the case closed. You have some important decisions to make, Mary. For Amanda's sake, I hope you make the right ones."

Celeste, Nora, and Agnes saw themselves out. Once they arrived at their vehicles, Celeste was unable to contain herself. "Is that it? We lit a match in there—what if it all goes up in flames once we're gone?"

Nora placed a hand on Celeste's shoulder. "Honey, as cruel as this may sound, we're not social workers. You're going to find yourself in situations that will be worse than this one. At best, those situations may break your heart. At worst, they'll leave you angry and doubting your faith. At this moment, our place in life is to do God's work by recognizing and identifying the presence of evil. There are others who are equipped to handle the containment and removal side of things."

Celeste grimaced. "Yes, I understand that, but it feels wrong to leave Amanda in that situation."

Agnes spoke up. "If you repeat what I'm about to say, you'll lose any trust I would've placed on you in the future."

Celeste nodded.

"I'm going to call the local Department of Health Services and ask them to do a wellness check on the family and to do it as soon as possible. It'll be an anonymous call from a pay phone at the gas station close to where I live. Before you ask, yes, they have a pay phone—I've used it before. You know as well as Nora and I do that we're not to make our work public. Father MacLeod handles that. Besides, I'm sure if I told the DHS we're empaths doing an investigation of demonic possession, they'd hang up on me."

Celeste grinned.

Agnes broke from the conversation and walked to her car. She paused at the door and asked Celeste, "We good?"

"We're good."

"Okay. See you at my place around six to write this up?"

Celeste waved. "See you then."

CHAPTER 2

"Father MacLeod?"

"Yes, Linda?"

"Mr. Lewis is here to see you."

"Thank you, Linda. Give me a minute, then send him in."

"Yes, Father."

Father MacLeod pushed back from his desk and exhaled loud enough for the sound to reach his ears. Mr. Lewis was here at the behest of the bishop; this did not bode well.

Possessing a tic that manifested itself whenever he was feeling uneasy, he fought an impulse—and lost. His right hand rose to his unkempt beard, squeezing both sides of the rat's nest as if he could shape its end to a point. He would often pull on the beard until the pain was too much to bear. He liked to do this in sets of threes. Linda had seen him tug away often, once quipping the reason he was bald was that he had yanked so hard on his beard, he pulled the hair down to his chin. His retort had her in stitches: "You should see my pubic hair—it's so long, I'm amazed my beard isn't stubble."

There was a courtesy knock, and his office door opened. Mr. Lewis stepped through without escort, closing the door behind him. He was elderly, well dressed, and rather thin. He clutched a file folder in his left hand.

"Father MacLeod. I'm Kevin Lewis."

The priest stood, held out a hand, and smiled. "Please, sit. The bishop tells me you have an interesting topic you wish to discuss."

Mr. Lewis hesitated, using the time to appraise the priest. A few moments later, he responded. "Yes, Father, I do."

"Well, then. I assume you're a busy man. Shall we get to the matter?"

What might have passed for a grin flashed on the old man's face. "I appreciate your tact. Allow me to follow your example. I am a wealthy man, Father MacLeod. I consider myself a philanthropist, one who employs due diligence when selecting recipients for my charity. I give extensively to those organizations that might somehow, someday, benefit me. For instance, one of these beneficiaries is my hometown, Goffstown, New Hampshire. I enjoy its tranquil setting and upscale nature. Those traits are beneficial to me and my family. But Goffstown does have problems that are immune to my largess. It suffers from the same societal ills that beset other small towns, issues money cannot fix. In addition, it also has a unique problem that I have been unable to solve. That problem is the Moore house." Lewis placed the file folder on Father MacLeod's desk.

The priest opened the folder, then gazed at his visitor. "This is a police dossier. How'd you come into possession of it?"

"As I said, I donate to those organizations that might benefit me in my own time of need. The town's small police force is housed in a new building in no small part because of my donation toward its construction. The chief is very grateful."

Father MacLeod stared at the old man for a moment before nodding. Thumbing through the folder's contents, he cringed. There were pictures of men, women, and children, seven in total—all dead. Some were mutilated, and many were missing body parts. The last picture showed a pair of severed legs on the ground. Local police reports and documents from the New Hampshire Attorney General's office accompanied the photographs. All the papers listed the location of the pictures at the same address in Goffstown.

Father MacLeod dropped the folder onto his desk. "Mr. Lewis.

These are gruesome photos, and I'm very sorry this is occurring in your hometown. But this is Haverhill, Massachusetts, not even close to you. Besides, we're a religious organization, not a homicide squad."

The corners of the older man's lips curled upwards. "Father, I know what you do here. Your office is a liaison to the Vatican on matters of the supernatural. To be blunt: demonic possession. I believe that address in the dossier, the Moore house, is haunted. I want your office to investigate it."

The priest was no stranger to politics or dealing with people of wealth—money had ways of gathering information and opening doors. Still, he was surprised by the old man's knowledge of his office. His funding did come directly from the Vatican, and his operation was known only to the Pope, a few at the top of his hierarchy, and his bishop.

"Mr. Lewis, I'm not sure where you got your information, but—"

"Cardinal Rosa."

The priest stared at the man. The cardinal was one of the Vatican's most trusted advisers.

"I've made sizable donations to Catholic charities. Cardinal Rosa and I have become well acquainted. Much as I'm doing with you now, I've presented him the facts on the Moore house. He directed the bishop to set up this appointment."

The priest leaned back in his chair. "What makes you think this house is possessed?"

"As you'll read in the reports, none of the deaths could be solved. They're all open cases. I should add that not all of the deaths connected with the Moore house are included in that file."

"How do you know this?"

The old man lowered his head. "Father, will you hear my confession?"

"What?"

"I'm requesting confession."

Mr. Lewis explained. "What I am going to tell you is a matter of illegal activity and sin."

The priest considered the request. He could deny it—it would be in his rights to do so, but that might create a new set of problems with the bishop. So far, his only opinion of Mr. Lewis was that of indifference. Hearing his confession might change this. If he was going to investigate, he needed to be impartial. However, he'd also need to be informed. Father MacLeod had yet to hear the older man's motivation for investigating the house, and a confession might bring it to light.

"Go ahead."

"That's it? No Latin? No prologue?"

The priest sighed. "If it makes you feel better, I can whip something up. I haven't heard confession in over twenty years. I have dispensation from serving mass as well as hearing confession."

"No need. You guarantee this stays between us?"

"And God. Yes."

The old man slumped in his chair. "My granddaughter is one of the people missing from that police report. She is a junkie, Father MacLeod. She disappeared two months ago. After hiring private detectives to find her, I learned the last time anyone saw Gam, she was looking to purchase drugs from someone inside the Moore house. I was informed it was unoccupied so with a police escort, I visited it. From the street, its facade unsettled me for some reason, but that did not deter me. I asked the police officer to remain outside, and I approached the house. Once I went inside, I grew more uncomfortable. Darting in and out of corners, shadows fluttered in my peripheral vision. Turning to them, they vanished. I heard noises but could find no source for them. It sounded like people sobbing, some of the voices, I thought belonged to children. Then, came the muffled laughing. When I heard my granddaughter screaming my name, I fled. Her voice did not have the inflection of someone begging for help, Father MacLeod. It was primal, evil. After leaving, I dug into the history of the house both documented and rumored. I came to the conclusion that the house was haunted, possessed by an evil spirit, so I contracted with two men to burn the damned thing down. Two days later a pair of unidentified men were found hanging from a tree a mile away from the property, their bodies burned beyond recognition. Based on missing person's reports and DNA, they were identified. They were the two men I'd hired. So, you see, I'm guilty of attempted arson, not to mention complicity in the death of those two men."

Father MacLeod leaned in. "Why didn't you just buy the house and have it demolished?"

"I've tried. The property is locked in an irrevocable trust. The taxes have been and continue to be paid."

The priest stared at Mr. Lewis for a moment, then gestured with his index finger. "Absolved."

The old man's head angled back. "That's it?"

"Well, say two *Our Fathers* if it makes you feel better. Look, I'm sorry about your granddaughter. It's a hell of a thing to happen. To be honest, your story, while sad and brutal, isn't conclusive enough to indicate possession. I'm sure you've pulled some strings and have me over a barrel. Moreover, if I say no, chances are I'm going to get a phone call or possibly a visit not long after you walk out that door. Am I right?"

Mr. Lewis nodded.

"I thought so." Father MacLeod hesitated for a few seconds. "I've got a team I send into situations for preliminary investigation. They're good—damned good. They're finishing an assignment near Boston today, so I can't call them until this evening. I'll have them look into the Moore house."

"What is this team?"

"Do you really need to know that?"

Mr. Lewis stared at him, impassive.

"Alright. It's a team of three women. They're empaths. They pick up emotions from people, and they're able to discern the history of objects and ascertain whether or not there was—or is—a presence residing in them."

"Women?"

"Yes," replied Father MacLeod. "Three former nuns who are now in the employment of the Vatican."

"I thought the Church considered these types of skills demonic in nature."

"All three left the Church because of that very thing. However, that isn't an obstacle for the branch of the Vatican that employs us. The women continue to serve God, and as a bonus, they're paid much more than the stipend they were receiving."

"Tell me about them."

"Why?"

"I want to know."

The priest considered the request. People like Mr. Lewis used information like currency. The more they knew about a subject, the easier it was for them to make deals. Father MacLeod had no idea what Mr. Lewis could do with the information; he decided to divulge only the basics.

"Agnes Levesque's the leader of the group. She's in her late fifties and from New England, as are the other two members. She's been working for us for over ten years, and she's very good at what she does.

"Nora Fournier is younger, but not by much. She's African American and has been working with Agnes for the past seven years. She's also very good.

"The last member is Celeste Roux. She's the youngest of the team, in her mid-thirties. She's new to the group." The priest smirked. "And I'm sure you already know all there is to know about me." He watched the old man sitting across from him process the information.

"Thank you, Father, for agreeing to look into this matter, as well for being forthright with me. I'll leave the police reports here with you. Please share them with your team. I hope to hear from you within a week's time. I do have one more request to make before I leave."

"And that would be?"

"Sending three women into that house alone would be ill-advised. I'd prefer that you accompany them."

Father MacLeod's hand went to his chin.

CHAPTER 3

Agnes stood on her tiptoes, reached up to the top shelf of the cupboard, and pulled down a half-empty bottle of Jack Daniels. Three fingers' worth splashed into a water glass. Both the bottle and the glass accompanied her to the living room coffee table.

"This one's yours," she told Nora. "I'm getting ice for mine."

Nora didn't wait for her to leave before taking a deep sip.

Agnes didn't blame her. They'd had a hell of an afternoon.

Agnes made her way to the freezer, her thoughts dwelling on the Millmans; more specifically, Mary. Would the woman do the right thing? Agnes had little sympathy for Mary—it was Amanda's plight that broke her heart. Agnes didn't have to use her empathic skills to know the girl's father was a controlling and self-centered son of a bitch. What troubled her was that Mary might have suspected the abuse on some level, and if so, did nothing to confirm or stop it.

Agnes also didn't need special abilities to see that Mary was non-confrontational—a sheep in an apron. She prayed the woman had the guts to get her daughter out of the situation permanently.

Agnes sighed, opened the freezer door, and dug out a fistful of ice chips from a bucket. She stepped to the cupboard and transferred the ice chips to a second glass.

Sheep in an apron.

Although Agnes didn't know Celeste or Mary very well, she couldn't help comparing the two. If this afternoon was any indication, she wasn't sure Celeste could handle it if things got rougher than they had today. It didn't happen often, but some investigations spiraled out of control. They didn't need another scenario like the one a few months earlier. One that had led to the loss of Catherine and necessitated Celeste joining them. Agnes and Nora needed the assurance that their backs were covered if the shit hit the fan.

"What'cha thinking about?" Nora asked with a crooked grin. Her glass was almost empty.

Agnes approached the table, set her glass down, and leaned into Nora. Their lips touched. Nora's arms circled Agnes' waist.

"Don'tcha know," she whispered into Nora's ear, "I'm always thinking of you?"

Nora leaned back, closed one eye and cocked her head. "Don't go bullshitting me, dear. You were thinking about what happened this afternoon. But, hey, let's wait until Celeste arrives before we get into it." Nora broke contact and refilled both drinks. She handed Agnes the glass. "If she's on time, she'll be here in five minutes. I'm going to pick up a bit."

As both women tidied up, the phone rang. Agnes walked to the landline carrying a few magazines. She fanned them atop an end table and answered the phone on the fourth ring.

There was a knock on the door. Nora looked into the peephole.

"Celeste," she whispered.

Agnes covered the mouthpiece of the phone. "Father MacLeod."

She spoke with the priest as she watched Nora let Celeste into the condo. Nora placed a closed fist near her ear and mouthed, "Father MacLeod," and Celeste nodded her understanding. They both sat on the couch, Nora with her glass, Celeste with her hands folded on her lap. The priest asked her to hold on for a moment as he had another call, so she turned her attention to the interplay between Celeste and Nora.

Celeste was making small talk and checking out the room when she noticed a cribbage board on the shelf under the table. "Oh," she remarked, "You guys play cribbage. I love the game. Hopefully you'll let me get a crack at it with you."

Nora's eyes lit up. "Yeah, the loser has to buy the winner an ice cream cone. I think Agnes must owe me hundreds of chocolate cones by now."

Celeste chuckled. "Wow, sounds like you're really good at it. Maybe you should be playing poker instead."

Nora's expression tightened. Glaring at Celeste, she retorted, "No. We don't play poker, and we never will." After a pause, her face softened. "Playing for ice cream is one thing. It's a fun way to pass the time. Poker is gambling, serious gambling. It can have consequences, and I will *never* be put in that position."

Taken aback, Celeste joked, "Well, I haven't played poker all that much, never cared for it. I guess that makes us two of a kind. Get it? Two of a kind?"

Nora sighed.

Celeste hit a nerve with Nora. Agnes had hit the same nerve in the past, but Nora's response had not been as restrained. Attempts to get Nora to talk about it had always failed. Agnes never pushed it, knowing that when the time was right, Nora would unburden herself.

The two women resumed their conversation, mostly talking about the décor of the room and how comfortable and homey it was. After Celeste declined Nora's offer of a drink, Agnes turned her back to the two women, but she could feel their eyes on her, waiting for her to rejoin them.

Father MacLeod returned to the call and asked how the Millman investigation had gone.

Agnes gave the priest a quick rundown of the meeting and promised him a report the next day. To her surprise, Father MacLeod told her not to bother to turn it in until the weekend. He had something more pressing for the team to address. She listened for ten more minutes. She didn't ask questions, instead took notes on the pad by the phone before finishing with, "See you tomorrow." She put the phone down, gazed up and noticed both Nora and Celeste staring at her; she'd forgotten they were there.

Agnes sat on a rocking chair at the opposite side of the coffee table from them. "I know we should discuss what happened this afternoon, but first, I need to tell you we've been assigned another investigation."

Nora's eyes widened. "So soon?"

Celeste spoke up. "Is this unusual?"

Agnes answered both questions with one word. "Yes."

Nora frowned. "When?"

"Tomorrow morning."

Nora sipped her drink. Celeste leaned forward.

Contrary to what she had read on the Internet, empaths could not read each other's emotions. While she had learned that people could learn to block her kind out, empaths, she discovered, had a natural ability to do so. She thought of it as a self-defense mechanism. The first time she had felt someone attempting to scan her, she reacted without thought, throwing up a mental shield against the intrusion. The action had been reflective and there was no way around it. She tried to scan Nora and Catherine several times and was never successful.

Although she could not probe either of the two women in her living room, Agnes had no problem deciphering the feelings of one of them. Nora was troubled, wary of tackling another situation so soon.

Celeste was another matter. She sat at attention, her gaze steady on Agnes. Though she was sure Celeste's fascination with the job would ebb quickly, she was impressed with her demeanor. The young woman wasn't taken aback by the new investigation. If anything, she seemed enthusiastic. Her eyes were soft but focused. *She's curious. She wants to know more.* What occurred at the Millmans' today might have frightened off any other new member of their team, but Celeste wasn't exhibiting any signs of fear. At least not at the present.

Agnes addressed both women. "Father MacLeod wants us to meet in Goffstown. It's in New Hampshire, right outside Manchester." She turned to Celeste. "I'll write the address down for you. You have GPS or a computer to get the directions?"

"Yes. I have both."

Agnes nodded. "Good. We're to meet him at 10:00 a.m. at the address, and—"

Nora interrupted. "Wait. We're meeting him at the site?"

"I know." Agnes' gaze shifted to Celeste. "In all the years we've been doing this, Father MacLeod has attended only two of our investigations. This one is rather involved, from what I gather."

Nora's hand shook as she gulped the contents of her glass. She poured herself another. Agnes frowned but refrained from commenting.

"We're to meet at a house. This home apparently has a name: it's called the Moore house. There have been several unexplained deaths at the site, all gruesome. He's sure the house is locked tight, so we're to do our sensing outdoors. If we pick up a demonic presence, we are to tell him and leave immediately. If that happens, we can all meet here afterward and discuss what we felt."

The atmosphere in the room became oppressive. The women were silent, frowning, their shoulders sunk. Nora and Celeste's eyes were dull and staring at a point somewhere beyond Agnes. She could guess where Nora's thoughts were, but she was clueless as to where Celeste's mind had retreated.

Her own thoughts went to their former team member, Catherine White. Visions filled Agnes' head: Catherine, strapped in her bed, thrashing and tormenting those who attempted to help her. She had been possessed, and the Church had done everything in its power to exorcise the demon.

Celeste broke the silence. "How many times have you come across an actual demon?"

The two older women locked eyes.

"Twice," Nora answered. "The first was four years ago. It involved a young boy. We picked up on it right away. The whole meeting couldn't have lasted more than fifteen minutes. Father MacLeod was with us on that investigation. He ushered us out of the family's home and took over. Though our involvement in the investigation phase was finished, Father MacLeod later informed us that the Church was successful in performing an exorcism on the boy."

Nora's voice lowered, and she spoke slower. "The second time was more than three months ago. That investigation wasn't so clear-cut when we arrived. The demon was smart. Both Agnes and I had a bad feeling before we even stepped onto the property, so we approached with caution. The other member of our team wasn't so inclined. She let her emotions get the best of her and the demon found its way in." Nora shook her head as if dislodging an image.

Celeste frowned. "What do you mean?"

Agnes caught Nora's discomfort, so she answered. "Much like this afternoon, a family reported odd occurrences to their local church. After the report went through the proper channels, Father MacLeod called us in. He was with us on that investigation, too.

"While we were uneasy, we hadn't picked up even a hint of a supernatural presence once we were inside the house. The subject was a teenage girl. We stayed in her bedroom for over an hour, talking with the girl and her parents. She was polite and answered all our questions, but her concentration seemed off as if she was hiding something from us. After our chat, the team met in another room to review the situation. While Nora and I couldn't detect a presence, Catherine said she had, but claimed she was unfamiliar with the sensation. Father MacLeod questioned her, and she admitted she couldn't tell if it was supernatural or not. He decided to wrap up the investigation with no determination made. While we were finishing, though, Catherine slipped back into the girl's bedroom. None of us noticed."

Celeste's eyes widened. "She went back there by herself?"

Agnes nodded. "Catherine violated two of the most important rules of an investigation—don't become emotionally involved with a subject, and never go it alone. We believe she took pity on the young girl and tried to discover what her issues might be. The demon had been in the girl all along. As mentioned, it was smart. Biding its time, it exited its young subject and possessed Catherine."

Celeste stiffened. "And what of Catherine?"

"She's being held in the same building as Father MacLeod's office. They have an area for this purpose, though we've never seen it. Members of the Vatican are with her, and they're working on exorcising the demon."

"Wait. You mean she's still possessed? After three months?"

Agnes sighed. "Yes. Some demons are stronger than others."

Celeste's hands came together, her fingers interlocking. She bowed her head to her hands. Closing her eyes, she mumbled a prayer. Agnes and Nora said nothing.

"Catherine screwed up," Agnes continued. "It didn't have to happen. If you're scared, Celeste, we understand, but you must also remember, we're doing God's work."

Celeste dropped her hands and lifted her chin. She stared at Agnes first, then Nora. Finally, she replied, "I'm fine."

Agnes smiled. "Since our plans for this evening have changed, we'll meet later in the weekend and write up the report on today's event—or should I say *two* reports, as we'll also have tomorrow's investigation to file. Why don't you head home, Celeste, get a good night's sleep, and we'll meet you in Goffstown tomorrow morning at ten."

All three women stood. Agnes jotted down the address of the Moore house and handed it to Celeste.

"Thank you," the young woman replied. "Okay, I guess I'll see you in the morning. Nora, can I give you a lift home?"

Nora squinted for a second, then opened her eyes wide and brightened. "No thanks, dear. I live in this condominium project."

Celeste's gaze went back and forth between her and Nora. She shrugged and stepped toward the entrance to the condo. Halfway out the door, she hesitated. "Have you thought how odd it is that out of all your investigations, Father MacLeod happened to be present at the only two where a possession took place?"

The reply came from Agnes. "Yes, dear, we have."

"Does it worry you that he'll be at tomorrow's investigation?"

It was Nora's turn to reply. "Yes, dear, it does."

CHAPTER 4

Celeste woke three hours before her alarm was set to ring. Vignettes of her meeting with Agnes and Nora had kept her tossing and turning. When she did manage to nod off, snatches of their conversations intruded into her dreams. She hoped a quick shower, and then a cup of coffee on the road would make her good to go for the meeting in Goffstown.

She was out of the apartment in twenty minutes.

Coffee from a local doughnut shop in hand, she plugged in her GPS, set the address, and hit the road. The radio stayed off. She wanted quiet time to sort her thoughts out before she arrived at the Moore house.

The official reason for her leaving the Church was her empathic abilities. She'd been told the same held true for her team. In Celeste's case, her expulsion from the Church was more involved, and she suspected the same to be true for Agnes and Nora. During her brief visit the previous evening, she hadn't picked up on any signs that something was off with them, but upon revisiting the situation now, she realized the two women were more than just team partners. For one, they were overly comfortable in each other's company. They frequently exchanged soft smiles and extended glances. Their body language—legs parted wide while sitting with arms draped over the top of their seats—also hinted at intimacy.

Celeste recalled Nora's response to her offer of a lift. Her facial expression had changed. The corners of Nora's mouth had elevated in concert with a softening of her eyes. At the time, Celeste had the impression her question was somehow amusing, but she'd been baffled as to why. Nora must've realized her expression was suspect and corrected it, but it was so quick, Celeste thought it forced. Reviewing the incident, she concluded that the two were lovers. Nora had mentioned she lived in the same building as Agnes, and it occurred to Celeste that the two might be sharing quarters. The Vatican provided funds enabling all three of them to live their lives in service to the Church. Most likely, Nora had a separate living space for appearance's sake.

When it came to Catholic doctrine, Celeste was *almost* a total conformist. Sex was the only issue that had her conflicted.

Sex with men was strictly forbidden in the convents, but it did occur and caused quite a stir when encountered. While lesbianism was also prohibited, a blind eye was usually turned to it by the superiors—if the parties were discreet. Celeste had never witnessed any sisters in her convent engaging in overt sexual practices, though the occasional flirting in the form of compliments or off-color jokes did occur. Based on the briefing she'd received from Father MacLeod before joining the team, Celeste was sure the two women had been in separate convents before their own partings with the Church. This might mean their affair began while they were members of the team. Aside from their empathic abilities, what could the two have done that was egregious enough to get them both expelled from the Church? To her way of thinking, attachments bound by love shouldn't have been the reason.

Celeste bemoaned that physic-empaths couldn't read each other's emotions. They had a natural ability to block scanning by their own kind. Too bad because it would've been an easy way to help solve the mystery.

Her thoughts turned to others she, and those of her kind, hadn't been able to read. While some people had a natural resistance to being scanned, others had learned how to deflect it. Father MacLeod was an example of the latter. Well, she assumed his ability to block her had been learned, as she'd never run across a male with empathic powers.

She wondered if male demons outnumbered female.

She'd never encountered a demon. There had been instances in lay society and in the convent where she'd picked up emanations of pure evil, but they'd always been of the human variety. Lust had been the strongest of these sins. To this day it was the one that stirred the most revulsion in her. An image of her former Mother Superior wormed its way into her mind, but she closed her eyes and concentrated on God's love. The old woman's image was replaced with that of a smiling Jesus, His burgundy-colored heart large, radiant, and centered on His chest. Celeste's white-robed Jesus had His arms spread out before Him, accepting of her and anyone else willing to embrace Him. She silently thanked her God for His love.

Google informed her that Goffstown was an hour away from the doughnut shop, but traffic was light. Celeste made the trip in fifty minutes. Two hours early, she thought to spend the extra time by getting something to eat. Crossing over a concrete bridge in the center of town, she came upon a diner called Travers Tavern and pulled into an empty parking spot in front. She was delighted to see it had counter-seating with old-fashioned steel napkin dispensers and real silverware. Chrome-trimmed stools with shiny red plastic seat pads lined the counter.

Preferring to eat in solitude, she perused the dining room. She smiled. *This diner does things right*! The wooden tables and chairs appeared rugged and every table had a linen tablecloth. Not only was it welcoming, it portended a quality meal.

A friendly-looking young woman in a white uniform adorned with an equally bright apron invited Celeste to sit down. The name tag on the girl's uniform read SANDI, and Celeste nodded, thanking her by name.

Celeste chose a table by a window and leafed through the menu. The waitress returned, poured coffee and took her order.

She sipped her coffee, her gaze drifting outside. Apparently, she wasn't the only one early for the meeting.

Across the street, in front of a columned building that must've been the town hall, two cars had pulled to the curb. One was a white Cadillac; the other, a large black sedan. Both drivers' doors opened. An old man exited the Cadillac. Father MacLeod, wearing his collar, cassock, and black trousers, climbed from the other.

The men moved onto the sidewalk, shook hands and spoke. A police cruiser pulled slightly ahead of the Cadillac in the street. The old man fished through his pockets, held up what Celeste thought was a ring of keys, and then walked to the cruiser with them.

"Excuse me."

Celeste sat back as Sandi placed a plate of French toast, baked beans, and home fries on the table.

"Would you like more coffee?"

"Yes, please."

Sandi filled Celeste's cup, placed a few small containers of cream on the table, and left her to her breakfast.

Before taking a bite, Celeste glanced back through the window. The cruiser was gone, and the other two cars were driving off. She chalked the meeting up to Father MacLeod's preparation for their visit.

She dug into her food. She was not disappointed.

Once finished, Celeste decided to walk off her meal, as there was still more than an hour before the meeting. Taking a left out of the diner, she headed south, past a Chinese restaurant and a bar. Beyond the bar, the concrete bridge she'd crossed earlier spanned a river. Intending to stroll along the river, she turned left onto a paved street running perpendicular to the bridge. She slowed when she spotted an awning hanging from one of the storefronts: *GOFFSTOWN PAWNSHOP*.

An odd feeling came over Celeste as she stared at the sign. She was picking up a sensation unlike anything she'd felt before. It wasn't malice or contentment. She couldn't describe it other than thinking something powerful was nearby. The feeling was strange for another reason—it came to her unbidden. Normally, she would have to concentrate on a subject to pick something up.

She walked in front of the store. The windows were tinted dark enough to prevent people from seeing in. Double doors at the center of the storefront had cameras set high atop them.

She stepped inside. It was not what she imagined a pawnshop would look like. Except for shelves lining the walls and a long counter to her left running the length of the store, the shop was empty.

This place is so big and there's nothing in the middle! A school could hold their prom in here.

Celeste strolled to the set of shelves lining the far wall. Instead of the junk she associated with these places, the items appeared to be works of art, and high quality at that. Oil paintings, vases, elaborate boxes, and items that she couldn't identify rested on the shelves. She reached for one, but before her hand could settle on the object, a voice from behind admonished her.

"Please, do not touch, Miss." A man, tall and thin, stood at the counter.

"I'm sorry," Celeste offered.

"That's quite all right. Is there something I can help you with?"

"I'm only browsing but thank you."

Celeste concentrated on the man. She probed, trying to pick up some kind of vibe. There was nothing.

The man sighed. "Look, Miss, I'm the proprietor. This may come off as presumptuous, and I mean no offense, but I'm sure most of my items would be out of your price range."

Though her empathic abilities revealed nothing about him, her natural instincts told her he wasn't the type to harm her. She smiled. "I understand, but would you mind if I looked around?"

He stared back. A little too hard, she thought; a little too long. She wasn't scared, but she was uncomfortable as she awaited his answer.

"If you must, but don't touch anything, please," he replied.

Celeste studied the objects on the shelves. All were old, she guessed centuries on some, maybe even older on others. Many had what she perceived as occult markings. The man at the counter interrupted her browsing

"May I ask why you're visiting our town?"

She turned to him. "How do you know I'm a visitor?"

"I've been in Goffstown a long time, and to be frank, not many local people stop by my shop."

"And why is that?"

The man smiled. "I'm not sure."

"How do you stay in business?"

"I have discerning clientele. They know how to find me."

She nodded, though his answer begged more questions. "I'm visiting Goffstown on business. I'll be meeting with a few people to look at an old house at the request of one of your townspeople."

"Ah. No doubt for investment purposes," he said. "May I ask which property?"

"The Moore house."

The man's face froze, then his smile dissolved. He didn't speak, and neither of them moved.

Celeste broke the stalemate. "Your reaction is peculiar, Sir. May I ask why?"

He stared at Celeste for a few more seconds. "First, may I ask the reason you're going to the Moore house?"

He knows about the Moore house!

She contemplated how much she ought to tell him. In the end, she decided to disclose as much as she could without divulging any identities and without mentioning her abilities. In return, she hoped he'd be more forthcoming. It wouldn't hurt to go into this investigation with extra knowledge. She explained her reasons for being in Goffstown.

The man listened without comment. Not once did he nod, lift a hand, or shuffle his feet. He hung on to her every word until she was finished, and then he shook his head, lowered his gaze, and bit his lower lip. "So, you and your team are going to The Moore house on behalf of a religious organization to investigate several unexplained deaths that occurred on the premises," he said, reciting the sentence in a flat, monotone voice as if reading from a textbook. The man shook his head like a father scolding a nasty child.

He spoke again, his voice softer, more relaxed. "There is much you're not telling me, and I guess you have your reasons. But, let me warn you, Miss, you would do well to stay far away from that house. You don't need to send a team there to tell you there's a supernatural shadow hovering over that property. The Moore house is evil. If you get too close, it will eat you."

It will eat you. The words hit her like a punch to her gut. While the previous day's conversation with her partners was disconcerting, it was nothing compared the brink of fear she teetered on now. Her mind filled with images of what Catherine White must be going through.

Pushing those thoughts away, she collected herself. "I have no choice; I have to go. It—it's my job," she responded, her voice low and shaky.

The man sighed. "This religious organization, is it Catholic?"

Celeste nodded.

"You're looking for evidence of possession? A demon?"

She nodded once more.

"You are playing with fire. You'll be burned." He hesitated a moment, then added, "Wait here."

He moved to the far end of the counter, turning the corner to get behind it. Stopping at a shelf containing several small boxes, he methodically read their contents and pushed them away one-by-one until he came to a box that satisfied him. He placed it on the counter. It was about two inches wide by ten inches long.

"Please, Miss. What's your name?"

"Celeste."

"Celeste, come here."

She obeyed. The man opened the box. Inside, on burgundy fabric, lay a cross made from ancient wood and inlaid with jewels.

"Celeste, this necklace was said to belong to a sixth-century English monk, named Cuthbert. Based on the tales of miracles performed in his name, your Catholic Church accorded him sainthood. One of those miracles was his ability to keep his own body from decomposing after his death at the hands of Danish invaders. The Danes took his body to Denmark and buried it there. Years later, he was exhumed and reinterred in England. It was reported that his body showed no signs of decomposition. Legend has it he was wearing this necklace when his body was exhumed. Thus, it may be believed the necklace will protect its wearer from bodily harm. Of course, this is all legend, but I've discovered over the many years I've been the proprietor of this shop, that faith is an enabler."

Celeste was fascinated by his story and the necklace but confused about why he was displaying it to her. "Is there a reason you're telling me this?"

"I'm going to loan it to you."

Once more she found herself unable to address the man. The offer was stunning. The necklace had to be worth thousands of dollars, most likely more. They had met no longer than fifteen minutes ago and here he was, willing to part with a treasure. Unless the necklace was a fake, and the story, too. His shop was full of items that appeared to be genuine historical artifacts, but she could see no security measures other than the cameras on the entrance doors, and those were aimed outside. Yet there was something about the man that begged her trust. He had listened to her explaining why she was in Goffstown and expressed no doubt about her story.

The man was obviously knowledgeable about the supernatural based on his comments about the Moore house and his history of the necklace. Additionally, he'd made comments concerning her safety. Another check mark in his favor was that he hadn't come on to her. He'd looked at her face during their conversations, not once glancing down at her chest. Even when she had worn her nun's tunic, she noticed the stares men had directed at her breasts. Had God delivered her an ally? She decided to press the man further.

"Why would you give me this necklace? You don't know me."

The man gazed at her breasts. His eyes remained on them for a few seconds and then he lifted his eyes to Celeste.

Her heart sank.

"Wear it under your blouse. Your shirt appears to be loose enough to conceal the cross. Do not tell anyone you have it with you." With emphasis, he added, "Tell no one." His voice returned to normal. "And, I am not *giving* this to you. As I said, it's a loan. I expect it back as soon as you're done with whatever you're doing at the property. As to why, there are two reasons. The first is that this is my town. The Moore house is an abomination—it is evil personified and a threat to my clients and my business. The other reason is that I sense you are a good person, but naïve, and woefully unprepared when it comes to dealing with the forces in that house. If the necklace has the abilities ascribed to it, it may be of assistance. I don't know you Celeste, but my intuition tells me you are who you say you are. For my own comfort, though, I would ask you to sign a standard purchase agreement. There is a stipulation that if you are not satisfied with the item, you can return it in five days without cost or penalty."

Celeste took the proffered necklace and contract. She slipped the necklace over her head and, as instructed, tucked it into her blouse. The fabric of her shirt pressed the cross against her skin, and as the man had noted, there was enough room for it to be hidden. She lifted her head, seeking approval.

The man was stone-faced, but he nodded.

She read the contract and let out an *EEK*.

"Well," he answered, "My services don't come cheap."

"I guess!" She produced a driver's license and filled out the form. The proprietor made a copy of the license while she wrote. "I guess if I don't return it you'll hunt me down."

He grinned. "Something like that."

Oddly, his smile put her at ease. "I have to go but thank you very much. I promise to return this to you later this morning or this afternoon when we've finished. If they ask to gather after the meeting, I'll return it tomorrow."

"Celeste," he replied, "Be careful."

"I will."

She strode out of the pawnshop, her left hand caressing the cross through her blouse.

The pawnshop owner watched the woman exit his shop. He thought her a good person, but weak. If the Moore house decided to target her, she didn't stand a chance.

The man's experience with the property was limited, but it was enough for him to keep his distance.

Though he was aware of the Moore house, his first encounter with the building had been a month earlier, when the patriarch of the town, Kevin Lewis, had asked his assistance in burning the place to the ground. Aside from the property's reputation, he'd agreed for a few other reasons. The man who'd asked him had purchased many items from the shop, all at a good price. As far as he knew, none of the items he'd sold Mr. Lewis had been used for nefarious purposes. Another reason, one that now caused him to fear for Celeste's safety, was the fallout of assisting Mr. Lewis. The two men he'd recruited for the arson attack had been murdered, and in a very unpleasant manner.

He had driven to the property afterward. The emanations picked up from the house were pure evil, and he'd left with no doubt that within its walls resided some type of malevolent presence. Celeste's visit had shed some light on its nature, a nature he was not presently prepared to deal with.

The owner had an assistant named Rex, a giant of a man the owner employed in any instances calling for brute force. Though he was reluctant to involve Rex in anything to do with the Moore house, he supposed it was best to advise him of the situation. While Rex was brutal and single-minded when it came to performing tasks, he had compassion for animals and innocent women who were victims of or might be exposed to violence. Celeste met one of these criteria. The

47

shop owner had no idea how far-reaching the Moore house evil extended, but he'd forewarn Rex and ask him to take additional measures to ensure the integrity of the pawnshop. By loaning the necklace to Celeste, he might be viewed as a collaborator with whatever she and her team were planning.

If so, he'd have to deal with the consequences.

CHAPTER 5

With only her thoughts to keep her company, Nora drove to Goffstown.

She was certain Father MacLeod was aware of her romantic involvement with Agnes, but that Celeste might not have caught on yet.

She and Agnes had decided to postpone the revelation until the investigation at the Moore house had been concluded. Celeste had been a member of the *Sisters of the Holy Cross*, one of the Church's strictest religious orders and, though she had been dismissed, it was unclear if she continued to devote herself to Christian doctrine. If so, the newest member of their team might be distracted by their affair, and now was not the time for such complications. After viewing the files Father MacLeod had sent over last evening, they all had to be cautious and at their best this morning. Though Nora hadn't mentioned it to Agnes, this investigation terrified her.

The successive photographs of dead bodies had been enough to send chills down Nora's spine, but her major reticence in this investigation stemmed from having viewed the first picture—the Moore house itself. It was taken from what she presumed was the road, and the moment her eyes had seen that file, a sense of helplessness had rippled through her. She'd froze in her chair, arms shaking. Fleeting visions of depraved sex acts and torture ran through her mind. She'd been unable to banish them. After a few moments, she didn't *want* to banish them.

Agnes' voice, coming from the bedroom, broke her trance. Upon hearing Agnes' call, the visions had ceased. Though uneasy, Nora had stood, her vision clouded, objects close to her slipping into the distance. She'd lowered her gaze to ground herself, and flushed when she noticed she was aroused, her nipples firm and sensitive beneath her blouse. After a moment her head had cleared, and she'd glanced back up at the computer screen. The picture of the Moore house was still there, but it no longer affected her.

Confused and frightened, she'd clicked out of the file and joined Agnes in bed. Agnes had been awake, about to cajole her into making love. There had been no cajoling necessary: after going through those files, Nora had craved her partner's loving touch.

Their coupling had turned out to be anything but romantic. Agnes was forceful; domineering. The woman's hands were rough as she roamed Nora's body, her fingers rigid as steel. Agnes' thrusts had been hurried, animalistic, and Nora was still sore as a result. When they finished, Agnes turned over without a word and was soon fast asleep. While their lovemaking had been frenzied and uncomfortable, a part of Nora had been turned on by it.

The adrenaline had kept her awake. As she'd lain there, unwelcomed thoughts had intruded. The belt buckle Agnes had found at the Millman's took prominence. That salacious image of a large-breasted woman cut too close to home. It was impossible to determine whether the woman on the buckle was black or not, but Nora couldn't help but think she was. Was this trinket in some way directed at her? Was that possible? Could it have some correlation with her shameful conduct in the past? She had kept that part of her life hidden from everyone; Agnes had no way of knowing, though it had been addressed during her initial interview with Father MacLeod. If it was linked to the Moore house, something powerful was intervening in her life. It could mean there *was* a demon involved. If it were the case, she might be way over her head in this investigation. She wasn't going to take any chances. If there was the slightest hint of possession involving the Moore house, she would report it to Father MacLeod, and then get the hell out of there.

CHAPTER 6

Celeste was the first to arrive. She parked her car at the curb and stood by the open door, waiting for the others. She used the time to study the exterior of the Moore house without mentally probing it.

Outwardly, it was no different than the thousands of other Victorians scattered across New England. It had been painted a Cape-Cod blue, and while it wasn't peeling, the color had faded. As an offset, the trim was dark blue, also dulled, but she could see no signs of rot or weather damage around the windows or roofline. The small porch was in good condition too—the floorboards weren't warped, and the stairs were nice and even. Though the house had been somewhat maintained, the yard appeared neglected. The grass was uneven and sunburned in sections. Bare spots indicated grub damage. For an abandoned building, it was in decent shape. With a little work, the home could be welcoming.

The only thing Celeste considered kempt was the front door, freshly painted a rich cranberry. Because its vibrancy contrasted with the rest of the house, she found her gaze continually drawn to it. Not deeply, but enough to pick up faint vibes. Photos from the file Father MacLeod had sent over the previous evening flashed through her mind. She shivered and decided to wait for the others.

The sound of cars approaching averted Celeste's thoughts. Two vehicles slowed and pulled up behind hers. Nora parked behind Celeste, and behind Nora, a police car pulled in. Her teammate exited and joined Celeste in the yard while the officer remained behind the wheel.

Nora glanced at the cruiser and then back to Celeste. "I wonder why he's here."

"Maybe he's just driving by. He saw me parked here, and when you pulled over, he decided to stop to see what's going on. Don't forget, there've been several deaths associated with this house."

"Yeah, probably," replied Nora, her voice trailing. "If he sticks around he might get quite an eyeful for his report."

Two more cars pulled in behind the cop. Father MacLeod and Agnes climbed out of their respective vehicles. They walked past the police car with a sideways glance and stood next to Celeste and Nora.

"Good morning, ladies." Father MacLeod's voice was gruff. "Here's what we're going to do. You—"

The door of the cruiser opened with a squeak, interrupting him. The officer was tall and muscled, his stride quick. His arms swung by his side, hands empty. Celeste recognized him as the officer Father MacLeod had spoken to outside the diner.

The officer spoke pointedly as he approached. "May I ask what you folks are doing parked in front of this property?"

The priest broke from the three women and, with his hand extended, walked toward the officer. "I'm Father MacLeod, from the Boston Catholic Diocese. May I ask your name?"

"I'm Officer Thad Jones." Staring hard at the priest, he shook the proffered hand.

The men were acting like they'd never met, but Celeste was positive this was the same policeman she had seen Father MacLeod with this morning. *What the heck is this all about?* She wanted to interrupt them, to ask why the charade.

"What's the matter?" Agnes asked.

What if I'm wrong? She would cause a scene for no reason and look foolish in the process. She decided to hold her tongue. "Um, nothing."

Father MacLeod glanced at her. "Are you okay? Something

bothering you?" he asked.

She absorbed the look without flinching, but he continued to stare.

Celeste inhaled and let it out slowly. "No, I'm fine."

The priest let his gaze linger a few more moments. With a barely perceptible shake of his head, he dismissed her and continued his conversation with the officer. "Officer Jones, we're here at the bidding of Mr. Kevin Lewis."

The officer nodded but said nothing.

"Your police chief, Donald Dodd, is aware that we're here this morning."

Office Jones remained silent.

"We're going to do a walk-around, say some prayers for those who have passed on in the house, and bless the property. We don't anticipate going inside."

The police officer broke his silence. "Well, Father, if you need, I happen to have keys to the front door." He raised the set of keys and grinned.

Father MacLeod returned a grin. "That's good to know. I don't foresee a need to enter the house, but we'll take you up on that offer if we have to."

The officer walked back to his cruiser, leaned against the hood, and watched them.

The priest faced the Moore house. "Okay ladies, we stay together. Do not engage until we've surveyed the property. We'll walk around the house, starting from my right. We are going to circle it and come back to the front. Only then will you give it a go. Everyone on board?"

The women voiced their assent.

"All right. Let's go. Remember, we all stay close." Father MacLeod led the way.

The yellowed grass had grown to mid-thigh, which made it difficult to see any obstacles or holes in the ground. It was switchgrass, dry and stiff, and as they walked it made whispering sounds like someone sweeping a floor with a corn broom. Celeste had dressed for the heat of the day, as had her teammates. The women wore skirts, blouses, and sneakers. Despite the heat and absence of rain, they stepped into areas of damp earth and small puddles hidden beneath the grass. Celeste heard the occasional *yuck* followed by a sucking sound as someone lifted a damp sneaker from the mud. Father MacLeod was the worst for it. His dress shoes and pants legs were soaked through. Celeste excused his utterances, though they were profanities.

Celeste felt nothing while passing by the right side of the house. As instructed, she didn't try. Agnes' and Nora's expressions were relaxed, so she assumed they were also holding back.

They rounded the corner to the rear of the house. A row of trees lined the far end of the property; behind them, woods stretched as far as the eye could see. If there had once been picnic tables, swing sets, or a garden in the backyard, there were no signs now. Had a family ever lived in this house?

Regardless, there *were* signs someone had been here recently.

Crime-scene tape draped the exterior of one of the first-floor windows. Below it lay a large area of trampled grass. The quartet approached the window. Flattened switchgrass, scuff marks in the dirt, a trace of red stains on the ground, and a recently cleaned portion of the wall under the window left no doubt about the reason for the yellow tape. A photograph from the file Father MacLeod had sent flashed in Celeste's mind. She diverted her eyes from the spot.

"Come on, let's keep moving," the priest ordered.

They continued along the back of the house, passing a small set of stairs leading to a rear metal door secured with a tarnished and scratched brass padlock. Celeste stopped. The markings on the lock resembled a mouth, its lips pulled into a grimace.

"It's secured from the outside," Nora said. "Somebody doesn't want people getting in there."

"Or getting out," Agnes added.

The three women exchanged glances. After a few moments, they walked to the remaining side of the building. They took notice of a steel bulkhead, also padlocked. The four of them pushed through the grass until they were once again at the front of the house. Father MacLeod led them toward the parked cars.

"I want some distance between you ladies and the house when you start. If there's a presence here, let's try to keep as far away from its influence as possible. As you saw from the files, a lot of bad stuff has gone down in this house, and we're here to eliminate one possibility. We don't know if it's a coincidence, if it attracts a bad element because of its location, or because of a demonic presence. If a demon *is* behind all those deaths, it's a powerful one, and I don't want you tangling with it."

Celeste sucked on her bottom lip. *What am I getting myself into?*

"Now, look at me, ladies."

She gave the priest her full attention.

"Before you start, I want you to face the house, line up side by side, hold hands, and close your eyes. I'm going to stand in front of you. If I notice any problems, I'll interfere. If you hear my voice, stop immediately. Though you may not detect trouble, your partners could be in distress. If one of you picks something up, tell me right away. It'll be enough, and I'll shut you all down. Do you all understand?"

Celeste nodded.

"Okay. Before we start, any questions?"

Agnes went first. "What're the odds that there *is* a demonic presence here?"

"Experience dictates that they're low, but not negligible. Demonic possession usually targets a specific individual, not an unrelated group of people. It can jump from one person to another, but contact is usually required. I know of only one case of multiple possessions without physical contact, and that only involved two people. We're talking about seven in this instance. I don't believe a demon is capable of that."

Hearing this, a weight fell from Celeste's shoulders. For the first time since the previous evening, she felt a modicum of relief.

"Why are you here, Father MacLeod?" Nora asked.

Celeste's spine stiffened at the question.

The priest blinked a few times and his hand went to his chin. He stared at Nora as he stroked his beard. Celeste was unable to read his facial expressions and couldn't decide if he was upset at the question or mulling it over. The previous evening's discussion about Father MacLeod's presence at two of their prior investigations had concerned Celeste. Apparently, it was on Nora's mind as well. Celeste leaned in to hear his answer, but the priest continued to ponder the question.

Finally, he took a deep breath and answered. "I was asked by a man in Goffstown to come. Mr. Lewis is wealthy and has plenty of political pull. I won't lie to you—aside from his granddaughter's disappearance related to the Moore house, he has another reason for us to be here. A reason I'm not at liberty to discuss."

Agnes shook her head. "I'm sorry Father, but we need more. Both times you've accompanied us on investigations, the results were positive for a demonic presence. The *only* two times we've discovered a presence as long as we've been a team. As you might gather, we're concerned about what awaits us this morning."

"I see." Father MacLeod responded. "You're connecting my presence to those two incidents." He inhaled sharply and let it out just as quick. "I can tell you, at the least, it was a coincidence. I can also tell you that, at best, it was God's will that led me to both those instances. As for this investigation, the sanctuary of confession is involved, and I won't betray it. If it makes you feel any better, the man who requested I be here had no idea this team existed. He has no intention of putting any of you, or me, in harm's way. All he desires to know is if the Moore house is possessed. If it is, I'll take it from there. Your job today is to find out. Any more questions?"

No one spoke up.

"Okay, let's begin," Father MacLeod ordered.

The three women positioned themselves facing the Moore house, the priest standing before them. With Agnes in the middle, Celeste to her left and Nora to her right, they held hands. Celeste gripped Agnes' hand with enough pressure to cause the woman to jerk. Celeste loosened the pressure and mumbled a soft apology.

"It's okay," Agnes replied. "Let's relax and get this over with."

"Yes."

Father MacLeod continued. "Now, ladies, close your eyes. That's good. I'm watching all of you. If you feel something, break your handholds and open your eyes. If you feel one of the others breaking contact, stop focusing right away. Call for me if you're in distress. I'll bring you and the others out. Ready?"

They all murmured agreement.

"Then get to it."

Celeste concentrated.

If the Moore house hid a demonic presence, it was doing a good job. Celeste couldn't pick up anything. Part of her was relieved, but it might mean she'd have to push harder. Her eyes closed tighter, and she focused on the darkness. She pictured herself stepping into it, pushing forward until she was isolated from her environment. She imagined herself a dimly lit star in a dark sky—an insignificant speck in an endless void—at one with God's universe. A lack of sound completed the scene.

Immersed in her mental projection, she called up an image of the Moore house. It appeared as it had when she first studied it from the safety of the road. She willed it closer. Its blue clapboards, the small porch, and the cranberry colored door loomed before her. She turned the house around in slow motion. After a full turn, she froze the image and focused on it.

Nothing. She could not pick up a single vibration from the house.

The image shook.

It slid away from her, disappearing into a point. A weight settled onto her shoulders, and her view spun like a pinwheel. She was tumbling, rushing out of the darkness. Flashes of light burst before her. She opened her eyes. Father MacLeod's face was inches from hers. He was staring at her, his lips tight and eyes wide. Another tremble passed through her—he was nudging her awake. She blinked away the confusion.

"Celeste!" She heard fingers snapping. "Come on, wake up."

She stepped back, shaking the fog from her head. Agnes and Nora were beside him, both alert, but frowning.

"Are you okay?" Father MacLeod asked.

"Ugh... yeah, I'm okay. What's going on?"

The priest sighed with relief. "So far, nothing. Agnes and Nora didn't pick up on anything from the house. It didn't take them long to conclude there's nothing there. But you were out of it for over ten minutes. We got worried and decided to break your concentration."

"Ten minutes? It couldn't have been that long. I just closed my eyes."

"It was." He fidgeted. "Actually, it was closer to fifteen. We decided to leave you be until we saw a sign of distress or you came out of it."

Nora interrupted, her voice tense as she shot a fierce look at the priest. "That's not entirely true. We wanted to pull you out earlier. Father MacLeod insisted we leave you alone. We relented—at first." Her tone turned angrier. "Agnes and I were worried. We finally demanded he bring you back." Softening her voice, she added, "If anything happened to you …" She reached out, taking hold of Celeste's hand.

Caught off guard by the sentiment, Celeste muttered, "I—I'm all right." Though she hadn't known Nora for that long, she was touched by her partner's concern. "I'm fine, really."

If Father MacLeod was offended or annoyed with Nora's interruption, he didn't bother to respond to it. As soon as Celeste confirmed her well-being, he asked her, "Did you feel anything?"

"No."

"Nothing? Nothing at all?"

"No."

The priest sighed. "Thank Christ."

The way he spoke had Celeste grimacing. It didn't sound like an exclamation of appreciation. It was more like a remark uttered when a burden is lifted. Agnes and Nora must've picked up on it, too: they stared at each other with similar scowls.

"Okay, ladies, our work here is done. Agnes, please file a report this afternoon at the latest. I have to head back to Haverhill to catch up on some things." He brushed by the women, taking hurried steps to his car. He stopped near the police officer, turned back to face the three of them, and bowed his head, making a frenzied sign of the cross. Finished, he waved and spoke loudly. "Oh, and thanks, ladies!" He didn't wait for a response.

As soon as Father MacLeod drove off, the officer left his cruiser and approached them. "Are you guys ready to leave now?"

Celeste, confused by the Priest's abrupt departure, looked to Agnes for guidance.

"Yeah," Agnes answered, "I guess so." She was staring at the parking spot the priest had vacated. She adjusted her gaze to the Moore house. "That black door creeps me out more than anything else about this house. I'm glad to take leave of it."

Celeste's head shot up. "Black door? What black door?

"Right there." Agnes pointed to the front door. "That one."

Celeste took in the door for a few seconds. "I don't see a black door. I see dark red."

Agnes frowned. She addressed Nora. "And you?"

Nora was staring at the door. "It's blue. Dark blue." Her voice was distant.

The police officer shook his head. "Is this a game? Are you ladies playing with me?"

"Why?" asked Agnes.

"It's green," he said, "And an ugly shade at that. It reminds me of vomit."

Celeste was aware of all four of them maneuvering, standing side by side to face the door. They all stared. *How can we all be seeing different colors?*

No one moved, until the door did.

CHAPTER 7

Departing from the Moore house, Father MacLeod headed south on NH Route 13 until it hit Route 3 in Bedford. He passed through the town of Merrimack, eventually arriving in Nashua, New Hampshire. Off the highway, he passed through an area of dilapidated houses, barns with caved-in roofs, and overgrown woods, until he spied his destination.

Despite what he'd told his team, he had no intention of going back to Haverhill.

Much like a patient visiting an oncologist and waiting for a diagnosis, the priest had been dreading with the worst outcome. In his case, demonic possession was *his* cancer. He'd survived an encounter with a demon once before, but like receiving a cancer-free diagnosis, he feared all it did was prophesy a recurrence. He lived with constant dread, waiting for the other shoe to drop. Turned out, Catherine White was that other shoe.

Catherine had been his responsibility and he'd failed her. He'd done everything he could to exorcise the demon from within her, but nothing had worked. Forced to summon exorcists from the Vatican, he'd waited with the hope they would accomplish what he could not. Catherine had periods of lucidity, and she used those periods to assist the exorcists in ridding herself of the demon. The priest shook his head at the memory of her tied to the bed—eyes large as half dollars, her mouth stretched impossibly wide, lips plump enough to burst, and infected lesions so numerous there was an absence of smooth flesh on her face. If anything like this were to happen to another member of his team, he wasn't sure he could handle it.

When the team had come up empty at the Moore house, he'd had to restrain himself from shouting with joy.

He should have pulled Celeste back sooner, but he'd wanted to be certain she'd had enough time to determine if the house was possessed. Based on the reports he'd received from her convent and on subsequent interviews with Celeste, he believed she had the strongest empathic abilities of the three women. With each new investigation—and patience—he would know for certain.

The results this morning had not only allayed his fear of a demonic presence, they'd encouraged him. He was wired, with a need to burn off the energy.

Arriving, he pulled into the parking lot at the far end of a two-story, 1940s-era industrial building. Standing in the center of a hardscrabble field, all four sides of the structure were clear of brush. Tree stumps and small boulders littered the area, accompanied by rusted machines once employed to die-cut the soles of men's work boots. Red bricks—weathered enough to be mistaken for black—made up the side walls. All the oversized windows along the façade were boarded over.

The priest counted the other cars sharing the lot. Five. The number was higher than he'd like. Though far from home, there was always a possibility he could be recognized. He slipped off his collar, removed his jacket, folded it, and tucked them into the well behind the front seats. He patted his left back pocket. Satisfied, he climbed out of his car. As he walked to the front door of the building, dust kicked up from dry ground and clung to his damp shoes and pants legs.

He stepped into a foyer with enough room to fit two people comfortably. Before him stood a closed door he'd been through many times. Made of steel and several inches thick, it was bare except for a black box halfway up the left side—an electronic lock.

"Lift your face to the camera, please." A digitally altered voice came from a speaker located in the ceiling. Father MacLeod stood still, staring into a small red light above the door, awaiting a prompt.

"Thank you," said the voice. "You may enter." A buzz sounded, and the door opened. When the priest passed through, the door closed on its own.

Father MacLeod gazed at the scene. He closed his eyes, breathed in deeply, and smiled.

"Welcome back, John Doe." The woman's voice, welcoming and seductive, opened his eyes.

"Please—call me John."

The woman chortled. "Of course: John. We are, after all, friends, despite our arrangement. Speaking of arrangements, I believe we have someone to your liking. She's new and possesses the trait you covet most."

The priest's eyes glistened as he nodded.

"I'll be right back," she assured him, sauntering to a spiral stairway at the back of the greeting room.

He gazed around the large room. The polar opposite of the outside, the interior of the building was immaculately clean with ornate furnishings. Period antiques complimented the décor which resembled a Victorian-era parlor. He'd ceased to be stimulated by the ambiance of the waiting room after his first few visits, but there was something here that never failed to excite him. The odor in the waiting room was exquisite. The smell of sex permeated the air. He had no idea how they accomplished it, but it had the desired effect on him. He was alone in the room—as was the policy of the establishment—so there was no embarrassment. His attention was called back to the spiral staircase by the clicking of heels.

The woman who'd met him at the doorway was followed by another. Father MacLeod held his breath when he saw her. She was young—he guessed no more than her early twenties—and wore a silk negligee that barely covered her ass. Her hair was long, fiery red, and fell in ringlets at her shoulders. When she reached the bottom of the stairs, he saw her legs were thin but shapely. Her breasts were enormous. The redhead held her place at the staircase while her madam approached the priest.

"Is she to your liking, John?"

His breathing resumed. "Are they real?"

"Of course."

"Then, yes. I like her a lot."

The woman smiled. "Shall we proceed then?"

The priest nodded. His hand went to his left rear pocket. He withdrew a wallet and counted out three hundred-dollar bills.

"I'm sorry, John, but this one is more expensive."

He didn't hesitate to pull out another hundred-dollar bill. The madam nodded, and, as was customary, held out her hand. The priest placed the cash in her palm. She folded it in half with one practiced hand and slipped it into a slot in her dress. She angled her head up and to the left, then nodded. He knew there was another camera there.

"Enjoy yourself, John."

Father MacLeod closed the distance between himself and his purchase and offered his arm to be led up the staircase.

CHAPTER 8

The front door of the Moore house inched open. Nora heard no hinges squeaking, wood moaning, or voices from the other side. Whoever was pushing it was in no hurry—if, that was, someone was actually behind it. Horror movie clichés came to mind, and the urge to flee taunted her. She couldn't be the only one who felt the need to run, but a quick glance revealed the others had remained in place, their eyes also drawn to the door. Her breathing slowed even as her pulse quickened. She stood with her teammates.

When the door opened halfway, she changed her mind. She wanted out of there.

In the time it took for her to blink, the door slammed against the wall of the house. The impact—as loud as the crack from rifle fire—had her screaming as she stepped away. Her teammates recoiled, colliding with her as they jumped back. They held onto one another as much to stabilize themselves as for security.

The officer remained where he was, gaze glued to the door, right hand at his hip, his fingers on the butt of his gun.

Nora wasn't one to scare easily. She'd seen things that would make the bravest of men cower. She'd been witness to the darkest of evils involving women and children. She'd participated in events that would've caused lay people to doubt their sanity. But while each investigation had had its challenges and dangers, none of them had affected her like this. The Moore house made her blood run cold—her skin prickled from the bottom of her spine to the tip of her head. Her chest felt hollow, as if all her emotions but one had been drained. Only fear remained, tainting her blood and spreading through her veins.

Her faith had always been adequate armor. Her God-given empathic abilities steeled her, preparing her for whatever was to come. If those abilities failed, she could count on Agnes or Catherine to back her up. The three of them had covered each other's asses since she had joined the team. This morning was different. Catherine was not among them, for one. And as equally distressing, not one member of her team had felt anything emanating from the Moore house. Investigating something that might be powerful enough to block out all three of them—to hide even the faintest evidence of its presence—had never happened before. It frightened the hell out of her. She looked to Agnes for reassurance. The right look from her lover would not only put Nora at ease but give her the strength and confidence for what might follow. But Agnes' eyes were locked on the door, as were Celeste's. Nora followed their gaze.

Nobody moved. Though Nora wasn't picking up on anything, she knew *something* had pushed that door open. As the seconds ticked past, she should've been relieved when nothing further happened. Her reaction was the opposite. Her arms and legs shook, the muscles in her face tightened, and her eyes widened. So great was her tension, her shoulders cramped. She had to leave this place. *Leave now!* She lowered her sights from the door, released her hold on her teammates, and stepped back. When Celeste gasped, Nora stopped.

A woman was in the doorway.

From where they stood she looked young, maybe in her late teens. Her jeans and blouse clung tightly to her body, betraying how thin she was. Though there was no breeze, the bottom of her long, stringy blonde hair fluttered about her shoulders. Head lowered, the woman shuffled forward two weak steps. Uneasy on her feet, she bobbed left to right. She slipped, falling backward, and raised a hand to hold onto the doorframe for balance. When she was stable, she raised her head.

Too far away to get a good look, Nora couldn't get a handle on her expression.

The woman stared at her audience for a moment and then slid backward, retreating inside the house.

The officer spun toward them. "I'm not positive, but I'm almost certain that was Mr. Lewis' granddaughter, Gam. She's been missing for months."

"Months?" Agnes questioned. "You must've been in this house many times since then."

"We have. Between the calls we've had from concerned neighbors about squatters, suspected drug dealing, and the recent death here, we've searched it from top to bottom many times. I was here just yesterday, and there was no sign of her," the officer explained. "It's possible she's been coming and going, and we've just missed her, but it doesn't add up. The front and rear doors have new locks on the outside, as does the bulkhead leading to the basement. All the windows are secure. I checked them all yesterday, and none were broken-"

"And when we walked around the perimeter minutes ago," Celeste interrupted. "We didn't see any shattered windows or glass on the ground."

The officer nodded. "You ladies stay here. I'm going in the house. The girl appeared dazed. She could be on drugs—or sick. You guys have cell phones?"

Agnes and Celeste confirmed they did but had left them in their purses in their cars.

"Good. If I'm not out in ten minutes call 9-1-1. Tell them to haul ass over here. Don't call before then for any other reason. If it *is* Mr. Lewis' granddaughter, I want to let him know first."

"Excuse me, but that doesn't sound like proper procedure," said

Agnes.

"Look," the officer said plaintively. "Mr. Lewis owns this town, and he owns the chief. I have my orders. If I want to stay on the force, I'm going to do what I'm told." His voice softened. "Just do as I ask. I'll come back out as soon as possible to let you ladies know if everything's okay. Depending on who it is, I can proceed from there. Okay?"

When no one spoke, Agnes answered for the team. "Okay. It's your town."

Nora watched the officer as he approached the front door. He scanned both sides of the house, his right hand hovering above his sidearm. Only when he was within a few feet of the threshold did he focus on what was before him. He crossed the threshold without looking back.

Knowing someone was responsible for the door's opening relieved much of Nora's tension. Though still unnerved, this was something she could handle. Once the officer took the girl into custody, they could leave this place. Whether it was possessed or not, she couldn't get away from the Moore house fast enough. The thought of going back to her condo—her home—put the faintest of smiles on her lips.

Agnes was the first to comment after the officer entered the house. "Well, that was certainly heart-attack fodder."

Nora appreciated the levity, even if it hit close to home. "Yeah, I don't mind saying it scared the crap out of me. I'll be glad when he pulls her out of there, no matter who the hell she is."

"You know," Celeste added, "I asked you guys yesterday if all your investigations were intense. You said they weren't. After spending these past two days with you, I'm not sure I believe you. I don't think I can...." Celeste's sentence died off. The officer was back at the front door of the Moore house. He was alone, waving his arm, motioning for the women to come to him.

CHAPTER 9

"Is he calling us over?" Agnes asked.

"Why would he need us?" replied Nora.

The officer continued to motion to them. After a few moments, Celeste spoke. "Maybe the girl's hurt, and he needs our help."

"Father MacLeod told us not to go into the house. We should listen to him," Nora said, nearly a whisper.

The comment stunned Celeste. *Could the girl have spooked Nora that much? Or does she know something she's not sharing with the team?*

Nora had been so calm at the Millman's investigation. Except for the bit about poker, she was the same the previous evening. After all Nora had been through and seen over the years, why was she so jittery now? Without being aware of it, Celeste's hand went to her chest, her palm resting on the cross beneath her blouse.

The officer's motions grew more frantic. He continued to wave them in, but now he followed it by jabbing his finger, pointing inside the house.

Agnes sighed. "We have no evidence that the house is possessed— in fact, our work this morning indicated the opposite. If that officer needs our assistance, we should help him. That girl could be in trouble, or maybe there are others in the house needing attention. Best case, the girl *is* Gam, and he wants to make sure we let him handle the situation. Worse case, he's calling us over to ask us, for whatever reason, to contact Mr. Lewis."

Celeste thought it over. She stepped away from the women, approached the house, and stopped after covering half the distance.

"Why do you need us?" she shouted.

"It's her," Officer Jones called back. "It's Gam. She's weak, and I need some help moving her to my car. Once we do this, you can be on your way." Without waiting for a reply, he ran back into the house.

"Well, that answers that. Come on, Nora, let's give him a hand, and then get the hell out of here," Agnes responded.

"Amen to that," Nora said, sounding more like she had the day before.

Celeste waited for the two to catch up to her. Once they were together, they walked to the doorway. Celeste peeked inside but didn't see the cop. "Officer Jones?"

There was no response. Raising her voice, she called him again.

"In here," came his reply.

"Well, let's go help the man," Agnes said resignedly.

Celeste led the way, with Nora bringing up the rear. Once they were all inside, Nora asked, "Which way?"

Bam! The front door slammed shut.

Celeste and Agnes pivoted to the door, but Nora yelped and ran straight to Agnes, clinging tightly to her.

"What the hell? What the hell?" Nora repeated as if it were a mantra.

Agnes struggled, trying to pull the woman off her. "Calm down, Nora," she pleaded.

Nora, wide-eyed, cried, "*What the hell is happening with that door?*"

"Hey! What's going on out there?"

Celeste's raised her head, her eyes following the voice to the top of a stairway at the far end of the room. Officer Jones stood, peering down at them.

"I thought I told you ladies to stay outside?" he said, descending.

"Oh God, no," Nora whimpered.

Celeste stiffened. "D-didn't you wave us in from the doorway?"

His face tightened. "What? No, of course not. I've been looking for that girl we saw in the doorway. I've searched the first and second floor but saw nothing. I was about to go up in the attic when I heard a door slam. What are you guys up to?"

Celeste shivered. Agnes was still, staring at the officer, the crow's feet surrounding her eyes more pronounced. Her hold on Nora, whose head was burrowed against Agnes' breasts, tightened.

"Officer." Celeste's voice was soft, pleading. "Please, tell us the truth. Didn't you come to the doorway, tell us you found Gam, and then asked us to help you?"

Officer Jones frowned. "Hell no—I just told you I didn't."

"We saw you. We heard you ask."

He stopped on the last stair and looked at them one at a time. Celeste thought he was waiting for them to admit this was all a joke. If he was, the looks on their faces were the only answer he needed to tell him they weren't kidding. Their frightened expressions must have been convincing—the corners of his mouth curled down, his back straightened, and he peered over their heads.

"That bang I heard. It was the front door?"

"Yes."

He took the last step, brushed past them, and walked to it. He twisted the knob but hesitated before pulling. Celeste, noting his hesitation, walked to his side. His hand gripped the doorknob, yet it rotated between his fingers.

"The hell?" he mumbled.

Celeste backed away, returning to her teammates. "I think we're in trouble."

Nora groaned.

"What's happening?" Agnes asked.

"The doorknob's not working."

"Probably broke when the door slammed shut," Agnes said.

Celeste shook her head. "No, that's not the problem."

Agnes' brow furrowed. The women turned toward the officer.

He stepped closer to the door, wrapped both hands around the spinning knob, and pulled. The door didn't budge. He braced his left foot against the wall for leverage, and then pulled on the door again. Celeste could hear his straining and grunting, but his exertion proved fruitless. After dropping his foot, he waved his hands around like they were on fire. *Friction burns*, Celeste thought. Shaking his head in disbelief, Officer Jones joined the three women.

"You ladies mind telling me *what the hell* is going on here?"

"It's the house." The subdued reply came from Nora. She let go of Agnes and moved to the nearest window. She inspected it, grabbed the bottom sash with both hands and lifted. It didn't budge. She pushed down on the upper portion. Same result. "I think," she hesitated a moment, then continued. "I think we're trapped in here."

"Wait. What? Are you saying the house is alive? That it's keeping us in here?" The officer sneered, but Celeste could tell it was for show. His voice was high, the words rushed—they betrayed his fear.

Nora nodded slowly, staring at the front yard through the window.

Officer Jones rushed to another window and lifted. It wouldn't open. He searched for sliding locks. When he found them, he muttered, "Shit." He hurried into the other rooms, repeating the same word, each time louder than the last. The sound of his fist punching a wall preceded his return. He dashed to the staircase, taking the stairs two at a time. More cursing and thumps against the walls. Celeste's shoulders tightened, and she flinched with each impact. Minutes later he descended at a much slower pace.

Agnes and Nora had remained silent as the officer searched. While Celeste knew they had to be as concerned as she was, their expressions were neutral, which helped keep her own fright in check. She once more recalled their reactions at the Millmans'. They'd been in a supernatural situation and reasoned their way through it. Surely, Agnes and Nora would figure this one out, take control, and get them all out of here. She was about to ask Agnes what they should do when the officer spoke up.

"I don't know what's happening here. I'm going to want answers when we get out, and I intend to get out of this damned house *right now!*"

The furniture in the living room was sparse. A sheet-covered couch was set against one wall with a sheathed recliner beside it, and a mahogany end table in a corner. The officer lifted the table and brought it to the window.

"Stay back."

The women moved to the other side of the room. He stood a few feet from the window, reared back, and threw the end table at it.

The women gasped as the table halted, suspended in midair at the point of impact.

There was no sound when the table struck. Neither the glass nor the wood cracked or shattered. Although it was the table that was frozen, Celeste was the one that shivered. The officer turned to them—his eyes wild, mouth open.

"How—how is this possible?"

"It's the house. It's possessed. By a demon," Nora answered, her voice monotone.

The officer's mouth snapped shut. He lined himself up in front of another window, slid the gun easily from his holster and aimed it at the window. "Screw this house," he mumbled and fired.

This was the first time Celeste had ever been in the vicinity of a firing pistol. She expected a loud bang—a crack that would resonate in her eardrums. Instead, the report sounded more like the whimper of a child's firecracker. *Did the house have anything to do with that?* She had no such questions when it came to the results.

There were no spider web cracks surrounding a small hole anywhere on the glass because there was no hole.

The three women followed the officer to the window. Celeste's shoulders sank when she noticed the bullet. Suspended horizontally from the window, its nose tightly against the glass.

"Oh my God," Celeste whispered.

"God's got nothing to do with this," Agnes shot back.

Officer Jones reached for the bullet.

"I wouldn't do that," admonished Agnes.

He glared at her. "Why not?"

"What happens if you touch that glass or the bullet? You want to be stuck?"

Celeste gave the officer credit: he didn't argue with Agnes or question her logic. He nodded, stepping back from the window.

The officer tried his radio, but it was dead. "You said you have cell phones. Call 9-1-1."

Nora pulled her phone from her pocket. Agnes and Celeste explained once again that their phones were in their purses, which they'd left in their cars.

Flustered, Nora said, "It's not working. I can't get it to turn on." She faced Agnes. "What do we do now?"

"We wait. We stay close to each other—real close, like holding hands close. We do *not* use our talents on the house. You two understand me on that?"

Celeste nodded, along with Nora.

"Something is playing with us. Something powerful. It has the ability to hide from us, to trick us into entering its domain, and to hold us here. To what purpose? I don't know. It could've assaulted us the minute we walked in, maybe even when we were outside. If those police dossiers are any indication, it has the power to kill us, but it hasn't done so. That's in our favor right now."

Officer Jones stared at Agnes, his head shaking. Once she had finished, he jumped into the conversation.

"I don't know what Chief Dodd and Mr. Lewis have gotten me into, but it's starting to scare the shit outa me. You talk about having talents, and something powerful having the ability to kill us. Can you tell me what the hell is going on?"

Agnes pointed to the chair. "Sit down, Officer. We'll tell you everything we know."

He removed the sheet covering the chair as the three women pulled the cloth from the couch. They all took seats, Agnes in the middle of the couch, her hands out to either side. Celeste took one hand, and Nora clasped the other. Agnes explained their empathic abilities, gave a condensed version of some of the cases they'd investigated, recounted the phone call she received from Father MacLeod last evening, and told him about the file they'd viewed.

"So," Officer Jones concluded, "When you ladies stood outside and then walked around the house, you were looking for some kind of supernatural presence."

Celeste nodded, and Agnes verbally confirmed it.

"You know," Jones went on, shaking his head. "Normally I would say this is all bullshit, like something out of a horror movie. But doorknobs don't take on a life of their own. Glass breaks when you strike it. Furniture and bullets don't freeze in midair. And all three of you say you saw me wave you in."

Nora interrupted. "We know it wasn't you, now."

The officer sighed. "I saw that file you said Father MacLeod sent you. I can tell you, I saw every one of those bodies first-hand. None of us could figure out who, or *what* in some of the cases, could do the damage that was done. I mean, what devours a man down to his hips—clothes and all—and then leaves a pair of legs on the ground? Hell, scavengers would have torn the body apart, birds would have feasted. Nothing went close to him, not even for a nibble."

Agnes said, "It wanted them to be found."

"What do you mean *it?* What the hell are we dealing with?"

"A demonic presence, Officer Jones."

"What the hell? A demonic presence? You guys are out of your minds!"

Agnes took a deep breath. "You've seen things here today that don't make sense. That body you described, how come it wasn't touched by animals? The very reason we're in this house is to detect a supernatural presence. You think this is all some kind of game concocted by us or Mr. Lewis simply to scare the hell out of you? Let me tell you something officer, this is no game, we're scared just as much as you are. Demons, the Devil, they're real. As soon as you get your mind around that, your chances of leaving this house increase."

The man's shoulders drooped. His head shook as he looked at the three women. "This is fucking crazy," he mumbled. He took a step back and raised his voice. "Okay, let's say you guys really believe this—that there is a demon holding us here—what the hell do we do?"

"Nothing," Agnes answered, and Nora choked on a sob. "We wait—and we pray," Agnes went on. "Wait for someone to notice we're missing and pray to keep it from hurting or possessing us.

"We'll fight this thing and win, won't we?" Nora said with a sad grin.

Agnes didn't have the chance to answer.

Officer Jones sat bolt upright and froze. His jaw dropped open, his eyes widened to their fullest, and he swung his head toward Celeste.

Unsure of what was happening, she squeezed Agnes' hand. The officer's head turned to one side and then the other, repeating and gaining speed.

He raised his hands to his head. "Make it stop!" he pleaded. "Make it stop!"

Crack.

The bones in his neck snapped. Celeste screamed, and Nora cowered. The rapid motion of his head increased until his features blurred.

He rose from the chair as if unseen hands had slipped under his shoulders and lifted him. His legs swayed like a hanged man's. Officer Jones' head continued its frenzied roil until the top of his scalp touched the ceiling. On contact, the spinning stopped. He dangled in midair, arms limp at his sides.

Celeste clung tightly to Agnes, who stiffened, but did not push her away.

Nora prayed.

"Our Father, in heaven, hallowed be your name...."

Celeste's lips moved, silently reciting the prayer along with Nora. When she finished the line, *forever and ever*, she bowed her head, said "Amen," and glanced up.

The officer glared down at her, his eyes changing—now egg-shaped and devoid of color. Their darkness was as endless as the void she disappeared into whenever she concentrated on her empathic abilities. There were no pinpricks of starlight in those black orbs. No sense of God's wonder. Only hopelessness. He opened his mouth. The cavity's bleakness mirrored his eyes.

Officer Jones descended from the ceiling. As he floated down, his gaze never left Celeste. His feet touched the floor and he stood, unstable, his mouth yawning wide, his head lolling. An invisible force pressed against the officer's back, jutting his midsection forward. He ambled toward her, shuffling one foot, then the other, until he was in front of the couch.

"*You.*" The man's lips never moved. Though he hadn't spoken the word, there was no doubt it came from him.

Unbidden, Celeste picked up on the demon. It wasn't an emotion or sensation she was feeling, but thoughts. *Can it read mine? Are Agnes and Nora hearing this inside their heads?* She observed her partners for a moment and then turned her back to the officer.

"*You. Why are you not like the others?*"

Celeste heard the sentence as a statement, not a question.

Agnes' voice filled the room. "In the name of Jesus Christ, I command you to leave these premises! In the"—her shaky voice belied the authority of the command.

"Shut up, bitch. I'll deal with you and your lover soon."

Celeste heard the otherworldly voice outside her head. There was no question that Agnes also heard it. The woman's jaw dropped, and she pushed further back against the couch.

Celeste took no satisfaction that her assumption about her partners had been correct. Instead, anger overpowered her fear. "What do you want from us?"

The demon ignored her. It raised Officer Jones' hand, rubbed his chin and pulled at it while gazing at Agnes and Nora. After a pause, he grinned.

"*You are a means to an end.*" He was quiet for a few moments, then added, "*In the meantime, I will enjoy all of you.*"

Officer Jones' body snapped back and away from the couch,

79

landing upright, seated in the recliner like a king on a throne. All the while, the demon kept its dark gaze on Celeste. After a moment, the body fell limp.

CHAPTER 10

Father MacLeod parked his car in the lot behind the building housing his office. It was a former post office—circa 1940s—with stately columns, wide steps in the front, and multiple loading docks in the rear. Heavy loads of mail had taken their toll on the pavement over the years. The parking lot was roughshod from frost heaves and cracks, and black paving chalk had prevented weeds from sprouting.

Over the past few years, the maintenance staff had struggled with the decay, but the patchwork was an eyesore. For the priest, it was also shudder-inducing. Those ebony, chalky tendrils grew more numerous each passing season. They were wider than ever, their reach expanding. The repairs reeked of advancing malevolence; only the sanctity of the Church held them at bay.

He knew the notion was ridiculous. The Church was so incompetent it couldn't make a dog sit with the promise of a treat. When it came to evil, the Church was good at one thing—mopping up, and with mixed results at that. Catherine White was a good example.

As he climbed the stone steps to the rear entrance, Catherine stayed on his mind—below him, in the bowels of the building, the exorcists sent by the Vatican were working on the young woman. He'd stopped praying for her; they didn't do much good. And hope? Hope was a bedfellow to prayer—a lifeline for the despondent; those too weak to take matters into their own hands. How many times had he heard someone utter the phrase, *I hope to God*? Well, he had news for those people. God intervened only when the urge took him. No, He couldn't be counted on for much. So far, God hadn't given a rat's ass about Catherine—or him, for that matter. Though the priest had to admit it would be nice if God did snap to attention and bestow a sliver of salvation to both of them.

Yet, he maintained his belief in God. Who wouldn't, in the line of business he was in? He had first-hand knowledge, a chair at the table, a bird's eye view—the metaphors were endless—that the soul lived on after death. The problem was, he had only seen one side of that coin—hell's dominion. Where were the angels that floated on high to provide guidance? Where were the twentieth-century miracles taking place? Did the term *second coming* only apply to porn movies? Why in the hell hadn't He cured cancer? Cleaned up the water in Flint? Aborted Hitler? Why hadn't He prevented a young priest from negotiating with the Devil twenty years ago?

The first floor of the building was full of life for so late in the afternoon. Walking down the hall, he tipped his head, waved hello, and spoke to those who acknowledged him. His smile was as dead as his soul. Entering his office, he pushed through, closed the door, and leaned against it. After exhaling, he raised his head to see his secretary staring at him.

"Good afternoon, Linda."

"Good afternoon, Father."

"Any messages?"

"Umm, yeah. I kept trying to call you, got voicemail every time. You should've called back."

He squinted his eyes. He hadn't heard his phone ring. Removing it from his pocket, he saw the screen was blank. He hit the power button to no avail.

I thought I charged this last night.

"Phone's dead. Sorry about that, Linda. What's up?"

"Mr. Lewis called. Three times and..." The landline rang. "Hang on a minute. Father MacLeod's office. Yes, Mr. Lewis, he just walked in.

Hang on."

Linda shrugged as she gave the priest a crooked smile. "He's on line one."

"I'll take it in my office."

He closed the door, sat, and stared at the phone. He had no idea how Mr. Lewis would take the news. Father MacLeod anticipated that the man would want specifics. He could be on the phone for a while.

"Father MacLeod. Can I help you, Mr. Lewis?"

"Yes, I hope so. What happened at the Moore house this morning?"

The priest wanted to put the appropriate spin on things, so the man would put the issue to rest. He responded in an upbeat manner.

"Well, as we discussed, I did attend the investigation with my team at the house this morning. We were there for around half an hour. I assume you know all of this, as the local police had a representative at the scene. I can report that the ladies didn't pick up on any demonic presence from the residence."

"I had arranged for the keys to the Moore house to be available to you. You saw me hand them over to the officer. Did you enter the house, Father MacLeod?"

After a pause, the priest replied. "No. We did a sweep on the outside."

Mr. Lewis was silent for a moment. "How did the investigation conclude?"

Father MacLeod's head inched back. "As I said, we found nothing. The Moore house is not haunted."

"That's not what I'm asking. What happened to you and your team after the investigation finished?"

Fear rippled up the priest's spine. *Does he know where I went after I left? Did he have someone follow me?* He forced himself to calm down. "I left as soon as the determination was made. I gave the house a blessing and then I left to attend to some appointments I had scheduled."

"You left before the others?"

What the hell is going on? "Yes, there was no need for me to stay. Why do you ask?"

"The officer who attended your investigation is missing."

"What?"

"His patrol car is still parked in front of the house. As are three other vehicles, which I assume belong to your team. Have you heard from them?"

Father MacLeod went numb. He leaned forward, resting his elbows on his desk. "No, I haven't, but I just stepped in. Has anyone gone inside the house?"

"Chief Dodd became concerned when Jones didn't check in. They tried his radio and cell phone; no answer on either. The chief drove there and saw Jones' vehicle parked on the road. He then attempted to enter the house, but all the entrances were locked. He tried the windows to see if anyone was inside, but he didn't see them.

"There was no sign of my team?"

"No. From what he could see, the house was empty. He was so concerned, though, he attempted to break one of the windows with the butt of his gun. When that didn't work, he fired a shot into it. The glass remained whole."

Father MacLeod mumbled, "Oh, shit."

"What was that, Father?"

The priest's free hand went to his chin. "Nothing, Mr. Lewis. What's happening now?"

"Chief Dodd is calling for a locksmith. If that doesn't work, he'll break the door down. The locksmith should be there soon. If they can enter the house, he'll call for back up. I want you there, Father

MacLeod, and damn it, I want you inside of that house if they can get you in. I'm not sure what's going on, but I'll be damned if I have the deaths of any more people on my conscience."

The priest sighed. "I'll be there. Give me an hour and a half."

"I'll meet you there."

The men hung up.

Father MacLeod rushed out the door. "Linda, have Agnes, Nora or Celeste called?"

"No, Father."

"Call them. Each of them. Whoever answers first, put them through to me right away."

"Yes, Father."

As the secretary punched the direct dial on her phone, the priest returned to his office. He fished out his charger from a desk drawer and plugged it in. The phone didn't light up. *What the hell is wrong with this thing?* He unplugged it and pocketed the phone with the intention of charging it in his car on the way to Goffstown. He sat in his chair, pulling at his beard. After a moment, he glared at the ceiling. *Why the hell can't you leave me alone?*

Linda's voice came over the intercom. "Father MacLeod?"

"Yes."

"No answer from either their home phones or cells. Do you want me to keep trying?"

"No."

The secretary cut off without a reply.

The priest stood, gazed around the office for a moment, and then walked out.

"Linda, if any of the three women call, tell them to try my cell phone. If they can't get through, they should call the Goffstown Police Department and ask for Chief Dodd and explain to him who and where they are."

"Okay. Do they have the number?"

"Look it up and give it to them. If they can't get me, tell them I'll call back as soon as I can."

He hurried down the marble steps leading to the parking lot but stopped before his foot landed on the last one.

Black veins crisscrossed the bottom step. They shimmied like worms struggling on a driveway in the afternoon sun. The inky lines rose from the step as high as half an inch before the marble appeared to suck them back down. The priest's ears pricked. Like a bag full of cats drowning, he heard their calls to be freed from the Church's grasp. Dark wisps materialized and floated over the veins and the scent of sulfur filled his nose. He raised his head to the parking lot. It was a sea of black writing tendrils. They were waiting. For him.

His body tensed and he closed his eyes. When he looked again, they were gone.

CHAPTER 11

The screams came from all directions. As sharp as knives, they sliced through Celeste's head, and she wondered which of her two teammates were responsible for them. Despite the pain, she was unable to pull her eyes from the possessed body of Officer Jones. She stood frozen, horrified by the awkward angle of his neck. The screaming ebbed, faded to an echo, and then rose again. It was high pitched and consisted of a single syllable that never varied.

Ahhhhhh...

The sound sent needles from the back of her head down to the curve of her back. The urge to comfort or confront the source of the wailing was overwhelming, but first, she had to fight the fear paralyzing her.

Celeste forced herself to close her eyes. After a moment, the seeds of control took root. The muscles in her upper body relaxed and her shoulders sagged. A heaviness overcame her, and her knees bent from the weight. With some effort, she angled her head toward Agnes and Nora.

She opened her eyes.

Nora had her arms wrapped around Agnes' midsection. Both women were shaking, their jaws clenched tight, their eyes wild and focused on the officer.

If their mouths are closed, who's screaming?

The answer came quickly. They were emanating from inside her head—from the part of her that wanted nothing more to do with dead men, demons, and the Moore house. She kneeled, covered her head with her hands and rocked her upper body in time to the screams. *Calm down, calm down, you'll get through this.* She repeated the phrase, again and again, letting the words bleed through her fear and blanket it. Soon, she heard only the mantra.

Celeste straightened and faced the two women. The movement caught Agnes' attention who made eye contact with her. Agnes exhaled deeply and nodded. Celeste was grateful that Agnes appeared to be aware of the situation, that she hadn't succumbed to shock. Nora wasn't faring as well. Her gaze remained on the body in the chair. Her head shook rapidly as if a continuing denial of the situation was enough to make it go away. Tears from overly wide and red eyes trailed down her cheeks. Celeste gently called to her, but there was no response. She positioned herself in front of Nora, but the woman stared right through her. Celeste called to her once more, but this time she placed a hand on Nora's shoulders.

Nora jumped at the touch. Her wild gaze shot to Celeste.

"Nora, it's me," Celeste calmly responded. "Come on, you have to snap out of this, we have to figure a way out of here."

Agnes removed Nora's arms from around her waist and took a step back. "He's gone for now, dear. Celeste is right, we need to stay calm."

Nora's head swiveled back and forth between the two of them. Finally, her panicked features softened and she lowered her gaze. Shoulders slumped, she let out a tired breath.

"I—I'm scared. I've never been more scared in my life."

Agnes wrapped her arms around her. "We're all scared, dear."

"I know, but this isn't like me to react this way. "

Celeste spoke up. "Nora, we need to do is stay level-headed, figure a way out of here or wait for help to arrive…."

A loud voice cut Celeste off.

"Ha!"

The three women shrieked, grabbed onto each other, and took two steps backward. Celeste looked to Officer Jones' body, but there were no signs of movement.

Nora groaned. "What are we going to do?"

Agnes who took control as she broke off from the others. "When help arrives," she said pointing, "I'd like to be next to those windows. I say we sit on the couch to wait, think this thing over. We should be able to hear them when they arrive."

Nora sobbed. "We won't last that long."

An hour had passed since the officer's death. In that time, Nora had done nothing but whimper and cling to Agnes. Agnes had never seen her so vulnerable, and she ached to protect her lover. As they sat on the couch, she cradled Nora tight to her breast, gently running her fingers through her hair.

Celeste was harder to read. She'd been quiet, but with the occasional movement of her lips, Agnes assumed the young woman's thoughts were racing. The demon had commented that Celeste was different. Was she trying to make sense of that statement? Initially, Agnes assumed the word *different* had something to do with sexual preference, but she didn't know Celeste well enough to come to that conclusion. While some sisters had joined the Church *because* of their attraction to women, many others had discovered their sexual orientation while in service. From what she did know of Celeste, the woman had strong faith in doctrine. Leviticus 18:22 popped into Agnes' head. *Thou shalt not lie with mankind, as with womankind: it is abomination.* While most of the scriptures addressed males when it came to homosexuality, the Church made it uncomfortably clear that it also applied to women. Though Agnes couldn't be certain, she doubted Celeste harbored same-sex desires. Then again, the woman *had* been removed from the Church.

Though it had never officially been broached, all of Agnes' teammates, present and past, had an unspoken rule: never ask the others about the circumstances that led to their leaving the Church. Father MacLeod had that knowledge, and he'd vowed during Agnes' initial interview never to divulge it to her partners. He'd followed it up by stating he would also respect her teammates' privacy. As close as she and Nora were, the subject had never come up, and she had no intention of having the discussion with her.

Nora clung tighter as if she were reading Agnes' thoughts. Agnes leaned over and kissed the top of the woman's head. Nora's right hand slid across Agnes' belly, and she paused there to rub it. She appreciated the intimacy and smiled, but then stiffened when Nora's hand cupped her breast. The fondling continued for a few moments before Nora's hand squeezed. Pain radiated through Agnes' breast, but as she pulled Nora's hand away, something moved in front of them.

Officer Jones' body.

Its head had straightened, and it stared at her with dead, black eyes. Its mouth had been forced into a grin.

It winked.

Agnes pushed Nora away, creating a distance between them. Recoiling, she pressed herself tighter against the back of the couch. The dead man closed his eyes and its head dropped, but the grin remained. Agnes thought it looked like a rag doll. *Puppet* might've been a better term.

"What's the matter?" Nora's voice was tinged with hurt.

Agnes peered into her lover's eyes and saw only innocence and uncertainty. *She doesn't know what she did. It's in her head, messing with her. Messing with me.*

"Nothing, dear," Agnes managed to say. "I got spooked, is all. Come back and lean against me. Try to clear your mind. Don't let the demon know you're thinking about it."

"Wait. Why? Did you pick up on something?"

"Yes." She paused. "No." Another pause. "Maybe. I don't know. Something just occurred to me, but I have to sort it out."

"If you can," Nora pleaded, "Do it fast, please. And let us know what you come up with."

Agnes pulled Nora closer. "Yes, dear. I will. Celeste, you okay?"

"Yes. Something happen?"

"Well, Officer Jones over there winked at me. Could be I imagined it."

"I doubt that."

"Yeah, you're right. It happened. I'm surprised that not much else has. Why hasn't it made a move on us?"

"I think it's waiting for Father MacLeod," Celeste answered.

Nora leaned forward. "Father MacLeod? Why would it wait for him?"

"I've been replaying the possession in my mind," Celeste answered. "I keep coming back to something it did before it forced Officer Jones' body into the chair. Remember when it said, "You are a means to an end?"

Agnes nodded. "Yes, and then it said it would enjoy all of us in the meantime."

Nora jumped in. "You said there was also something it *did*. What was that?"

Celeste went on. "Before it answered me, it did something with his hand. You remember?"

Agnes thought a moment. "I do. It rubbed the officer's chin."

"It didn't just rub it. It pulled at it. Who does that remind you of?"

"That's not much to go on," Agnes said. "It could be a coincidence."

"Maybe. Maybe not. I've been running this through my mind for the last hour. On the two previous occasions, you've experienced possessions, Father MacLeod was present, and he was here for this one. Earlier, when we finished our investigation, Father MacLeod was in a hurry to leave. His relief at our outcome was almost over the top. Looking back, I think he embraced it as a personal victory, not a spiritual one."

"So, you think there's some kind of relationship between the demon and Father MacLeod?"

Celeste didn't answer right away. After a few moments, she said, "Yes."

"The Cavalry is here." The voice came from Officer Jones' direction. All eyes settled on him, but his body remained limp.

Agnes walked to the window. A locksmith's van was pulling up to the curb. She also noticed another police cruiser parked behind their cars.

"Hey, come and look at this!" Her voice was light, the tone hopeful. Celeste and Nora joined her.

The locksmith met up with a police officer at the rear of the van. After removing a toolbox, they strode toward the front door. Agnes waved at them through the window, but neither responded. Celeste and Nora joined in, jumping and screaming, hoping to get their attention.

"Why can't they see us?" asked Nora.

"It's blocking us," answered Celeste.

"Well," added Agnes, "It's not blocking everything."

The locksmith had stepped to the window. His eyes were focused on the table affixed to the glass.

Agnes could hear their conversation.

The officer said, "Yeah, this is some weird shit right here. Let's get this over with."

Minutes later, Agnes heard the whirring of a drill. The three of them hurried to the front. They could hear the drill wheezing as the bit pressed against the metal.

Agnes shook as she waited for freedom. She saw Celeste and Nora, their eyes trained on the lock, leaning forward in anticipation.

The wheezing stopped.

The bit did not extrude from the lock. The door remained closed.

Agnes heard the men.

"Chief, I've never seen this before. The drill bit's melted."

"What? How can that be?"

"Don't know. It's carbide, that lock should have a hole in it by now."

"You got more drill bits?"

"Yeah."

"Let's try the padlock on the back door, and if that doesn't work, we'll try the one on the bulkhead."

The voices faded. The three women moved to the back door. They heard clicking, and then the drill started. Less hopeful, the women waited again.

The results were the same.

In the quiet after the drill was turned off, the locksmith moved the padlock and pressed his eye close to the hole where the doorknob was supposed to be.

Nora bent low and shouted, "Help us! Please help us!"

The locksmith's eye moved left to right a few times, then disappeared.

"Can't see anyone inside there, Chief. Just an old kitchen."

"Okay, let's try the bulkhead."

Nora pounded on the door. "Don't go! Please, get us out of here!"

Agnes didn't expect a reply.

Celeste asked if they should go into the basement and wait by the bulkhead. Agnes was quick to respond.

"I have no idea what's in that cellar, and I'm not sure the lights are even turned on in this house. It'd be the perfect place for the demon to screw with us. Anyway, we'll know right away if those two get in, but I'm not holding out any hope."

"Yeah, that makes sense," Celeste replied. "I'm going to find the door that leads downstairs and stand by it. If they do make it through, I want to make sure they can hear us."

The three women found a door off of the hallway that led to the cellar. Agnes opened it, glancing at the walls on either side of the stairs. She flicked a light switch. The cellar remained dark. "Like I said, we stay up here."

Though muted, the familiar whine of the drill drifted up to them. It soon stopped. The three of them waited. A *thunk* against the bulkhead vibrated through the cellar and up the stairway. It was followed by another, and then a series.

Nora identified the sound. "They're trying to hammer the lock off."

The pounding stopped. They heard no squeaking of hinges, no sunlight brightening the cellar, just a long silence. Hurrying to the front windows, they saw the locksmith and the police officer walking across the front yard to their vehicles.

Nora slapped at the window. "No! Don't leave us here!"

Agnes was relieved Nora's hand didn't stick to the glass.

Celeste mumbled, "Well, I think that's one more piece of evidence."

"Evidence?" Agnes asked. "Of what?"

"That it's waiting for Father MacLeod. It's not going to allow anyone in, or let us leave."

Agnes absorbed Celeste's comment. Then she spoke. "Speak of the Devil."

Father MacLeod rushed past the line of cars parked in the street, toward the locksmith and cop. Before he reached them, another vehicle pulled in behind him. An old man in a suit exited the car. Taking hesitant steps, he walked toward the Moore house.

CHAPTER 12

Father MacLeod ignored Mr. Lewis and approached the police officer. "What happened, Chief? Did you get in?"

"No. The drill bits melted. *They freaking melted!* Three of them. We tried breaking one of the locks and didn't even scratch the damn thing," answered the chief, his voice shaking.

"Melted?"

"Yeah. And that's not the only messed-up thing about that house. Go look at that window to the left of the front door. On the inside, there's a freaking table sticking out of it. It's suspended there, on the glass, without support. I was here earlier and tried to break the glass. I even shot at it. The bullet bounced off. And that does *not* look like bulletproof glass."

The locksmith left the officer's side and opened the rear doors of his van. The priest and the police officer watched silently as he tossed the toolbox inside. He closed the doors.

"I'm outta here. Don't ask me to come back," he shouted to the chief, slipped into the van, and drove away.

Behind the priest, Mr. Lewis commented. "It would appear the locksmith was not successful."

Father MacLeod didn't respond.

"Are they inside?" asked the old man.

"We looked in the windows, but didn't see anyone," the chief said. "They could be upstairs or in the basement, but we didn't hear anyone. If they're in there, they're locked in tight."

Mr. Lewis regarded the man. "Let's take another look, shall we?" The old man walked to the front door without waiting for a response.

Father MacLeod and the chief followed.

There was no sign the lock had been tampered with, but there were slivers and gobs of metal on the floorboards. No one bothered to try the door.

The chief pointed. "Over there is the window I was talking about." He stepped toward it, the other two following.

Once they reached it, Father MacLeod froze. He could see Agnes, Celeste, and Nora, banging on the glass, pleading for help. Stunned, the priest quickly regarded Mr. Lewis and the chief. They were stone-faced; both studied the glass, their eyes on the table. *They can't see them,* Father MacLeod realized and returned his attention to the women. Though all three were screaming and weeping, he couldn't hear them. He studied their lips—Celeste was repeating *help us,* while Agnes shouted *Father MacLeod* over and again. Nora's lips were alternately tight and twisted open, soaked with tears. His own eyes watered. He reached a hand up to the women.

Agnes, Celeste, and Nora went still. The priest saw the fear etched on their faces. The women slowly turned.

Behind them, Officer Jones rose from his chair, his motions jerky, his stance uneasy. He shuffled out of view, towards the front door.

The priest stepped back from the window, his gaze shifting to the entrance. Mr. Lewis and the chief took note. They stood on either side of him.

Cackling exploded inside Father MacLeod's head, the volume escalating, the laughter's echo careening through his skull. His hands went to his ears as he fell to his knees. He screamed in pain and slammed his head against the grass to dislodge the sound. His hands went to his ears, and blood pooled in his palms.

In time, the cackling stopped—the ringing in his ears its only remnant. Dazed, he stood and stared at the door until the ringing subsided, but now a voice arose, low and guttural.

"Welcome to hell, priest."

Father MacLeod backed a few paces, separating himself from Mr. Lewis and the chief. "Move," he hollered. "Get away from the house. Do it now!"

The two men didn't question the order. With the priest leading, they rushed toward the street. When Mr. Lewis slowed, the chief grabbed his arm and pulled him along. Father MacLeod stopped on the grass, shy of the cars, and the others followed suit. Breathing heavily, they faced the building.

The three men held their breath and remained still, as the front door of the Moore house inched open. Officer Jones stood in the doorway, knees bent, head lowered, leaning against the frame for support.

"Jones! Jones! Are you okay?" Chief Dodd called to the officer.

Father MacLeod placed a blood-stained hand on the chief's arm. "That's not Jones."

"What the hell are you talking about? That's Jones; there's no doubt in my mind."

"He's been possessed. He might even be dead, from the way he looks."

Mr. Lewis spoke up. "Chief, you know something's not right about that house. The reason Father MacLeod is here is that since my granddaughter disappeared, I've suspected the house is possessed by something—I don't know what. But please, Chief, listen to the man."

"No offense, Mr. Lewis, but that's crazy talk. I have an officer over there who appears to be in trouble. He's one of my men, and I'm going to him." He didn't wait for a response. With his hand on the butt of his gun, the chief hurried to his officer.

Father MacLeod followed the man's progress.

The police chief climbed the steps, approached the open doorway, and stopped in his tracks. Father MacLeod heard some words from the chief but couldn't make them out. However, he *could* hear the response from Officer Jones.

"Welcome to the party, adulterer."

The chief stepped back. The priest saw the butt of the pistol rise out of the holster, but before the chief could remove the gun completely, the demon struck, wrapping a hand around the chief's throat. It happened so fast, it took Father MacLeod a moment to process it. The chief was lifted from the porch and tossed into the Moore house. Officer Jones followed, and the door slammed shut behind him.

Father MacLeod and Mr. Lewis exchanged a glance. Their attention quickly returned to the house when two gunshots rang out. Mr. Lewis gasped, and the priest closed his eyes.

The door to the Moore house opened, the doorway empty. Father MacLeod and Mr. Lewis ran to the street. When they arrived at the priest's car, both looked back at the house.

"He's not coming out, is he?" Mr. Lewis asked, breaking the silence.

The priest shook his head. "No."

"Let me ask you something, Father. When we were all standing by the window, did you see something we didn't?"

The priest lowered his head and spat on the ground. "Yeah."

"What did you see?"

Father MacLeod focused on the window. "My team is still in there. They were banging on the window, begging for help. I couldn't hear them, but there was no question they were in distress. I also saw Officer Jones' body sprawled in a chair. I thought he was dead. When he rose and shuffled to the door, I got a good look at him and confirmed it."

Mr. Lewis sighed. "We now have two police officers trapped inside the Moore house. It's only a matter of time before this place is saturated with more police and possibly the media. To be honest, Father, I don't know if that's a good or bad thing."

The priest faced the old man. "It's a bad thing. The demon will likely kill everyone inside, and I can assure you the deaths will not be linked to supernatural causes. The killings, like those in the past, will be unsolved and attributed to either suicide or murder. Your quaint little town is going to be on every news show and featured in every tabloid in the country. After the attention fades, it will kill again. The demon must be exorcised, Mr. Lewis. It's the only way to stop it."

Both men were startled by the front door slamming.

"You were in obvious pain after looking into the window, but neither the chief nor I felt anything. Now that you're a distance from the house, it appears that its influence is weakened, or even gone. Let me ask you two things. Is this demon targeting you? And is its influence dependent on proximity?"

Father MacLeod avoided eye contact. "To answer your first question, I don't think it's personal if that's what you mean. My collar is reason enough for it to, as you put it, target me. Secondly, yes, the demon's reach is limited. In past cases, the influence of a demon has been closely centered on its host. There is an exception. A demon can impart evil to an inanimate object, and he can have that object materialize in any location he chooses. The object itself is benign—it can't physically cause possession, destruction, or death. However, if someone touches the object, the demon establishes a link with that person. It can read their minds, discover their fears, and manipulate them to a certain extent. This manipulation usually takes the form of nightmares or hallucinations. Eventually, the infected person is led to the demon by suggestion."

"Would a hypodermic needle be one example of an inanimate object?"

"Yes."

After a few moments of silence, Father MacLeod opened his car door.

"Where are you going?"

"I think you're right, Mr. Lewis—we don't have much time. There's someone I need to talk to before I go into that house."

"How long will it take?"

The priest shook his head. "I'm not sure. Four hours at the earliest. Is there something you can do to hold off more police presence?"

"I'll try. But first," Mr. Lewis said, turning his back to Father MacLeod, "There's someone I need to talk to, as well."

CHAPTER 13

Ignoring the warnings, Chief Dodd rushed to assist his officer. He stepped onto the porch and stopped in his tracks. The priest's words echoed in his mind, *he might even be dead.* One look at Officer Jones left no doubt in Dodd's mind—the man *was* dead. Sores, oozing a black oily liquid, covered his skin. Blisters had exploded around the officer's mouth. The man's nose was flayed, the cartilage exposed. As gruesome as it was, it was Jones' eyes that scared the hell out of the chief. They were dark pits, their depth endless.

The dead man smiled. *"Welcome to the party, adulterer."*

The chief's spine froze. *How does he know?* he wondered.

He pulled his gun, but it never made it out of his holster before Jones' hand clamped onto his throat and lifted him off the porch. Eyes bulging and gasping for breath, the chief's hands went to his neck. His view of Jones receded, and then everything around him was in motion. The pressure on his neck disappeared as a solid wall of white rushed toward him. Drywall crumbled, and shards of pain exploded from his collarbone as he felt and heard the bones in his left shoulder snap. He fell to his ass on the floor, crying out and reaching for his injured shoulder.

Behind him, the front door of the Moore house slammed shut. Brain-fogged, he gazed around the room. Despite the pain and confusion, his instincts were intact, and he searched for his officer. He didn't see Jones, but three women were cowering by a window—the priest's team.

He found it odd that they weren't coming to his aid, huddling close to each other instead. One was crying and the other two, their eyes widened with shock. Only they weren't looking at him—it was if he wasn't there. All three had their gazes locked above him. The chief tilted his head back.

Officer Jones stared down at him; the dead man floating upside down, his face hovering inches from the chief's. Dodd couldn't drag his gaze away from Jones' eyes. The blackness within, shifting and spiraling into emptiness. The chief felt himself slipping away into that inky vortex.

No! the chief's mind screamed, resisting. He concentrated, pushing away the pain and willing his eyes to close. He battled the vortex, his consciousness ebbing and flowing. During his lucid moments, thoughts of his family anchored him. On the verge of giving in to the darkness, images of Beth, Officer Jones' wife, naked and on her knees, flashed before him. He tried to sweep aside the guilt and eroticism, clinging instead to thoughts of his own wife and daughter. He knew he'd succeeded when the tension fled his body and pain returned to his shoulder with a hostile vengeance. Head hung low, he took heavy breaths, waiting for his mind to clear. After resting a few moments, he lifted his chin.

Officer Jones' wife called his name.

Halfway across the room, Beth knelt before him, her generous breasts hanging low and heavy. Her knees were slightly parted, granting him a glimpse of her sex. Fingers gently probed her cleft, leaving a glistening trail on her thighs. The woman's lips were a deep red, forming a promise in the shape of a perfect O. Curled auburn hair framed her face, partially covering feral eyes.

"*Donald,*" she purred.

He couldn't look away.

"*Donald, let's leave this place. He's gone: it's just you and me now. Oh, the things I want to do to you.*"

Beth had never looked so good. The pain in his shoulder had somehow lessened, no longer enough to prevent his arousal. Thoughts of his family, the three women in the room, and Beth's dead husband faded—the only thing on his mind was feeling those perfect lips between his legs.

"Come closer," he ordered.

The woman crawled toward him on all fours. The chief heard muted shouts, coming from a distance.

"No! It's not real! It's the demon!"

A murky memory of three women standing by a window coalesced inside his head. The shouting continued, and the image became clearer. *The priest's team.*

He refocused on Beth as she crawled towards him. She was different than he remembered. This Beth was facially perfect. The Beth he was familiar with had mild chickenpox scaring about her cheeks. The Beth before him had plump, enviable lips, but the lips he'd so often kissed were thin. He had fondled and sucked upon Beth's breasts plenty of times; they were in no way as bountiful as those of the woman crawling toward him.

"Stop!" he ordered.

She did. Rising off her hands, she leaned back, sitting on her calves. She pushed the curls back from her forehead, revealing her wide, soulless eyes, now as black and empty as a starless night.

The chief drew his gun and pointed. When she laughed, the chief fired twice, but her laughter continued.

The woman leaped. There was no time to react. She landed with her knees straddling his torso, her face inches from his. She tilted her head left and then right, birdlike, as she took measure of him. He pushed his head against the wall as the perfect O of her lips grew larger, widening and expanding, finally overtaking her features until her face looked to be all mouth. Row upon row of teeth tightly lined the circumference, continuing backward and down, disappearing into the darkness of her throat. Her tongue, blistered, and as black as her eyes, caressed those teeth.

Dodd tried to avert his gaze, to look away, but her voice immobilized him.

"Come," she said. *"I have a special place for you, Chief."*

Their faces touched.

CHAPTER 14

Finished with feasting on Chief Dodd, the demon conformed into its earlier, sexier incarnation of Beth Jones. It refocused attention to Celeste and her teammates. Although Celeste abhorred having anything to do with the demon, she kept her gaze on it. The alternative was worse in her mind—a view of the chief's bloody and broken body. The demon had consumed the man's head down to his neck, and now it stood over its meal, glaring as if daring the three of them to object. While Celeste had been repulsed enough to gag while the demon feasted, she'd kept her wits about her, as did Agnes. Nora screamed through the ordeal until she couldn't scream anymore. Once her voice failed, her terror had manifested as sobs, and she once again buried her face against Agnes.

Despite the wincing, screaming, and wailing of the three women, the sounds of snapping bones and rending of flesh had risen above their din. Celeste had covered her ears with her palms at one point, and they stayed there until the demon was sated. She'd kept her eyes open throughout the ordeal even though she was desperate to close them. If the demon came for her, she didn't want to be taken by surprise. She would not go quietly into that dark abyss.

The demon's gaze moved past Celeste to the window. Its eyes, although black, burned with fury. Lifting a delicate hand, it pointed a slender finger to the glass.

"He's gone," spoke the demon.

She and Agnes turned to look out the window. Father MacLeod and the old man were nowhere to be seen. Celeste craned her neck; Father MacLeod's car was also gone.

"Why would he leave us?" Agnes whispered tearfully. "He knows we are in here."

"Because he's a coward," the demon responded. "He's sacrificed others at my altar before—"

"No." Celeste interrupted. "He wouldn't leave us unless he had a reason. He'll be back."

A grin formed on the demon's lips. "I've got all the time in the world, but I can't say the same for you three."

The demon turned its back to the three women. As it walked to the hallway, the woman's visage faded. It vanished on her fourth step with a sucking *pop,* near the wall beside which the chief's body lay. Blood, bits of bone, and scraps of flesh and clothing absorbed into the floor, disappearing from sight.

Celeste and Agnes stared at one another.

"I know what you're thinking," said Agnes, "And no, we didn't imagine it."

Celeste inhaled loudly and exhaled just as noisily. She shook her head. "No, I guess not."

"What do we do now?" Nora's eyes were puffy and red from sobbing. She stepped away from Agnes.

Celeste's heart went out to her. Watching men die was certainly not in their job description.

"I don't know. I'm sure Father MacLeod will be . . ." Agnes started to answer but lowered her gaze to the floor.

Celeste felt a tremor through her shoes. The vibrations were light, more of a tickling sensation than anything else. They faced each other, uncertainty clouding their features.

"This ain't good," Celeste said.

Agnes agreed. "Let's go sit on the couch and get off the floor."

The three women walked to the couch and sat in the same

locations as earlier, their legs tucked under them. Celeste could still feel the tingling through the couch.

Agnes instructed them to hold hands.

"Remember, we have to stick together. Don't let it break us apart," Celeste added.

"Celeste, why do I feel better when we're holding hands?" Agnes asked after a few moments.

"Yes, I feel the same," Nora said "It's hard to explain, but it's like we're putting up some kind of defense."

"I—I don't know," Celeste replied. "I don't feel any different when we're holding hands. Maybe it's psychological?"

"No," Agnes stressed, "It's more than that. The demon said you are different. Is there something about you that sets you apart from us? It senses that. Think. Do you—"

Celeste's torso jerked forward, her head snapping back. A view of the ceiling morphed into one of the floor. Her forehead connected with something hard and the pain was immediate. She raised a shaky hand to her face and rubbed above her left eye. She took in her surroundings. Agnes was on the floor to her left, as was Nora, on the other side of Agnes. The women groaned, and Celeste was relieved when both women began moving. Above and behind the two women, the couch hovered, suspended three feet in the air, tipped forward and still in motion.

"Crawl!" Celeste shouted.

Agnes and Nora slid forward, neither taking the time to get on their knees. The couch slammed to the floor, pieces flying in all directions. The floorboards split beneath the couch, creating fractures that traveled beneath and beyond the three women and continuing to the wall and the chair that held Officer Jones' body. The dead man's black eyes were fully open and trained on Nora. Before Celeste could warn her partner, pain wracked her body. Countless electrically charged needles pierced her skin, stealing the breath from her.

Cries arose to her left, where Agnes and Nora convulsed on the floor. Celeste struggled to stand. The pain in her body abated, but the stinging, needle sensations in her feet persisted, though her sneakers appeared to provide some insulation.

"Stand up!" she hollered to her teammates. "Get your exposed skin off the floor."

Celeste wrapped her arms around Agnes' waist and lifted her to her feet, then repeated the effort with Nora. The three stood there, shaken, confused, and breathing heavily.

A loud report like a shotgun blast exploded beneath them and the cracks on the floor began to multiply and elongate. The sound of wood breaking intensified—the shotgun blast morphing into automatic-rifle fire. Portions of the floor crumbled and fell inward, creating holes like jagged toothed maws. Celeste and Agnes, the tips of their shoes perched precariously on tattered shards of wood, leaped to safety. They could only watch as Nora, her eyes frantic, her hands desperately clutching, fell through the splintered floorboards and down into the basement.

"Nora!" Agnes screamed.

The splits on the floor shuddered and shifted as if hearing Agnes' voice. They lengthened and widened, redirecting their course towards the two remaining women.

"Run!" yelled Celeste.

Agnes' gaze went from the hole Nora had fallen through to Celeste, the older woman's eyes wide and blinking rapidly. She looked once more into the hole, turned and sped past Celeste into the hallway.

She's going to the basement door, Celeste realized and attempted to follow, but another resounding crack split the air and a new hole opened between her and the hallway, blocking her pursuit of Agnes. The house pitched and groaned as more holes appeared.

Searching for a path to escape, Celeste found only one — one she dreaded. She hopped across the spreading cracks, heading toward the stairway. As her foot landed on the first step, she understood what had happened.

The demon had split them up.

CHAPTER 15

Mr. Kevin Lewis lingered in front of the pawnshop's glass doors, back stooped, both arms hanging limply by his sides. A reflection of a tired old man stared back at him.

His research into Father MacLeod had led him to believe the man was seriously flawed, but he couldn't blame the priest or the Church itself for the circumstances that now brought him back to the shop.

Mr. Lewis had been an atheist since grade school when his parents forced him to attend catechism on Saturday mornings. They were poor, God-fearing people of Welsh descent, and while they didn't have the money to send him to Catholic schools, they were insistent he follow their religious leanings by sacrificing his weekend mornings to the Church. He had spent his Saturdays being taught dogma, and his Sundays practicing it at mass. It didn't take him long to understand that it was all myth—stories made up to appease conformists and to provide for the further enrichment of the church coffers. This knowledge served him well. He learned from the priests that self-righteous indignation was a powerful tool to sway the uninformed, and failing that, fear was an effective motivator to induce compliance. In other words, he got rich by bullying the average Joe and making empty threats.

The seeds of his fortune had taken root when he signed up as a life insurance agent. When calling on new customers, he wove horrific tales of husbands decimated from cancer and how their surviving spouses were financially stranded. When words weren't enough to seal a deal, he would go for the jugular, pulling out photographs of skeletal patients and of women and children living in shelters.

The income from selling life insurance was good, but it involved working too many hours for the return. He moved onto the secondary loan market, specializing in payroll advances and used car financing in the largest city in New Hampshire. Manchester was a certifiably blue-collar town with its shoe factories and textile mills. Their uneducated employees made them perfect marks for high-interest loans. His commissions were substantial, and he was soon flush with cash. But it wasn't enough. Tired of making his bosses rich, he founded his own business, a second-mortgage lending company. He was ruthless when it came to collections, which in turn led to him owning an abundance of real estate. He leveraged that real estate into industrial properties and cleaned up during the Ronald Reagan boom years. Investing those proceeds into the stock market had made him an extremely wealthy man before he turned fifty.

Fortunately, his business acumen had led to a robust social life. It was during a holiday business gala that he'd met Amanda. He had fallen for the young woman over drinks at the bar, and after a short courtship, they married. It had taken her years, but Amanda had been instrumental in changing his opportunistic view of people. While he never came around to viewing others as his equals, he had become more compassionate and considerate of their circumstances.

Having a family had a lot to do with this change in perception. His marriage had produced a son, who would eventually thrive in his father's real estate business. This left Mr. Lewis more time for leisurely activities. In turn, his son provided him with a beautiful granddaughter, who proved to be as endearing to him as his wife. The child was beautiful, intelligent, and she loved him as much as he loved her.

With his gaze fixed on the pawnshop's doors, an aphorism came to him—*karma is a bitch*. Though his gains were legal, they were morally ill-gotten. Many people, many families had suffered because of his greed, enabling him to enjoy his later years wanting nothing and surrounded by family. He had attempted to assuage his guilt with philanthropy—with some success—but he had to admit, even *that* served a purpose. Appeasing a God he did not believe in had never been a consideration on his path to redemption.

Now, the bill for his earlier excesses had been served. His granddaughter was missing, presumed dead. His skepticism in the supernatural shaken. After the events of the past two days, he had no doubt there was a seat at a table in hell with his name on it, because if demons existed, there could be no doubt in his mind that God did as well.

He had no idea how redemption worked—or if God even took it into account. Would He perceive his actions now as atonement, or would it be viewed as an attempt to purchase a *get out of jail free* card? Either way, he was determined to do whatever he could to save those three women; this he knew was imperative if there were any hope for his salvation.

The shop doors parted as he pushed his way through.

The pawnshop owner was leaned over at the middle of the long counter, his elbows resting on its surface, his chin nestled in his clasped hands. The man was staring at him, a bemused expression on his face.

Was he expecting me? Lewis wondered. He knew the man had gifts, but he didn't think precognition was one of them.

The owner nodded. "What can I do for you, Mr. Lewis?"

Lewis raised an eyebrow. "You knew I was coming?"

"No. I have cameras on top of the doors. I saw your face when you walked in. You have a worried look."

After a pause, Lewis said, "I need help, but I'm not sure what kind."

"Oh?"

"Yes. It involves the Moore house again."

The man closed his eyes for a moment, taking a deep breath. "Does this involve Celeste?"

"You—you know her?"

"Yes, she was here this morning. Tell me what's going on."

Lewis filled him in, starting with his initial visit to Father MacLeod, and concluding with the sounds of gunshots that had come from the house less than an hour earlier.

"You've heard my story, now please, tell me about Celeste's visit here."

The tall, thin man complied. Though the pawnshop owner's story was not as involved as his, Lewis did find one aspect of the story intriguing.

"This necklace you gave her—"

"Loaned her."

"I'm sorry—loaned her. Do you think it will offer her, and hopefully the others, a measure of protection against the demon?"

"It's impossible to verify the effectiveness of all the items I sell. I research everything, sometimes to the point of exhaustion; nonetheless, I offer no guarantees. Based on feedback and first-hand knowledge, I can tell you I've never sold an item that did not live up to its reputation or description."

"So, they, or at least Celeste, might be afforded some protection."

"I believe so." The man lowered his eyes. "But as I mentioned, no guarantees."

"What more can we do?"

The pawnshop owner sighed. "This is a demon we're dealing with, Mr. Lewis, a purview best left to the Catholic Church."

"You've heard where that has led."

"Yes." The man paused for a few seconds. "I'm not religious, but I've learned there are entities beyond this realm whose origin or existence cannot be logically explained. Not many things scare me, but demons – they're something else. I've seen the movies. I've read the books. I've never dealt with a demon myself, but some of my customers have. Those customers are all dead."

"Are you telling me you won't help?"

The man stared hard at him. "A demon can't be killed. From what little I know, the best we can ever hope for is banishment, to send it along its way—or back where it came from. From what you've described, this demon is entrenched in the Moore house. An exorcism is the only way to remove it that I know of."

"We don't have time for an exorcism. There are three women in that house, and their lives depend on quick action. We have to get them out of there first, and *then* have the Church perform an exorcism."

Moving to the end of the counter, the proprietor surveyed a shelf on the wall. He moved a few items, then stood still. He gazed at an item at the back of the shelf, frowned, and returned to within a few feet of his visitor.

"You need to find out the name of this demon, and gather any other information you can."

"You'll help, then?"

"Yes."

"I'll call Father MacLeod. He told me he was going on an important errand, so I may not be back in touch with you for a while."

The pawnshop owner handed him a card. "I'll be here. The phone number for the shop is on that card."

They walked to the exit, and Mr. Lewis stopped at the doors. "You were going to say no, then you changed your mind. How come?"

"I want my necklace back."

The pawnshop owner was at a loss on how to proceed. Before he could take any action, he needed to know the demon's name. During Mr. Lewis' visit, he'd searched a shelf for a set of reference books that dealt with demonology. He'd acquired those years earlier for a client who had never collected his purchase.

Three of the books were ancient, *Demonology of King James I*, *The Grand Grimoire*, and *The Grimoire of Pope Honorius*. They were originals or first editions, highly sought-after by book collectors and occult practitioners. The fourth was a widely available book called the *Dictionary of Demons*, which was included in the set at no extra charge.

He reflected on his conversation with Mr. Lewis. Despite the seriousness of the situation, he'd given the man a flippant answer when asked why he was agreeing to help. The old man had cocked an eyebrow at his answer. Apparently, Mr. Lewis wasn't buying it. The old man was astute.

Not only had the pawnshop owner been aware of a presence in the Moore house for the past month, he'd felt its influence growing beyond the confines of the building. Over the last few weeks, his customers had appeared ill-at-ease when discussing business inside the shop. While general inquiries could be discussed over the phone, he always insisted serious discussions be handled in person or with a representative.

Of those he had recently met with, many were overanxious, jittery, and concluded their business quickly. Others had confided that they were inexplicably drawn to his store—people searching for items that could cause immeasurable harm to others. Those potential customers were assessed within minutes and told they had been misinformed about the nature of his business. At first, he chalked these incidents up as unrelated coincidences. But after another disturbing occurrence earlier that week, he now considered them all possibly connected.

Three days earlier, he'd tried—and failed—to change the location of the pawnshop. As proprietor, he was gifted with the ability to pull up stakes and locate elsewhere, instantaneously, without a loss of basic services. He wasn't sure how the process worked, but the bills and taxes delivered to his post office box would always be marked with the latest address. There was one limitation to this supernatural ability—the shop couldn't be moved outside of Goffstown. Locals were vaguely aware of the existence of the business, and their reaction upon seeing it in a new location was either indifference or mild confusion. He used this ability sparingly, usually after a prolonged interaction with a local who might portend police involvement, or if he perceived a credible threat to the business. Recently, after an episode involving his associate, Rex and a traveling nightclub called Painfreak, he'd decided to move again. Though his own involvement in the Painfreak incident was minimal, he wanted to err on the side of caution. Only it didn't work this time; the pawnshop remained in its present location. Further attempts yielded the same result.

It was a simple, offhand remark from Rex that completed the puzzle for him. Rex, over 400 pounds of pure muscle, feared nothing. But the hulk was visibly shaken when the pawnshop owner asked him to check the Moore house for unusual activity. "I'd rather not," Rex had responded. "There's something bad living in that place."

What was in that house that had Rex, of all people, so intimidated? Mulling it over, he suspected he had the answer.

Mr. Lewis had contracted with him to burn it down because he thought the building was haunted, and that the house had something to do with his granddaughter's disappearance. After the discovery of the two dead arsonists, his customers had started acting strangely. Could his involvement in the attempted arson have made him a target? If the house was indeed haunted, he'd never heard of a ghost with such a reach and capable of causing him this much trouble. He made his way to the front doors, locked them, returned to the counter and waited impatiently for Mr. Lewis to provide him with a name.

CHAPTER 16

Nora moaned, the nerves in her right leg screamed. She was on her back, with a lump beneath her, extending from her butt to lower spine. She rolled her shoulders forward and arched her back, trying to ease the pressure. It helped, but the relief was minor. She took deep breaths through gritted teeth, focusing on the crux of the pain. The worst was coming from her knee. It was intense, constant, but there was also a throbbing elsewhere vying for attention.

Spasms developed from arching her back; she wouldn't be able to hold the position for long. She willed her leg to move and regretted it instantly as what felt like a thousand paring knives hacked away at her knee. But the lump shifted, bringing some relief, and giving her the courage to try again. This time, she was successful. The lump was gone, but she had bit her tongue trying to cope with the pain. Her mouth filled with blood and she choked on the taste.

She sat up slightly, wiping away tears and spitting red phlegm out the side of her mouth. When her eyes had run dry, she was clear-headed enough to assess her situation. Though her view was constrained by darkness, some light fell into the basement from the tattered floor above. She pushed herself into a full sitting position. Arms outstretched for support, Nora leaned back on them and assessed the damage to her legs. Her left leg appeared uninjured, resting straight out on the floor. Her right leg was another matter. The kneecap was twice its normal size and twisted to one side. Her calf and foot were at an unnatural angle, pointed toward her crotch. When her gaze rested at the tip of her sneaker, she understood the source of the lump against her back.

Oh God, help me, I can't feel anything below my right knee.

Her arms ached—they wouldn't support her weight much longer. Her choices were to lie exposed on the floor or find something to lean against, so she could see if anything was coming for her. She didn't want to be anywhere near the hole in the floor in case Officer Jones or more debris came crashing down, she decided to try to make it to the wall behind her. Lifting her bottom off the ground, she slowly pushed backward. Her knee screamed from the pain, but she gritted her teeth and dealt with it. She continued to slide backward until her back contacted something solid. It was hard and smooth, so she leaned against it and took deep breaths.

The light was much dimmer against the wall and she could barely make out her right leg. Dragging her body backward had straightened it somewhat, but even in the darkness, she could see the swelling had spread beyond her knees. She needed to find a way out of there, and soon.

If she was to think clearly, she had to externalize the pain. She concentrated on Agnes and studied the hole in the ceiling. *Is she still up there?* There was no visible activity, and she heard no sounds. A sudden image of Agnes, dead, flashed in her mind, and Nora choked a sob.

No, she can't be dead! I'm sure she and Celeste are coming for me.

"Don't count on it."

Nora stiffened. The words were taunting, assured. Her first reaction was to search the basement for their source, but the limited light from the hole did not allow access to its darkest corners.

"Does your leg hurt Nora? It must hurt quite a bit," the voice mocked her.

With a shiver, she acknowledged the voice originated inside her head. "Agnes, it's here, down in the basement. Please, I need you," she whimpered.

"Agnes can't hear you anymore."

God, please. Nora cupped her face, her tears returning.

"He can't hear you either."

Nora recalled Celeste's warning about letting the demon know what she was thinking. She tried to block him out, to make her mind go blank.

"It's too late, Nora. I'm already inside. Let's look around, shall we?"

A heaviness overtook her, her chin dropping to her chest. Her head bobbed several times. She fought back. Determined, she raised her head, focusing on keeping it level. It worked: her tiredness subsided but her view had changed—she was no longer in the basement, but sitting in a kitchen chair, her leg uninjured.

No. This can't be happening. I don't want to be there again.

Sitting across from Nora at the other side of a table were Sheri and Sandel. Sandel appeared every bit the same adorable toddler that Nora remembered. The girl seemed healthy and displayed no outward signs of abuse. Her mother, on the other hand, had bruises on her left cheek and both arms. Sheri was explaining to her daughter why Nora was visiting.

"Sister Nora is here to check on you, Sandel, to make sure there are no bruises on you." Sheri's eyes closed, her lips tightening. She opened them and smiled at her daughter. "Sister Nora wants to make sure

you haven't fallen off your bike or tripped and bumped into anything."

The girl nodded and replied, "Yes, Mommy."

Sheri addressed her visitor. "I can tell you, Sister Nora, that Sandel is fine. Sandel, stand up and show Sister Nora your arms and legs."

The toddler slid from her chair and approached the nun.

Despite the surreal nature of the situation, and the mother's obvious leading and coaching of the child, Nora inspected the girl's arms and legs.

"Thank you, dear," Nora said. "Can you pull your shirt up for me?"

Sheri lowered her head. "Sandel, do as she asks."

The young girl complied. After a few moments, Nora told her to push it back down.

"Sandel, please go to your room—I have to talk to Sister Nora."

Her daughter nodded and left the kitchen.

Nora stared hard at Sheri. "It looks like he's leaving her alone, but I can't say the same about you."

Sheri didn't reply. She frowned, and tears

formed. "We can't leave. He says he'll find us
again and kill us both this time if we try."

"Come with me then; the Church will take
you in."

"No," said Sheri. "The police said that the
last time, and he found us. He's got
connections with the police, he pays them off
and cuts them in on his drug dealings. He will
kill us both if we ever leave him again. We
need money, Sister, not empty promises.
Money to get far away—somewhere he can't
find us."

"Where is he now?"

"Upstairs. He's got the guys over. It's
Wednesday, poker night. He runs the games.
They play for big stakes. If he wins,
everything is fine until next Wednesday. If he
loses, nobody here is safe."

Nora struggled to keep from replying. None of this was real. The
demon was forcing her to re-live that day, a day she had tried so hard
to forget. But she couldn't stop herself from responding.

"I'm going up there."

"What? Why?"

"To play."

"Are you crazy? He might hurt you for
just interrupting, never mind his
embarrassment at a nun breaking up the
poker game. And if he lets you play, what do

you think will happen after you leave? I'll tell you what, he'll take it out on Sandel and me!"

Nora hadn't been fazed by Sheri's reaction.

"You said they're playing poker, right? If I can get you the money, will you and Sandel leave?"

"What? You're a nun! You gonna pray it from them?"

Nora could not control her smile. "No. I'm going to play them for it."

"You? You know how to play poker? These guys do it all the time. There's no way you can beat them. Do you even have a stake?"

"Yes, I know how to play poker. I was brought up by a dad who not only taught me but let me play with his friends until he didn't play anymore. As for a stake, I'll ask them to front me."

"What will you use for collateral?"

"I don't know," answered Nora, "But I'll come up with something."

"Just because you played poker with your dad, what makes you think you can beat these guys?"

Nora's smile widened. "I have an edge."

Sheri got up from her chair, pacing the

kitchen. "This is crazy! You're going to get yourself killed, and probably me and Sandel, too!"

Nora stood and began to approach the stairs. "Don't worry, it'll be fine."

Nora was shaken to her core. She was a puppet, without control of her actions and voice. It wasn't real—it couldn't be real. But she could smell the lingering odors of Sheri's cooking, and could almost taste the remnants of flat beer in the bottles that were stuffed into an overflowing garbage can by the sink. The linoleum under her shoes squeaked when she neglected to pick up her feet.

She'd made the worst decision of her life that night.

Dealing with abused women had taken its toll on her. As the Church human services liaison for the police department, Nora had seen too many abused women, too many families torn apart by the violent actions of husbands and boyfriends. With a social system that was unequipped or unable to help them, she couldn't count the instances of violence that had rendered women crippled, both physically and emotionally. This had been an opportunity to help at least one of them break free of the cycle.

In hindsight, Nora knew that her own cockiness had much to do with her decision. She'd been so certain she would win that money. It took years to deal with the aftermath of that night's decision.

Nora climbed the stairs.

When she reached the top, she heard voices to her right. She followed them into a large room.

Five men sat at a round table, their

cigarette and cigar smoke fogged the air. Cards flew from a man facing her. It was Barry. When he saw her, his hands froze, and his face reddened.

"What the hell are you doing here?" he demanded.

The other four men turned to look at her.

"Is that a nun?" one of them asked.

Nora had been wearing street clothes, a long, plain black dress, but had donned her white cap and a crucifix hung from her neck. There was no mistaking her profession.

Barry's face reddened more. "Never mind her; she's here to meet with Sheri."

The men turned their attention back to the card game.

"Excuse me," interrupted Nora. "I'd like to be dealt in."

Once again, Barry froze. All heads turned in her direction.

"What? This is a man's game, woman— no place for the likes of you."

Nora smiled. "Afraid you'll be beat by a nun?"

The men guffawed. One of them spoke. "Come on, Barry, let her in. Her money is as good as yours."

Barry stared at Nora. "You got enough money to ante?"

"No, I'll need you to spot me."

"You got anything to put up?"

"I'm a nun—you see any deep pockets in this dress? Besides, I've taken a vow of poverty."

The men laughed again.

Barry looked her up and down. He smiled.

"Okay, I'll spot you $500.00. You lose it, I own you until it's paid back."

That comment alone should have been enough for her to rethink her decision. Nora had been so sure of herself, she hadn't taken the time to consider what it would mean if she lost.

She nodded agreement.

Barry grinned. "Take a seat."

Dread swept through her as she saw and felt herself taking a seat at the table. The memory of chair pressed hard and unforgiving against her bottom, the tobacco smoke made breathing difficult, and the sounds of shuffling cards echoed in her ears. She knew none of it was real. That it was all an illusion—visions planted inside her mind. If its aim was to torment her, the damned demon was succeeding. Every word, every movement, every detail was as vivid as it had been that night. She'd relived it so many times, for so many years, there was no doubt of its accuracy. The demon was mining her brain.

Wordlessly, Barry counted out twenty-five twenty-dollar bills and tossed them to her.

"Hello, Sister, my name's Bob," a man to

her right introduced himself. "The game is five-card stud. You can discard two, three with an ace, but of course, you have to show it. Ante is twenty dollars. Any questions?"

Nora shook her head, and the game resumed.

She lost the hand, and then the second one. It was on the third hand that she let her skill—not her Dad's poker lessons but her other talent—kick in. It was down to Bob and her. She was sitting with three of a kind, sevens, and she was sure it would be enough to bump the pot another twenty dollars. Bob was amused, saw her, but then raised another fifty dollars.

She studied him and picked up that he was uneasy. There was doubt in his mind. He was bluffing.

She saw his raise.

Bob threw the cards on the table, face down. "It's yours," he said, without emotion. There had been enough in the pot for her to recoup what she'd lost, and then some.

The game went on through the evening hours. She continued to concentrate on the men whenever she had a hand she thought strong enough to win. She won many more pots but was wise enough to lose a few to divert suspicion. By midnight, the original six players had dwindled down to three—Barry,

Bob, and herself. She and Bob had most of the winnings, but Barry had enough to stay in the game.

Bob dealt the next hand. Her five cards consisted of three twos, an eight and a nine. She discarded the nine and Bob tossed a card her way. When she lifted it, her heart accelerated; another eight. She had a full house. She glanced up at her opponents.

Barry stared at his cards. He discarded two. "I'm in." He sighed, throwing twenty dollars on the table.

Bob nodded. He threw in a twenty, then added four more. "I'm bumping it to one hundred."

Nora concentrated on the man. To her horror, she couldn't read him. She tried again with the same result. She turned her ability on Barry. He was noticeably unsure of himself. He was no threat. She squirmed in her seat, and then faced Bob. She closed her eyes, focusing harder. Nothing. What the hell was happening? When she opened her eyes, he was smiling at her.

"Are you in?" Bob asked.

She thought for a moment. "Yes. I'll see your hundred, and I raise you five hundred."

Barry studied his hand, then stared daggers at her. "I'm out." He threw his cards on the table.

*The smile never left Bob's face. "Look, it's
just you and me. What do you say, all in?"*

Nora wanted to cry, scream, get up from the chair and run. She
couldn't. She was trapped in this basement. Helpless.

*She mentally added up her winnings so
far. There had to be over three thousand
dollars sitting in front of her. It might be
enough to get Sheri and Sandel to safety and
give them a head start, but six thousand
would be even better. She was sitting with a
full house. The odds were with her. She
pushed her winnings to the center of the
table. Bob did the same.*

"What do you got?" he asked.

*She placed her cards down, face up. "Full
house. Twos over eights."*

*Bob nodded. He sighed, throwing his
cards down. Four tens.*

The years that had passed since that night did nothing to diminish
her shock. The emptiness that filled her body now mirrored that
original moment.

*Nora lowered her head and a short sob
escaped. Bob scooped the money from the
table. He arranged it neatly, then folded it.
He placed it into a small leather bag he had
pulled from the floor. He tipped an imaginary*

hat to Barry and walked over to her. He leaned down and put two fingers to her chin and pulled her face to his.

"When I was very young, my mother could read my moods. It was almost as if she could see what was in my mind. When I got to around ten years old, I could actually feel her poking around in my head. Then, when I was around thirteen, a weird thing happened. I found I could block her out. It didn't even take that much effort. Soon I didn't even have to concentrate: it just happened automatically, and she never tried again." He straightened. "It's funny, I forgot what it was like to have her poking around up here." He pointed an index finger to his head. "Until tonight, that is. Goodnight, Sister Nora."

He left the room with his bag over his shoulder.

"Well, Sister, that's twice you screwed up tonight."

She'd forgotten Barry was there. "Twice?"

"Yeah. One time was betting it all on the last hand. The other time was not paying me back the five hundred dollars when you were flush."

The thought had never occurred to her.

"You owe me, woman, which means I

own you. Decent whores go for around a hundred dollars a night. Looks like I own you for five nights."

"No." She shook her head. "Please, no. My vows forbid me."

"You made a deal, and I aim to hold you to it. I'll tell you right now, if you don't, Sheri and her brat will suffer. They'll disappear again, but this time nobody will be able to bring them back."

What had she done? There was no way she could live with herself if she was responsible for the death of Sheri and Sandel. She nodded in defeat.

"There's an empty bedroom, end of the hallway on the right. Go in there, strip. I want a look at what's due me."

She'd done what was demanded—to which she had agreed. Barry hadn't touched her, but his comments had been brutal, degrading.

She almost lacked the strength to dress and leave the room. His parting words had only served to drag her further into the hell of her own making. He had instructed her to return the next evening at seven when they would really get down to business. Nora didn't think it was possible to feel more worthless, but she was wrong. On the way out, the expression on Sheri's face when

Nora passed her in the kitchen would forever burn in her memory. The woman's eyes were as large as a doe's; empty, moist. Nora couldn't decide if Sheri's vacant gaze had more to do with what Barry had done to her upstairs, or what awaited Sheri and Sandel after she left.

It was in that instant Nora had an epiphany. She'd committed many sins this evening, but this one was as egregious as Judas's. Because of her foolish bravado, Sheri and her daughter might never escape the clutches of her husband.

When Nora was home at the convent, she had prayed Sheri and her daughter would not suffer a fate similar to that of Jesus. After hours of asking God for guidance and pleading for forgiveness, the feelings of helplessness and guilt remained. Nora had come to a decision, one no less self-centered than the one she'd made earlier. The repercussions from this decision would last an eternity. She understood she was the one who got herself into this mess, and no one else, including God, was going to get her out of it. She made the necessary preparations, starting with a phone call to Sheri.

The next evening, she knocked on the door of Barry's house at the appointed time and waited. When he answered, she saw

Sheri standing a few feet behind him. Sheri nodded.

Barry had a glass in his hand, filled with a smoky colored liquor. He was unsteady, his eyes glassy.

"You made it, bitch," he said. "Good thing, too, because I meant what I said about Sheri and the brat." His free hand reached out and squeezed her breast. "Come on in, let's get this show on the road." Leering, he added, "And just so you know, Sheri's going to join us."

Nora shifted her gaze to Sheri. A quick sob escaped the woman's mouth. Sheri nodded once again.

"Where's Sandel?" Nora asked.

"At a friend's house for the night," Barry slurred. "Never mind her, let's go."

He grabbed Nora by the hand and led her to the staircase. Sheri followed behind them. Barry stumbled on the first step and liquid spilled from his glass. Letting go of Nora, he grabbed onto the handrail. "Follow me," he ordered and climbed the stairs, bumping into the handrail and the opposite wall as he made his way. When he reached to top, he stood and waited for her and Sheri to join him.

Once they were side by side at the top of the stairs, Barry laughed. It was ugly, filled *with phlegm and lust. Sheri maneuvered behind him. Nora watched without surprise or remorse when Sheri pushed Barry down the stairs. The man never said a word as he tumbled head over heels.*

When he landed on the floor, Sheri descended the stairs. She checked for signs of life and frowned. Nora watched her step from view, into the kitchen, and then return with a plastic bag. Sheri placed it over Barry's head and secured it around his neck with her hands. For ten minutes neither Nora nor Sheri moved. Sheri checked once again to see if Barry was breathing. Confirming the man was dead, Sheri walked back to the kitchen, and then returned empty-handed.

Nora stared at Barry's lifeless body. She had imagined revulsion from guilt would overwhelm her when this moment arrived; instead, a hollowness overcame her.

"Sister Nora, we have to finish this."

Nora walked down the stairs. "How did you drug him?" she asked

"I went into his stash, took three of the Blue Devils, ground them up and put it into his bourbon."

"What are Blue Devils?"

"A barbiturate. Amobarbital. He was already drunk so I'm guessing he didn't notice anything. The drug slows you way

135

down. I'm not sure he could have done anything to you if it got that far."

"Did you take his money?'

"Yeah. I put it somewhere the police won't find it if they go looking, I left some though." Sheila put her hand on Nora's shoulder. "Let's finish this."

The police arrived three minutes after Sheila had placed the call. The ambulance a minute later. She had explained to them that Sister Nora was over for counseling and that they heard Barry fall down the stairs. Sheila had been careful not to give too many details, ones that could trip them up if there was any suspicion.

Nora needn't have worried. Barry was a renowned drug dealer, and though he bribed the police to stay in business, they had no love for the man. If they did check his blood and find the depressant, they would conclude he used some of his own wares. Satisfied with Sheri's alibi—after all, she was with a nun at the time of the murder—the police left satisfied.

Nora had seen Sheri a week later at Barry's funeral. Other than a sincere hug and a few words of encouragement, they had no further contact. Nora had been interrogated once since the funeral, but nothing ever came of it, although she did learn that Sheri and Sandel had left the area without leaving a forwarding address.

Erring on the side of caution, Nora waited two months to confess her role in the scheme to the convent's Mother Superior. The day after her confession, she was asked to meet with the

Reverend Mother again. At that meeting, Nora was directed to leave the Church for the good of all parties, and she'd agreed.

Nora stared off into the darkness of the basement. She had struggled after leaving the Church. During the daylight hours, she was secure with her actions. She justified them with the certainty it was the only way. Sheri and Sandel were presumably in a safe location, and Barry would never harm another woman or child again. Those impressions comforted Nora and served as armor against doubt. It was only after sunset when the nightmares crept into her head that she thought otherwise.

It was only in darkness when her certainty was supplanted with second-guessing, that guilt set in.

It was only in the evening's deepest shadows when horrific visions of damnation and eternal suffering plagued her, did she label her actions a sin.

It was only in the blackness of night, as she lay in bed staring toward the unseen ceiling, that she considered her solution, which was—murder.

She had hoped joining Father MacLeod's team would mitigate any punishment God would deliver onto her. Redemption had been her only option to escape eternal damnation. Father MacLeod understood her need, and he had given her an opportunity to pursue it. But, as her unfocused eyes gazed into the basement, she wondered if it was enough.

"Ha! Ah, Nora, you'll never be able to make good on your sins in your god's eyes." The voice inside her head was jovial, falsely sympathetic, and cruel. *"You gambled, broke your vows, and participated in a murder. You really fucked up. A spot in hell had been reserved for you the moment you sat down at that card game. I'm here to collect your soul. By the way, nuns hold a special place*

at our table."

Nora's body shook and she flailed her arms, hoping to ward the demon off. The movement ignited spikes of pain in her leg and she cried out.

"Aw, Nora, don't act that way just yet; we're not finished here."

Please God, I can't take any more—let this be over with.

Nora raised her head and froze. Captured in a circle of light falling from the holes in the ceiling, she saw a man standing in the basement. He was naked, facing away from her.

No, no . . .

The man turned to face her.

Barry.

A yellowish glow enveloped him, his eyes blacker than the darkness in the depths of the basement. The corners of Barry's lips rose in a lecherous smile, his penis also rising in concurrence, pointing accusingly in her direction.

Time for you to make good on your bet," he said.

CHAPTER 17

Father MacLeod came to an abrupt stop at the bottom of the marble stairway leading to the old post office building. The black vines obscured the white and blue hues of the stone, their darkness rippling over the long rectangular steps. An image of a spider web beckoning prey flashed through his mind. People walking over the stairs took no notice, making it clear he was the only one who could see them. Something was fucking with him, but he wouldn't be cowered. He climbed, and as he approached the top step, he saw that the vines progressed no farther.

It can't go into a holy place. At least, that's what he hoped. He rushed to his office.

"Linda, have there been any calls?"

"Good afternoon to you, too. There's a message from Mr. Lewis on your phone."

The priest nodded, slipped into his office, and closed the door. At his desk, he opened the bottom drawer and pulled out a bottle of Glenfiddich. Wrapping his lips around the neck, he swallowed, the amber liquid dribbling out of the sides of his mouth. He wiped his lips, capped the bottle, and returned it to the drawer. Withdrawing a small vial filled with a clear liquid marked *Lourdes*, he inspected it to ensure it was full, pocketed it, and then listened to the message.

He'd do what he could to get the name of the demon. He took a deep breath and left his office.

"Linda, I'm going downstairs. Don't tell anyone where I am."

She nodded without looking up at him.

The door to the basement was located at the far end of the hall.

Passage through the doorway was secured by a keypad, where he punched in a six-digit code. He heard a click, pushed the door open, and descended the stairway. At the bottom, he paused before a dimly lit hallway with water-stained walls and a cement floor with numerous cracks that betrayed the age of the building. His destination loomed ahead.

On either side of the hallway, equally spaced, heavy oak doors led to small rooms. From past visits, he knew they all stood locked and empty—except for the fifth room on his right. To the side of that door stood a desk. Seated there was a nun dressed in full habit, a large crucifix hanging on her chest.

"Hello, Sister Bernice."

"Hello, Father."

The priest stood close, casting a shadow over her. "How is she today?"

The woman's face was neutral. "Doing well today, Father."

"Is she lucid?"

The sister hesitated a moment. "She was earlier."

"Are they in there with her?"

She shook her head. "No. They left for the night, about an hour ago."

The priest sighed in relief. "I need to speak to her."

The nun stared hard at him. "You know I can't allow you to go in there without the exorcist's permission. I've got my orders. Besides, Father, you've been drinking, I can smell it on you."

The priest grinned. "I can assure you that I only had one sip, and that was to fortify me for my conversation with her. As for your orders, you report to me, Sister Bernice, not them."

Her eyes lingered on the priest's.

"Look," he continued, "I don't want to do this any more than you

140

want to let me. The thing is, I have no choice. Three women are engaged with a demon at this very moment, and their lives depend on whatever information I can get from her."

The nun broke eye contact. Both her hands went to her crucifix and clutched it tightly. After a few moments, her gaze returned to Father MacLeod. "If something goes wrong in there, I'll be in serious trouble, Father. You tell me you're doing God's work, so I have to believe you. I'll pray for all of you. Punch in six sixes."

The irony wasn't lost on him. "If anything goes wrong, tell them I ordered you to give me the code. Is it the same to leave?"

"No, it's six nines."

"Thank you, Sister. The last time I was here, there was a box of dust masks on the table—they're gone now."

"Yes, there was no need for them."

He reached for the digital lock.

"I hope God is with you, Father."

He punched in the numbers. "Me, too."

The door opened, and he stepped into Catherine White's holding room.

His last visit, a month earlier, had sown the seeds of many nightmares. The urge to gag had overcome him when he'd entered the cell, which stewed in a cocktail of pungent odors: sweat, urine, infection, and unwashed genitalia. The taste that had wormed its way down his throat, combined with the stifling heat of the room had him retching and reaching for the door. He'd left the room to ask for a mask, taken a few minutes to walk off the upset, and then dabbed the mask with a few drops of lavender oil from a bottle he'd spotted beside the box. After pulling on the mask, he'd taken a deep breath and re-entered the room.

Catherine had been screaming and cursing in tongues, alternating between Greek, Latin, and French. She had been naked, her body covered in sores that oozed a foamy yellow fluid. Brown festering boils spotted her face. A large one beside her nose erupted, spewing a viscous umber tinted pus that dripped onto her lips. Her head had been shaved clean and placed in a brace. A strap had run tight over her forehead to restrain her from fracturing her neck. Her wrists and ankles strapped taut to the corners of the bed frame.

The exorcists had tied a leather strap over her stomach to prevent her from levitating and breaking her back. Her legs had been parted wide, her vulva shaved, though he had questioned the need aloud to the exorcists. Her mattress had been stained by vomit, feces, and blood. He'd left the room shaken, vowing not to return until the exorcists were successful.

This day's visit was different; Catherine's transformation was startling.

She was restrained, but the straps on her wrists were connected to the bed frame on either side of her hips. The straps to her ankles had slack in them, enough so she could close her legs. The restraint over her waist was gone, as was the binding for her head. Fuzz adorned her scalp. She wore a nightgown, and while it was flimsy, it covered her from neck to mid-thigh. The mattress was unsoiled. More startling, her face was clear, and there was a smile on her lips. It was a sad one, but considering her situation, the priest was grateful to see it.

"Father MacLeod! I wonder what brings you here." Her voice, though weak, had the lilt of humor.

The priest grinned. "First, how are *you* doing, Catherine?'

The woman sighed, then the smile returned. "I'm beating it, Father. It's still there, but very weak. Every day I get a little better. They tell me it'll be over soon."

Father MacLeod frowned.

Catherine squinted at his reaction. "You don't seem pleased."

"I'm happy for you, Catherine. It's just that something's come up, and I need your help."

The woman's face stiffened. "What do you want?"

"I need to speak to the demon inside you."

Her eyes widened and she shook her head. "No—ask of me anything else but that."

"I wouldn't ask if it weren't important."

"What could be so important you would want that damned thing to come back out?"

"Agnes and Nora are in trouble. Serious trouble. Their lives, maybe even their souls, are in jeopardy."

Catherine closed her eyes. "Tell me."

The priest filled her in on the details of the team's investigation. When he finished, he went to her side and placed his hand over hers. "I wouldn't ask if I didn't think it would help them. There's another player in this that might be of aid to me. From what I understand, he's involved somehow with the supernatural. He's asking for the name of the demon that torments the team. You're the only hope I have of finding it out."

Catherine opened her eyes. "You have no idea what you're asking of me. I've been in hell for the last couple of months, and I mean that, Father—in actual hell. It's real, and even more evil and terrifying than we've been taught."

"I wouldn't ask you if there were any other way."

Catherine gritted her teeth. She looked away and then brought her gaze back, locking eyes with the priest.

"When it comes, it's all over me, Father. It burns my skin, violates me. I know it's not real when it happens, but I can feel it tearing at my arms and legs. It plucks my eyes out, holds them up, and I swear to God

I can still see out of them." Her voice drifted. "It makes me watch what it does to me." After a pause, Catherine's voice rose. "Insects burrow into my skin, Father. My body ignites and the flames dance over me while they consume me. Creatures tear me apart, even as they use me. It shows me friends and family members doing horrible things to others, and to each other. The suffering is never-ending. Through it all, it either tells me there is no God, or it insists He exists but doesn't give a shit about me. All I have to do, it says, is renounce Him. Then all the pain, all the suffering, all the visions will stop."

Father MacLeod's gaze went to her restrained hand. It was small, delicate, and it trembled under his.

"But, you know what?" Catherine went on. "I never did. I won't renounce God. Demons are the kings of lies, the kindling used to stoke evil." She sighed. "There were periods when it vanished. I had brief moments of relief. When I was alone in my head, I'd ask myself why it was going through all the trouble to convince me God wasn't real, or that He had abandoned me. Why ask me to reject God if the Devil had me already?"

The priest raised his head. "Tell me, did you come up with an answer?"

Catherine nodded. "Yes. You see, I was convinced I was going to hell for what I did. Even after you asked me to work for the team, I didn't think I could be saved. To be honest, I had hoped at best that I could mitigate my punishment. But I was wrong. As the exorcists drove it farther away, closer to the hell it came from, I came to realize there was hope for me. This is a test. A way for me to acknowledge my sins, to pay for them. I am not a lost soul. There's a place for me in God's kingdom. This conversation is further proof I'm right. They showed me your sins, Father. Not just the ones I was involved with. If what it showed me was true, you're in the position I was. I want to tell you now, Father, there is a chance to be saved."

Father MacLeod's tore his hand from Catherine's. He stepped back, eyes wide and mouth open. "Catherine, whatever it showed you, you have to dismiss it. You yourself said demons were the kings of lies."

She sighed, tilting her head back. "I did. But I've always thought the most effective lies were the ones based on truth." The woman met his gaze. "It doesn't matter whether it was the whole truth or not: what I'm trying to tell you is that redemption is possible. Have faith."

If he had the time, the priest would've made more of an attempt to discuss or dissuade her of the notion. Instead, he smiled. "If you believe that, then you understand why I've asked you to do this."

Catherine's face tightened. She remained silent for almost five minutes, an eternity for the priest.

"I'll do it for Agnes and Nora, as well as the new woman—"

"Celeste."

"Celeste. I'm going to try to keep it under submission, not let it take complete control over me. I'm not sure if I can. It's very weak, so I have a chance. When you get what you need, you have to bring me back. Call to me. Pray for me. Do whatever you have to but bring me back."

He nodded. "I will, Catherine."

"Thank you. Please, place the restraints on my stomach and forehead."

The priest hurried to do as she asked. When she was secure, he stood by the door and waited.

When the demon returned, the lights didn't dim. There was no smoke. He couldn't smell anything out of the ordinary.

"Hello, Father," it said. "You here to deliver on your promise?" It wasn't Catherine's voice.

CHAPTER 18

Agnes twisted the cellar doorknob and yanked with all her strength, but it wouldn't budge. "Nora," she screamed, pounding on and kicking at the door. She leaned forward, pressed her forehead against the wood, and sobbed hard enough to make her shoulders hitch.

"*Agnes.*"

She stiffened. The voice was male, soft, yet loud enough to catch her attention. It was distant as if someone had called her from the next room. The only person alive in the next room was Celeste, and it definitely wasn't her. She backed from the door, looking to her left. No one stood in the entranceway. Whoever it was had to be in the living room.

Agnes was certain her name had been called, but what if she had been mistaken about the caller's gender? What if it were Nora, in the basement, distraught, and hurt from the fall? Agnes knew it could be the demon, but what if it wasn't? She listened. The house was unnaturally quiet.

She took hesitant steps toward the living room. The cracks in the floor ended at the threshold to the hallway, near where she stood at the room's entrance. There were too many for her to jump over to get to the hole Nora fell through.

Officer Jones' lifeless body remained crumpled on the chair. Celeste was nowhere in sight.

"Nora?" she shouted. There was no reply.

The only way Agnes could get to her partner was through the door leading to the basement. She'd have to find something to hammer the doorknob off, and if that failed, she'd have to somehow destroy the door. With that thought, she turned to head back down the hallway, but it was no longer there.

Her mind clouded. When it cleared, she was in a bedroom, instantly familiar. She now wore street clothes, her arms stretched up and out before her. Both her hands held onto the small, delicate fingers of an African American woman. Though she knew who she would see, Agnes looked at the woman's face. Agnes closed her eyes and tears gathered.

Agnes shook her head. "No! You bastard. No. Get out of my head!" She repeated the phrase over and again, hoping to chase it away. "Get out of my head—get out of my head—get out of my head—"

"Too late, lezzie, I'm already here and I'm not leaving until I have some fun with you. Let's see what brought you to me, shall we?"

"Get out of my head!"

There was no reply. Agnes waited a few more seconds before opening her eyes. When she did, she found herself seated at the dais table during a dinner banquet.

> *Casual conversation echoed through the hall and assaulted her ears. She was dressed in her habit, but those on either side and in the audience were dressed in formal wear. Women wore exquisite evening gowns accented with pearls, gold bracelets, and diamond rings. High heels straightened their stances, and, in some instances, flaunted brightly painted toenails. The men were decked out in tuxedos, all of them black, with color-matched bowties.*
>
> *A loudspeaker sprang to life with two taps. A man she knew to be the head of the*

local Better Business Bureau implored the guests to sit. It took a few minutes, but once everyone was seated, the man addressed the crowd.

"Tonight, we are here to honor Mr. Jim Arsenault," the speaker said, proudly.

Agnes knew this was an illusion, a trick of the mind. Worse, she knew where this scene was headed.

No! Please, God, don't make me relive this.

But she had no control over the vision; she was forced to participate in the re-enactment.

The speaker went on reciting all the good deeds Jim had accomplished, most of which involved giving various charities boatloads of money. When the oration was over, he called Mr. Arsenault to the podium. Jim gave a self-deprecating, humor-filled speech that went over well with the crowd. Toward the end, he acknowledged his wife, Linda, for all her support. Linda was seated next to Agnes, and the two made eye contact.

Agnes sobbed. *Why didn't I see it in her then?* There had been no sparkle in her lover's eyes, and despite a generous quantity of makeup, Linda couldn't hide her fatigue. Thinking back on it, Agnes understood she'd made a horrible mistake. She had mistaken resignation for fatigue.

Linda stood to enthusiastic applause. She gave them a halfhearted smile, then mouthed, "Thank you." When Linda sat down, Jim then praised the work of Sister Agnes, the Church's outreach director, for creating the Loving Children's Society and for her tireless work in fundraising. Embarrassed by the spotlight, she stood, bowed once, and sat back down.

They ate dinner on the dais, taking the time to acknowledge anyone who came by to congratulate them or thank them for their service. Agnes had occasionally reached under the tablecloth to stroke Linda's thigh. Her efforts were not reciprocated. The most she received in return was a slight smile or a nod. Agnes thought nothing of it, as they were in a public setting. For her own part, she found the surreptitious fondling playful and erotic. A hint of things to come, she'd hoped.

After dinner, the band started up and the attendees danced and mingled. Agnes was alone with Linda, and it gave her the opportunity to talk to her without being overheard.

"Linda," Agnes said, "Can I stop over this evening, after the ceremony?"

"Yes," came the reply. "We have to talk."

Agnes smiled. "I know. I'm going to the head of the convent tomorrow to renounce *my vows. I won't mention us, so please, don't worry. I'm not sure how long or what's involved, but—"*

"Wait," Linda interrupted. "Let's discuss this later tonight. Jim is packed and will be on a flight by one o'clock, so please, come after that."

Before Agnes could respond, Linda was approached by a local merchant to discuss what he claimed was a matter of importance. She excused herself, leaving the table to talk with the man.

"No, why can't I stop this?" Agnes screamed.

"Oh, come now, Agnes," the voice in her head spoke, *"We're getting to the good part, aren't we?"*

Agnes knew she was standing in the hallway of the Moore house, but the vision was so real. Why was this charade necessary? The demon said something about finding out what had led her to this point, which would back up what Celeste had said earlier—*the damn thing gets into our heads and uses that information to terrorize us. Is there a way to stop it from digging around?* She closed her eyes and concentrated on pushing everything out of her mind.

"Agnes."

She opened her eyes.

She was outdoors, on the front porch of Linda's house.

Not quite an hour earlier, the gala had ended. Jim said his goodbyes, giving Linda a quick peck on the cheek before hurrying off. She made her way through the crowd and her eyes met Agnes'. After a nod, Linda made the rounds to thank everyone and say her own goodbyes. Agnes slipped out of the hotel ballroom without making conversation with anyone.

In one of the guest rooms the event had provided, Agnes changed out of her habit into street clothes. She packed her church garb into a canvas bag and walked out of the hotel without being recognized. She killed time driving through the city. Thoughts on how to approach Mother Superior preoccupied her for the next forty-five minutes. She parked the car a block away from Linda's house, walking purposely to her front porch. After a glance behind her, Agnes opened the unlocked door and stepped inside.

Despite the time that had passed, in spite of her affair with Nora, Agnes was crushed at the vision. She and Linda had been lovers for almost a year, and to say their affair had been complicated was an understatement.

Linda was married to a successful businessman who was a community icon. As his partner in business and marriage, Linda projected the façade of a loving and supportive wife. In the eyes of the public, they were considered a team in every respect.

Agnes had no idea why Linda had initially approached her. Try as she might, and she did so several times during their lovemaking, Agnes hadn't picked up on anything from Linda. The woman had a natural ability to block her out. It hadn't bothered Agnes; she knew Linda's love for her was genuine—she didn't need an empathic ability to verify it. When she'd asked Linda why she had chosen her, the answers were usually cute, evasive, or even flippant, yet they were always reassuring.

Equally baffling at the time was why Agnes let herself be seduced. While Linda never fully explained her reasons, Agnes had come to terms with hers—Linda had been the only woman who'd ever expressed a desire for her. Agnes had been aware of her sexual orientation since her early teens. She'd kept it suppressed, thinking something was wrong with her. Battling weight problems also contributed to her introversion. The boys in school weren't that interested in her, which had come as a relief. The young Agnes lost herself in books, mostly autobiographies, which led to religiously-themed reading. When she'd announced to her parents that she wanted to become a nun, they weren't surprised; they applauded the decision.

It had been a poorly thought-out choice.

Though Agnes had thrived in the religious environment, she struggled to suppress her sexual desires. Living among women did not tamp down those yearnings. It took Linda's interest in her to give her courage to pursue her lifelong fantasy.

Agnes called out to Linda, who responded from another room and then walked in to greet her. She had changed from her elegant formalwear to sweatpants and a T-shirt, both of which clung tightly to her body. Agnes thought she'd never get enough sights like this—until she caught the expression on her lover's face. Her eyes were red, and her frown was set deep. They both sat on the couch, and Agnes leaned forward, taking her hand.

"What's the matter?"

"Don't renounce your vows. We can't be together."

Stunned, Agnes let go of Linda's hand. "What—what're you talking about?"

Averting her gaze, Linda went on. "Jim and I have been embezzling funds from the charity accounts. We've been discovered, and it's only a matter of time before it hits the news media. We're both looking at some serious jail time, Agnes. Jim didn't leave the event to go to a business meeting—he's going out of the country. I'm supposed to leave tomorrow and meet up with him."

Agnes froze. So many thoughts went through her mind that she couldn't sort them out. She never would've thought it possible for Linda to be involved in something like that. Then, one thought came to the forefront.

"Linda," she asked, "Is the Loving Children Society one of those charities?"

A sob erupted from her lover. "Yes," she answered, in a soft voice.

"You stole money from the charity I'm

involved in? I—I—" She couldn't finish the sentence.

"Jim embezzled from the Loving Children's Fund because of you. He thought that having someone from the Church as a spokesman would prevent anyone from looking too closely at the finances. For additional insurance, he asked me to become friendly with you in case you noticed."

Agnes' mouth dropped open. "Wait, are you telling me the reason we became lovers was so you could steal from the charity?"

Linda locked eyes with Agnes. "Yes. I mean no! No! I didn't plan on going that far with you, but it became obvious you were attracted to me in a way that went beyond friendship. I thought it was cute at first. As I worked alongside you, as I got to know you more, I developed deeper feelings." She lowered her head. "At first, I admit, it was thrilling, exotic. I had never made love to another woman before."

Agnes shook her head. "Still, you were betraying me the whole time."

"Yes, and it was killing me. When you said you were going to renounce your vows, I was stunned. I never meant for it to go that far."

"But it did." Agnes bit her lower lip. "And now I could be thrown into jail because of *you."*

The tears returned to Linda's eyes. "I'm so sorry. If I had known what was to become of us, I never would've agreed to this. Whether you believe me or not, Agnes, I care deeply for you. And, I promise, I've made arrangements; soon, everyone will know that you weren't involved."

Agnes stood. She gazed down at Linda, who stared back with eyes that begged for sympathy. The emptiness in Agnes turned to rage. "Sure, you'll tell everyone, but only after you get caught. Before then, I'll be dragged through the mud, accused of embezzlement." Agnes left the couch, walking to the front door. With her back to Linda, her last words to the woman were loud and anguished. "You know, I placed you above God. I was willing to leave the Church and spend the rest of my life with you. Damn you! I feel like a fool. I hope you burn in hell." With another shake of her head, Agnes walked through the door, not bothering to close it.

"Please, Agnes, wait!"

Though it was all a game the demon was playing, the pain in her heart was as heavy and penetrating as it had been that evening. She willed herself to return to the couch in Linda's living room, to figure out a plan that included the both of them.

Nothing changed.

The tears flowed. She made her way to her car, but strode past it, needing time to process what had happened. She replayed the conversation in her mind, comparing it with their intimate moments. Upon reflection, she was positive Linda loved her, which made the betrayal even more difficult to comprehend.

Agnes struggled with her decision to leave as she had. A sliver of remorse slipped into her heart. While she was mulling over her reaction, it occurred to her that her lover might also be suffering terribly. Could Linda have been confessing all of this so that, with Agnes' help, she could figure a way out of this mess? Agnes had invested so much in this relationship: she needed to know. She changed direction and started walking back to Linda's home.

The door was open. Agnes couldn't remember if she'd closed it or not. She slowed as she approached, craning her neck to look inside. Seeing no one, she stopped and cocked an ear. There was no sobbing, no rustling about—it was dead quiet. Moving into the living room, she looked for Linda. Again, she came up empty. Gathering her courage, she went through all the rooms on the first floor; they too were deserted. She stood in the living room, deciding if she should call out to Linda or check out the second floor. A loud thump above hastened her decision. She rushed to the staircase, climbing quickly. At the top, a sound came from the master bedroom—the bedroom where they'd made love so many times. It had sounded like a sob. Ignoring her fear of an intruder, she rushed to the bedroom. The door was closed. She pushed her way into the bedroom.

Her lover stood on a chair in the center of the room. Around her neck was a noose, the other end secured around one of several oak beams traversing the ceiling. Linda teetered on the chair. There was almost no slack on the rope. Her eyes were closed, but she opened them when she heard Agnes approach.

"Linda," Agnes pleaded, "Please don't do this."

The woman's face was red, her eyes puffy, her makeup smeared. "I—it's the only way, Agnes. I don't know what else to do."

"It's not! We can fix this together." Agnes took a deep breath. She noticed an envelope on the bed. "Is that your goodbye note?" she asked. "Was it meant for me?"

Linda's eyes widened. "No. I didn't know

you were coming back."

Agnes picked up on the nervous tone in Linda's response. She picked up the envelope. It wasn't addressed, but it was sealed. She took one more glance toward Linda, then tore the envelope open. The contents were short; it all fit on one page.

When she finished reading it, her eyes burned with fury.

"You," Agnes spoke loudly. "You lied to me. Jim had nothing to do with the embezzlement. It was all you."

Linda nodded. Tears rained down her cheeks. "Yes. I fell in love with you, Agnes, but I can't let him take responsibility for my actions."

"I could've helped you with this mess, Linda. I would have been there for you."

"I didn't think you would. And then, when I told you, you walked out on me. I thought you were leaving me for good," Linda sobbed. "Now that you're back, maybe we can work this out."

Agnes gave an uneasy laugh. "I read your letter, Linda. You were emphatic that Jim had no part in your schemes. The thing is, you told me you were going to let everyone know that I also wasn't involved in them. There's no mention of that in here." Agnes held the letter up. "In fact, the only mention of me is

"... and please forgive Agnes for her part in this."

"I'm so sorry, Agnes. I was angry at you for the way you left. I understand now that this is wrong in so many ways. It's a coward's way out. Let's start over, figure this thing out together."

Agnes' face softened. She stood by the chair. "What then?"

Linda smiled. "We'll work it out somehow."

Agnes folded the letter, shoving it and the envelope into her back pocket. She stood silent for a minute. Then she walked toward the bedroom door.

"Agnes, where are you going? Agnes?"

"I'm going to call the police, let them cut you down and save you. This is going to end badly for me no matter what I do. I'm implicated as it is, and if I help you to get out of this embezzlement scheme, I'm an accomplice. The safest thing for me to do is to walk away and tell them what I know."

Arriving at the door, she turned back to Linda. The woman was staring at her, stunned. Seconds later, Linda bent her legs and jumped from the chair.

"No!" Agnes started for Linda, but she pulled back when the woman's decent jerked to a stop with a loud crack. The snap of her *neck sent tremors down Agnes' spine and through her legs. She froze, unable to look away. Her vision narrowed; everything except for the outline of her lover's body faded to black. Agnes' eyes followed the suspended corpse as it swung back and forth beneath the beam. A minute passed, and when the swaying stopped, the dead woman slowly twirled at the end of the rope.*

Agnes approached the body. She stretched her arms out and grasped the dead woman's hands. Despite her fury at Linda, tears rolled down her cheeks.

The vision faded and Agnes was back in the hallway. Her body was numb after reliving the event. She stood still, her shoulders slumped, and her head bent low. She'd called the police minutes after Linda's death to report the suicide. At the police station, she told them she stopped by her friend's home after the charity event to discuss the fundraiser. It was then that she found Linda hanged in her bedroom. Agnes made no mention of their being lovers, having been present when Linda died, or of the note. The next day she confessed all of it to the priest in charge of her convent and then renounced her vows. He did not dissuade her. She was investigated for fraud for almost a year following Linda's death and was eventually cleared of wrongdoing.

The voice in her head returned. "So, you drove a woman to suicide. You could have saved her. Talked her down, and then helped her. Your self-interest came before another's welfare. Aren't you special."

"Yes," she replied, "And I understood I would have to answer for that."

The demon laughed. "And you thought doing all this work with Father Fornicator would get you back into God's good graces?"

She thought it odd the demon referred to Father MacLeod that way. What was the connection? Had Nora and Celeste something to do with it?

"I got news for you," it went on. *"God doesn't give a shit about your penance. You're going to hell, Agnes, and I'm going to speed you along your way."*

Her head shot up at a sound in front of her. Someone was at the far end of the hallway. It was a woman. Her head was down, but there was no mistaking who it was. The noose around her neck and the rope trailing down her body confirmed it. The woman's raised her head and Agnes saw her face. It was purple, with eyes as dark as the deepest night. The woman spoke.

"Hello, Agnes. Have you missed me?"

Agnes' stiffened. "No," she whispered, "It can't be!"

"Oh, but it is. It's wonderful here. You're going to love it. We can finally be together, where we belong. Agnes, we're going to spend eternity together."

Linda stepped forward.

Agnes backed away, shaking her head and holding her breath. Focused on the demon, her left foot came down, but there was nothing solid beneath it. As she fell through the floor, the ceiling receded, and the demon spun out of view.

CHAPTER 19

"Hello, Father. You here to deliver on your promise?"

Father MacLeod ignored the demon's question. He studied Catherine's face, finding no visible indications that the woman was possessed. This either reinforced her notion that the demon was weak, or proved he was deceivingly cunning.

The priest stared directly into her eyes. "I wondered who you were," he said. "I suspected it was you, but if I used the wrong name in the rite, it could've made it even worse for Catherine. Your question about my promise told me all I need to know."

There was no response.

"You have very little presence left," he continued, "And now I know your name. By calling you out during an exorcism, I could banish you here and now. But I need an answer first."

"Quid pro quo?" asked the demon.

"If that's what it takes to get the information I need."

Catherine's eyes squinted. *"You'd let me stay inside this woman?"*

"Like I said, if that's what it takes."

It laughed. *"I can't trust you. You've already broken one promise to me, not to mention breaking all your vows to your god."*

It was Father MacLeod's turn to laugh. "That's rich, a disciple of the Devil not trusting *me*." His face tightened as he leaned toward the demon. "I'm not going to banish you if I get what I want. I'll keep your name to myself and let Catherine's exorcism continue as it is. You'll have more precious time in that vessel. More than you'll have otherwise."

The demon went silent. After a few moments, it nodded. "Ask your question."

Father MacLeod's tone hardened. "There is another like you, not far from here. It has killed many, and it's currently tormenting three more women. I need to banish it."

The laugh it emitted was loud and gravelly, echoing off the cell-like walls. "Yes, I know this demon. One higher tier, very powerful. You stand little chance, even if you have its name."

"Tell me."

Catherine wore the demon's smile, its grin expanding wider than humanly possible—the corners of her lips rising to just below her eyes. A thin, dark tongue forced its way between her lips and flickered obscenely.

"I know what you did with this one, Father."

The priest remained silent.

"You fucked her like a pig. You kept on doing it to her, even when she didn't want you to. Oh, you had your fun. Taking her in every hole, making her suck your dick. You want to know something, Father? Images of you two fucking often enters her mind. What if I told you she pleasures herself to those visions?"

The priest shook his head. "It was you who made me the way I am."

The demon spit. A glob of dark mucus flew the distance between them and clung to Father MacLeod's cheek. He wiped it away with the back of his hand, brushing it off against his pants.

"Ha! Priest, you were already vile before we met. I simply nudged you a little further. A bonus, shall we say, after you agreed to the deal. Only you didn't keep your side of the bargain. I had that young boy's soul—he was mine. You renounced your god, said you'd do anything to save that child. The deal was struck: you promised me two others in his stead. I am owed one more soul."

Guilt slammed Father MacLeod. He struggled with its weight.

Memories of his own mother's phone call begging him to do something flashed through the priest's head. He saw his nephew tied to a bed, emaciated, near death. The boy's eyes were wide, the white sclera dark red, his irises black. Cracked lips, caked with yellow crust stretched into a grimace revealing rotted teeth. The skin on his nephew's face erupted in bulges that slithered back and forth from his forehead to his chin. Father MacLeod would never forget the sounds the boy made. They were raspy, mocking, the volume rising and lowering at the demon's whim. In between the taunting, the priest heard his nephew's voice, pleading for help.

The young boy was close to death, and there was no time to battle the Church bureaucracy to conduct an exorcism. Though forbidden from performing one on his own, Father MacLeod initiated the rite. In the span of two hours, he performed the ritual repeatedly. It was ineffective. Frustrated and afraid, he resorted to personal pleas to God. They went unanswered. When the weakened boy's body convulsed with blood pouring from his nose and ears, Father MacLeod knew his nephew wouldn't survive the trauma for much longer. He called on the demon, asking it to reveal itself. If God wasn't interested in saving the child, the priest would take matters into his own hands. Unlike God, the demon responded to his plea. A bargain was struck. His nephew would be freed. The compensation: two souls. He had made good on half the debt, delivering to the demon a homeless man Catherine had brought to the Church for assistance.

Father MacLeod bowed his head. "You were taking my nephew. I had to do something."

"And you did. You gave me one soul years ago. You covered your tracks well with that one. I picked up the story from this vessel. Ha! You told her the man was sent to a Church-related facility for the homeless. I wish you could've been there when I showed her how you took him away and then dropped him off at the bottom of a bridge in some shit town. She saw what those men did to him. You owe me another soul, priest. Four years is too long to wait."

Father MacLeod's eyes burned with fury. "You took Catherine."

The demon's smile returned. "But she was not your offering."

The priest returned the smile. "You know, you screwed up. You reached out to me when you went after my nephew. I'm an exorcist— an exorcist who knows what the hell he is doing. The thing is, I got a good look at you then. I heard your thoughts, I could see what you were, and...I discovered your name." He paused a moment to let his words sink in.

"I wondered from the start if it were you inside Catherine, but I had no way of knowing. I couldn't risk using the wrong name during the exorcism. The last thing I wanted was to have two demons living in her. I didn't know for sure it was you until you asked about my promise. I know who you are now, and I can send you back."

The demon studied the priest through Catherine's eyes. "You need something from me. You won't do it if you want the higher demon's name."

"How will I know you'll give me the demon's *real* name?"

"How will I know you'll let me stay in this vessel after I give it to you?"

The priest peered down at Catherine's body and nodded. "Fair enough. I give you my word that I won't banish you from this vessel. After I get the name, I'll open myself up to you. Let you see for yourself that I'll do as I say. But if you go any further, I'll not only stop you, I'll send you to hell."

The demon took a moment to consider Father MacLeod's words. "You intrigue me, priest. You're willing to prolong the suffering of this vessel, one you've had a relationship with, for three other women.

Those three women must fuck well. I'll be making note of them."

The priest raised his fists. "Give me the name!"

"Once again, we are bargaining, priest. I'll give you the name. I expect you to deliver on your word fully this time; if not, when we meet again you'll rue the day. And don't forget, you still owe me one more soul."

Lowering his hands, the priest demanded, "What is its name?"

"Belphegor."

Father MacLeod's countenance fell, and he took a step back. *Belphegor.* A shiver chilled his spine and his knees grew weak. This was bad.

A sharp sound at Catherine's side diverted his attention. Both wrist straps were broken, and her arms were rising. She raised her head and the band across her forehead snapped with a loud *crack.* The restraint over her chest severed in two.

The demon sat up, closed and reopened Catherine's eyes, revealing coal-black pools void of pupils, the malefic grin still on her face. "I'm not as weak as you thought," said the demon.

"Maybe not, Asmodeus," the priest answered, "But weak enough."

At the mention of its name, the demon flinched.

The priest reached into his pants pocket and removed a small vial. He screwed off the lid and shook the contents toward Catherine's body. When the liquid contacted her skin, the demon screamed. Puffs of steam clouded the air, and the smell of burnt flesh filled the room.

"I cast you out, unclean spirit . . ." Father MacLeod recited, beginning the exorcism. He approached the demon while digging into his other pants pocket and pulled out a crucifix. As the priest spoke the ritual, he placed the wooden cross against Catherine's forehead.

"No!" The demon howled in agony and rage. It remained still, unable to remove the crucifix. "You gave me your word!"

The priest continued with the ritual. Near its conclusion, he paused. "My word, as you have seen, means nothing, demon." He resumed, uttering the few remaining stanzas of the rite. "Begone, in the name of the Father, Son, and the Holy Spirit. Be gone, Asmodeus, back to Satan and the hell he has dominion over."

Catherine's body flopped down onto the mattress. Her eyes were still dark as she focused them on the priest. The demon spoke in a feeble voice. "How? We've been watching you. You have lost faith in your god."

Father MacLeod's eyes were bright, his grin cruel. "I don't have to have faith in Him. I only have to have faith in the ritual."

Catherine's eyes closed.

The priest lifted her left eyelid, then let it drop. He did the same to her right. They were both back to normal. He removed the crucifix from her forehead and, using holy water, made the sign of the cross in its place.

While he was sure God had abandoned him some time ago, Catherine apparently still had some pull. He figured she should be okay from there on in. He walked to the door and took one last look at her. The familiar feelings of arousal stirred as he gazed at her legs and what sat between them.

We did have fun for a while, didn't we, Catherine? Sighing, he punched six nines on the keypad and left the room.

Sister Bernice sat at the desk, peering at him with a frown. "Is Catherine okay?"

Father MacLeod nodded. "Yes."

The nun sighed, relaxing her shoulders. "Thanks be to God. Did you get what you needed, Father?"

"I did. Thank you, Sister."

"Can you save those women?"

"I—I don't know. I'm going to try. Can you go in there and make her comfortable? You can remove her leg restraints. She shouldn't be a problem anymore. I'm sure the exorcists are going to have some questions. You can tell them I was here."

Sister Bernice did not reply.

"I'm not going to ask you to lie, but if you can, please keep the part about Agnes, Nora, and Celeste out of it. I don't want them involved with the exorcists at this point. I'll fill them in later."

Father MacLeod didn't wait for her answer, but he did hear her say, "I will," as he walked down the hall.

Back in his office, he called Mr. Lewis. "Tell your contact I have a name. You have a pencil and paper? Okay, now this is important: do *not* speak the name aloud. Never. Tell your contact not to, either. Got it? Good. I'm going to spell it out for you. B-e-l-p-h-e-g-o-r." Mr. Lewis began to recite the name as he wrote it. "No! I told you not to say its name out loud! What the hell! You want to make this even worse than it is?"

There was silence on the other end of the phone.

"Look, this demon is powerful," the priest went on. "It's a higher demon, said to be the closest to Lucifer. You don't want to be calling its attention to you. It's imperative you tell your contact this."

Mr. Lewis emphasized that he would.

"I'm going back to the Moore house. Tell your guy to meet me there in two hours. It's going to be dark, so bring flashlights for all three of us."

The priest hung up. After considering some of the potential disasters that could transpire at the Moore house, he made one more phone call. When finished, he reached for the bottle of scotch. He gulped down two swallows. He let the liquid burn in his belly as he pulled on his beard.

CHAPTER 20

The pawnshop landline rang.

Customers who had heard it would often remark how it was reminiscent of phones in old movies and television shows. Located on a shelf underneath the shop's counter, the vintage device—original to the 1960s—sat out of view. While the proprietor had made some upgrades as concessions to the times, namely installing a plug cord so he could use a modern phone jack, he preferred its bulky, worn appearance over modern digital handsets. The raised push-buttons made calling slower, and its aqua color was hideous enough to raise eyebrows, but he was comfortable with it. Truth was, he took comfort from old and obsolete objects. He made his living off them.

The handset was snatched before the fourth ring was complete, and as was his practice, he waited for the caller to speak first. After several seconds of silence, a tinny voice called out to him.

"Hello? Hello? Are you there?"

It was the call he'd been waiting for. "Yes. I'm here."

Mr. Lewis was on the other end. "The priest called me back," the old man said. "He wants to meet with you in about two hours at the Moore house."

"Did he give you a name?"

The old man was quiet for a moment. "Yes," he said hesitantly, "But I'm not supposed to speak it out loud, and neither are you. He was quite firm on that. Do you have something close by to write it down? I'll spell it out."

"Hang on." The proprietor searched the shelf for a pencil and paper. He moved a few items aside—rusty knobs, grease-stained rags, a coffee can that contained blue metallic stars, and a stack of year-old newspapers. His fingers brushed against a pencil and he removed it, along with a newspaper from the top of the stack. "Okay," he said, "Spell the name."

"B-E-L-P-H-E-G-O-R. Remember, don't say it out loud."

The owner copied the letters onto the newspaper as they were read to him. When finished, he silently read what he had written. The name meant nothing.

"You still there?"

Nothing. "*Hello*? Are you still *there*?"

"Um, yeah, sorry," he replied. "I'm still here."

"You know," the old man said, lowering his voice, "I don't even know *your* name. All this time we've been doing business and I've never learned it."

"Look," the owner said, cutting the man off. "If I only have less than two hours, I've got to get working on this. Call me Smith for all I care."

"Okay, I understand. I'll also be there. Father MacLeod asked me to bring flashlights, so I've got to stop at the hardware store. It's near to you. You want me to swing by after and pick you up?"

The pawnshop owner rolled his eyes. He didn't need Lewis watching over his shoulder. "No. I'll meet you at the Moore house." He didn't wait for an acknowledgment, returning the handset to its cradle. He proceeded to the end of the counter where the occult books were laid out.

Half an hour later, the man closed all four books. He gathered up the few notes he'd taken and brought them to his computer. As expected, the internet provided information on the demon, but he had no idea how accurate it was. One of the sites mentioned that Belphegor was so vile he could only be summoned with excrement. Despite the seriousness of the situation, an obvious joke came to mind about how shitty this demon was. Dismissing the claim, he clicked away from the site before he traveled down a rat hole of puns.

There was one piece of information he'd gleaned from the texts that the internet sites confirmed—that the appointed enemy of Belphegor was Saint Mary Magdalene. But this wasn't as straightforward as he'd hoped.

There was some confusion as to whether this saint was the same woman who had stood by Jesus as he was crucified and the one from whom Jesus had exorcised seven demons. Many websites strongly hinted these were two separate Mary Magdalenes. If that were true, the pawnshop owner faced a dilemma. Which one was the demon's enemy?

Artifacts belonging to the exorcised Mary Magdalene were readily obtainable. Their significance was not lost on the apostles, who had collected as many of her possessions as possible. Over the years, many of these were acquired by the Catholic Church and placed in storage. Those not claimed were available through back channels. There were enough in circulation to devalue them, and worse, to enable cheap counterfeits. The pawnshop owner had a wooden serving bowl that was purported to have belonged to her, but he couldn't obtain a respected authentication on it. It sat on his shelves unsold. The bowl had been included in a lot he'd purchased on behalf of a customer. His client took what he wanted but had no use for the bowl without proper certification.

If there were indeed two Mary Magdalenes, he might be out of luck. Even if the bowl were authentic, it could belong to the wrong one. There was no time to seek an authenticated object connected to either of the women. Though he had no idea what power the bowl could possess over the demon, if it *did* belong to the right Mary, it was all he had to work with.

A bothersome notion crowded his thoughts. Owning this bowl appeared to be fortuitous. While he was often fortunate enough to own objects that clients might be desperate for, the outcome of this situation was far too serious to be determined by luck. Was he somehow being played? During his conversation with Celeste, he'd mentioned that the influence of the Moore house was growing. Had it reached the pawnshop? Had it reached him? Could the demon have discovered the presence of the bowl, and be using it as a distraction? If this were true, he had no other supernatural method to combat the demon—that would be up to the priest and Mr. Lewis.

However, he did have one other type of assistance at his disposal.

Rex was often called on when a situation required extreme strength or when it was too dangerous for the owner to handle on his own. The problem with Rex was that on occasion, he could be mentally unstable. He had changed after following a client's wife into a nightclub called Painfreak. When he returned from the club, he'd brutalized the client's wife, and then killed the man.

Rex was aware of the changes inside of him, and he'd come to the pawnshop owner seeking relief from his physiological torment. As his mentor, he did what he could for Rex. For the most part, he was successful, but Rex did suffer from relapses, leaving carnage in his wake.

The giant agreed to meet up at the Moore house, but only after he finished a task at hand.

He found the wooden bowl and stuffed it into a plastic grocery bag. The less attention called to it, the better. Before leaving the shop, the owner set the alarm. After hearing a confirming beep, he stepped through the front doors and locked them. Standing in the street, he stared at the storefront.

Who would take over the business if I died?

CHAPTER 21

The sounds of cracking floorboards chased Celeste up the stairs. She held onto the handrail tightly as she sprinted, until it split in her hand. It was pulled from her grip, and the weight of the rail threatened to take her with it. Her hold relaxed, saving her from tumbling down into the chaos, but she lost her balance and landed hard on her knees. She cried out, reaching to grab a stair above her. She rolled up onto her toes to ease the pain to her knees, straining to hold herself up on all fours. She glanced toward the living room where ragged fragments of wood sailed through the air. The shrapnel embedded into the surrounding walls with soft thuds. More holes opened along the floor, creating miniature tornados that sucked in debris and whirls of dust.

Nora's down there!

The staircase shook, sending vibrations coursing through her body, and making her hair dance before her eyes. She focused on the top of the stairway. She needed to get up there, *now*. She pushed off with her toes and struggled up the remaining stairs until she reached the second-floor landing. Thoughts of Agnes and Nora caught in the carnage below caused her to turn around. At the bottom of the staircase, Officer Jones stared up at her. His eyes were wide, empty, and pitch black; his grin enormous. He stepped onto the bottom stair, which vanished beneath him, yet he hovered over the jet-black chasm that appeared under his feet. Jones took another step; the second stair disappeared.

Celeste stood and scanned the hallway; one door to her right and three to her left, all closed. Choosing the last door on her left, she rushed to it, entered the room and slammed the door shut behind her.

She twisted a simple lock on the handle and then turned to survey the room for something to push against the door. The bedroom was empty.

"Oh, come on! How 'bout some fucking furniture?" she entreated the ceiling in frustration.

She hurried to the only window in the room, brushed back the curtains and yanked upward on the lower sash, but it was jammed. Visions of the table and bullet embedded in the window downstairs flashed in her mind and she presumed there was no way she was going to open or break this one, either. Daylight was nearly gone, and the room was bathed in shadow.

She slumped to the floor, sat with her back against the wall and cradled her head in her hands.

A blow to the door snapped her head up.

The doorknob moved. The lock held.

There was a long silence. Celeste stared at the door. She couldn't look away.

Another blow startled her.

The middle of the door wavered, and the wood stretched, pushing inward toward her, its shape like that of a closed fist. Inches above it, the wood also transformed, this panel looking more like a face. As it protruded forward, she recognized it...Officer Jones.

"God, please, save me!"

Surrounding the face, deep fissures sprouted. A sound like logs burning in a fire pit followed as the seams grew. The door bulged outward, the fissures growing wider at the strain. A crack as loud as a felled tree rang through the room. Celeste covered her face and eyes, tensing, waiting to be hit with debris, but moments passed and she felt no pain. She lowered her arms. All that remained of the door were splintered shards clinging to the hinges. Wood fragments covered the floor in front of her, but none within three feet of her. The body of Officer Jones stood in the doorway. His dead, vacant eyes glued to hers. Behind him the hallway was no longer visible; all she could see was black.

The demon stepped forward.

Celeste's heart pounded. She drew back against the wall, and when she could go no farther, she raised her arms as shields. Eyes squinted, teeth gritted, she waited for the demon to take her.

It stopped in front of her where the spread of debris ended, and though the demon tried to push closer, he was not able. It stood still, head cocked, staring at Celeste. It remained motionless a minute, and then lowered itself to the floor, sitting cross-legged in front of her.

"Well," it said, "You *are* different."

Though Celeste knew it was the demon who sat before her, she couldn't help but think of Officer Jones. There was no doubt in her mind the man was dead. Was his soul still earthbound, trapped in his body? Did it travel to God's heaven? Or was the demon's power so great the man's soul was delivered to hell? She mentally recited a prayer for the officer, asking God to forgive him for any sins he may have committed. She kept her eyes open and focused on the demon while she prayed. It didn't look away from her.

Why didn't it take me? Why did it stop there? Why does it think I'm different?

The answer came to her. *It's the necklace.*

Her body relaxed as hope took root. She thought back to her visit to the pawnshop and the owner loaning her the wooden cross. His thoughts about the necklace protecting the wearer from harm *were* true. She hoped she'd get the opportunity to tell him if she ever saw him again. Her hand rose to her cleavage, but she stopped herself and let the cross lay flat over her heart. The demon didn't seem to know why she was protected, and she saw no reason for it to have that information.

Even with the necklace, she was still trapped. The demon had physical power over the house and everything in it. It could open a hole beneath her if it so wished, or it could make the ceiling fall. She doubted the necklace would prevent its weight from crushing her. From what she'd witnessed, the demon could cause everything around her to disappear, leaving her afloat in a black void. Maybe it could do those things, but why hadn't it? It sat, staring at her, allowing her to live. At least for the moment.

Celeste fought the urge to grasp the necklace. If it were indeed protecting her, she would take advantage of his lack of knowledge for as long as she could. She had no idea how to respond to the demon, or if she should even engage it. Hoping a prayer might offer some defense, she started reciting the Lord's Prayer out loud. "Our Father, who art—"

"Cut the shit, Celeste." Its voice was even, almost parental. "Invoking *Him* will only irritate me further at this point, and you don't want to do that. I may not be able to see what's going on in that head of yours, but I can still make your physical presence uncomfortable."

Celeste did as she was told. "What do you want?"

"I had planned to fuck with you before I dragged you down into hell like I did with Agnes and Nora," the demon answered.

At the mention of their names, Celeste swallowed hard.

The demon laughed. "Yes, they're mine now, as you'll soon be. You're all foreplay. It's like having appetizers before the main course. Your leader, the priest, is on his way here, and that's when my fun actually begins."

Celeste blinked. Her earlier suspicions that Father MacLeod was involved with the demon were correct. Had the priest known he was the demon's quarry? If so, why did he send the team to the Moore house? Would the demon explain it to her? If Father MacLeod was on his way, maybe he had a way to exorcise it. She had to buy some time.

"How come you don't talk like a demon?" she asked. "You talk like someone from our time, not like someone centuries or millennia old."

Officer Jones grinned. "That's a thing with you Catholics. All your demons are as ancient as the scripture you quote. Much of what you've been taught about us is as fanciful as the piety of the saints you worship. Reformed holy men versus the unrepentant fallen. Have you ever thought, Celeste, that the modern Church has no problem bestowing sainthood on men and women who've passed on fairly recently, but when it comes to demons, we're regulated to the Dark Ages? Take Josef Mengele, for instance. He was even called *The Angel of Death*. Wouldn't he fit the definition of a demon? I can tell you Mengele is one of us, and he is thriving."

Her face tightened. "What? You're saying Mengele is one of hell's demons?"

"Yes. Satan is especially proud of him. The Angel of Death is responsible for serial killers Michael Swango, Maxim Petrov, Harold Shipman, and Anders Hansson. All were medical professionals, all were possessed by Mengele."

Celeste leaned forward. "And you? What of you? Are you saying that you've lived in recent times? That when it comes to evil and possession, you have a specialty?"

The demon ignored her questions. "Have you noticed you can see me clearly? The sun has set and there's darkness surrounding me, yet light radiates from you. I don't think you notice it." It paused for a moment. "You're much different than the others. There is more to you. I don't understand...but I will."

She took her eyes off the demon to glance around the room. Her view was not impeded by the lack of sunlight. However, she didn't see herself as the source of any powerful emanations—to her she appeared normal. She craned her head to the window. Where the heck was Father MacLeod?

"He's on his way."

She redirected her gaze to the demon. "I thought you couldn't get into my mind."

The demon shook Jones' head. "You looked at the window. I'm also guessing you believe you're stalling me."

She had no reply. Strangely, the demon went silent. After minutes of staring at each other, Celeste was compelled to ask, "Why are you waiting for Father MacLeod?"

"I want him to watch when I eat your soul."

Its words froze her. Could the demon harm her while she wore the necklace? Had it figured a way around it? Was it bluffing? Keeping her eyes on the demon, she lowered her head and asked, "Why?"

"We have time, so let me tell you...."

CHAPTER 22

Mr. Lewis pulled up to the curb; no one else had arrived yet. He considered leaving the car and standing in the yard to wait but based on his conversations with the other two men, this demon was powerful. Mr. Lewis wasn't sure the damn thing couldn't reach out to him while he sat in the car, but based on their earlier visits, he thought he'd be safer here. The moon was full and the night cloudless, giving him a clear but shadowed view of the house. He kept watch.

Five minutes later, another car pulled in behind him. The pawnshop owner exiting the vehicle; Mr. Lewis grabbed the flashlights and opened his door. As he got out of his car, he noticed the man was clutching a bag. He approached him, handing over a flashlight.

"What do you have in the bag?"

"Something that may or may not help us. I need Father MacLeod's advice on it. Where is he?"

Mr. Lewis shook his head. "I don't know. He told me he was on his way."

The man sighed. "We don't have much time." He gazed at the house. "It might already be too late."

The old man nodded and turned to the house. "Yeah, it's awful quiet. I almost expect to hear screams coming from it."

"Maybe the screaming is over."

Mr. Lewis shuddered. "I hope not. I want to save those women and get rid of that demon. After that, one way or another, I'm going to demolish that damn house."

They heard Father MacLeod pull in behind the pawnshop owner's vehicle. He climbed out of his car and walked to the two men. He held a book in one hand and what appeared to be a small vial in the other.

"Gentlemen," he greeted. To the pawnshop owner, he said, "You wanted the name of the demon because you thought you might be able to assist us with it. You got the name. Now, what kind of help can you offer?"

"I'm not sure what value this may be." The proprietor opened the bag and withdrew a wooden bowl.

The priest glared at him. "What the hell am I supposed to do with that? Serve him a salad?"

A flash of anger surged the store owner's eyes. "It may have belonged to Mary Magdalene. She—"

The priest interrupted him. "I know who Mary Magdalene is, or should I say, are. You do know there were possibly two Mary Magdalenes?"

The man nodded.

"Do you know which one this might have belonged to?"

"I can't be certain, no."

"Even if it did belong to the one who is said to be the arch-enemy of the demon, *what am I supposed to do with her bowl*?"

The man sighed. "I don't know. I thought it might help."

The priest returned the sigh. "Okay, bring it in; who knows. You gentlemen ready?"

Mr. Lewis nodded, but the man who said to call him Smith needed more time.

"I'm waiting for my associate to join us. He should be here any moment. Give him five more minutes. He'll be able to help us."

The priest sneered. "How? What's he bringing? Forks?"

A grin appeared on Smith's face. "You'll see."

CHAPTER 23

Celeste thought she heard car doors and hoped it was Father MacLeod bringing help. The demon didn't react to the sounds, so maybe it didn't hear them. Or maybe it didn't care. She prayed it was the former and prodded the demon to distract it. "Yes, tell me the story."

"Time is endless where I come from," it began. "We have no way of knowing how much has passed until we come back into this world. For those destined to suffer eternally, they're always in the moment. They have no perception of a 'later on,' an 'afterward,' a 'tomorrow.' Their torment is constant, unending, with no comprehension of future escape. Others such as myself are the fortunate ones. We have Satan's blessings. We are the tormentors, those who have excelled in doing the Devil's work while we lived. We hold a special place in his kingdom. Though I had no way of knowing how much time had passed until I came back to this world, it appears I pledged my devotion to Satan ten years ago.

"I made a bargain with Satan before I entered his kingdom. I requested to come back so I could fuck over those who had wronged me while I lived. I promised him souls. I was mentored, and I ascended to the unholiest of ranks by a demon who had been banished back to hell by an exorcism...."

"If Satan was going to collect those souls anyway, why did he need you?" Celeste interrupted.

"There's no guarantee a soul will be delivered to him. Redemption is possible in your god's eyes. I'm ensuring that those who are on Satan's path stay there."

"What does all this have to do with the Moore house and Father

MacLeod?"

Officer Jones' body tilted forward. "Impatient? Though your priest has arrived and is standing outside, we still have some time."

Adrenaline surged through Celeste. Father MacLeod was here! *It's planning something. But what?*

The demon leaned back. "Fifteen years ago, I was of this world. My child took ill, acting strange. I became convinced she might be possessed. When a behavioral specialist couldn't diagnose her problem, I persuaded my wife to contact an expert on demonic possession."

Celeste's eyes widened. "Father MacLeod."

"Yes. The shit bag agreed to meet with us but insisted it be at our home. He took more interest in my wife than he did my child. I would catch him checking out my wife with more than simple appreciation. She was built, Celeste, built like Nora—busty, voluptuous. Speaking of Nora, I can assure you MacLeod is well acquainted with her body."

Celeste gasped; she couldn't help herself. Pushing aside the shock, she thought about the accusation. What were the odds of Nora having an affair with a man? Then again, the accusation came from a demon, a master of lies.

"I don't believe you."

"Let me into your mind, I will show you."

"That's not going to happen."

The demon's eyes drilled into Celeste and a scheming smile transformed his face. "One day, I came home to find my daughter sitting in front of the television set, and that hypocritical fuckhead in bed with my wife. She was sitting astride him, in the throes of passion, submitting to him in a way I had never experienced as her husband. She was too lost in her frenzy to notice me standing there, but MacLeod saw me and just smiled. The cunt put his hands on my wife's thrusting hips and smiled at me."

Celeste lowered her head at the image.

"God had forsaken me. Mocked me. I never told my wife I had seen her with the priest. Instead, I spent more time with my daughter. I was right. She was possessed, and the child shared with me the wisdom and sweet promise of Satan. I spent years delving into Satanism, real Satanism, not the play-nice shit you find on the Internet. I made contacts with the right people and learned the rituals. I surrendered my soul. After I moved my family here, I struck a deal with Satan. I killed my whore wife and daughter as an offering. Butchered them in the basement. I joined up with both of them in hell."

How many deaths was this demon responsible for? Celeste recalled the contents of the police folder sent to her computer the previous evening, which seemed so long ago. Those deaths were a lure, a way for the demon to get Father MacLeod to this house.

"The time is now, Celeste. Follow me downstairs."

She felt safe there, against the wall, wearing the necklace. "No."

Officer Jones' body suddenly stood, yanked upright as if attached to strings. "It seems I cannot physically or mentally touch you, but the same isn't true for our surroundings."

The floor beneath Celeste groaned as cracks formed in a radius around her. They expanded across the floor and toward her like dozens of small black snakes.

"If you don't follow me, I'll meet you downstairs."

The floor groaned louder, pieces falling away. A vibration hummed through her bottom, her body sinking about half an inch into the floor. She yelped and scrambled away. More of the floor fell, leaving a three-foot gap. She stood and faced the demon.

"I'm not walking into that void." She said and nodded to the hallway.

The blackness beyond the doorway vanished, and the interior of the house came back into view. A sickly hue of yellow light illuminated the hallway.

"I want the asshole to watch what happens," the demon said as if reading her mind. "I'll savor the expression on his face when he sees what I do to you and your two friends. Now, follow me."

CHAPTER 24

Agnes craved sleep. Her head lolled as she struggled to keep her chin off her chest. If she let it fall too far, pain from her right shoulder assaulted her with the ferocity of a pit bull. She thanked God she was lying on her left side. The torment originated at her collarbone, radiating down to her elbow, below which, she couldn't feel a thing. Arm movement, no matter how slight, begat thousands of knife-like jabs.

Where the hell am I? The pain fed her confusion. She couldn't concentrate, and the surrounding darkness was no help. Her thoughts clouded and her head dropped. Snapping it back up, she cried out in pain.

"Agnes?" Someone called her name.

She forced herself to think clearer, to focus through the pain. Images flooded her mind. In an instant, it all came rushing back to her, culminating in the confrontation with the demon in the hallway. She recalled the visions it cast, how it mined her memories and caused her to relive them. Wincing, she saw Linda leaping off the chair, then remembered the dead woman calling for her to join her in hell. The last image she recalled was of the ceiling as she fell through the hole on the floor.

"Agnes?"

Was it Linda calling to her? *No! Please, don't let it be Linda!*

"Agnes! Are you okay?"

No, it wasn't Linda. "Nora, is that you?"

"Yes, Agnes. Oh, thank God, it's you! There was someone else here. I—I think he's gone now."

"Where are you?"

"I'm behind you. I'm hurt, hurt bad. It's my leg."

It sounded like Nora. But what if it wasn't? There was no way to know without having a good look. Still, she longed for it to be her partner—it would mean Nora was still alive. An idea came to her. "Nora, if you can, clear your mind. If you can't, think about kittens, flowers, anything but the situation we are in. I'm going to ask you a question. You will need to answer it right away. No hesitation at all. I'm going to give you a few seconds before I ask it. You okay with that?"

"Yes."

Agnes silently counted backward from thirty. When she reached zero, she asked, "Nora, recite Ephesians one-seven."

"In Him, we have redemption through his blood, the forgiveness of our trespasses, according to the riches of his grace."

Agnes choked up, letting out a loud sob. She couldn't be sure, but she hoped that scripture wasn't on the top of a demon's tongue. Nora didn't hesitate with her answer, and she recited it with grace and authority. "It *is* you. Thank God you're alive."

Nora let out a grunt. "Yeah, I'm alive, but I feel half-dead. Your turn, Hebrews nine-twelve."

"He entered once for all into the holy places, not by means of the blood of goats and calves but by means of his own blood, thus securing an eternal redemption."

Nora broke down. Her sobs carried through the room.

"Look," Agnes said, "I'm going to try and slide over to you. I can't turn over—my shoulder's probably broken—so you're going to have to tell me if I get too close to your leg. Can you see enough to tell me if I do?"

Nora managed a *yes* between sobs.

Agnes took a deep breath—knives slashed at her chest. She shifted her weight and pushed off with her legs. Her body moved mere inches, but she was that much closer to her partner. Shoulder on fire, she plowed through the pain. Like a woman dying of thirst with an oasis in sight, she found her way to Nora.

"Stop!" Nora's voice was low, weak. "Turn to your left, and then keep pushing back until you reach the wall. It's another four feet or so."

As Agnes pivoted, she couldn't suppress a groan. Taking another deep breath, she slid her knees up and pushed off with her heels. It was slow and painful, a sticky dampness saturated her clothing, but she continued until her head bumped something solid.

"You're at the wall, Agnes. Can you sit up?"

There was no way she'd be able to lift her upper body and lean against the wall. The best she could hope for was to turn onto her back. It had to be done quickly, too—if she attempted a slow rollover, she wasn't sure she could handle the pain. She had no other option if she wanted to see her lover again.

One...two...three!

"Ahh, oh God, that hurts!" Agnes almost blacked out. She internalized the pain, imagining her shoulder as a foreign body, detached from hers. Between the squinting and tears, she was blind. She heard her lover calling to her, but Nora's voice alone wasn't enough to pull her through the agony.

It was a touch that eventually calmed her enough to battle the pain. Nora laid a hand on her hip, consoling her as she rubbed. If she had needed any more proof Nora was really beside her, this was it. With her good hand, she wiped away the tears and turned her head towards her partner. The look of concern on Nora's face almost brought her to tears again. Instead, she smiled. "Hey there, Babe."

Nora's face relaxed, and she let out a small breath. "Hey there, yourself."

They gazed at each other for a few moments. Though grateful for the chance to see Nora once more, Agnes was sure it would be the last time. "I think we're in the kind of trouble we can't get out of," she said.

"Yeah. It's going to get us, one way or another. I'm bleeding out at my knee, it soaked into your clothes as you slid toward me, and it's only a matter of time before I pass out, or worse." There was a pause, then, "Hey, you got a minute?"

Agnes chuckled. "I think I can spare you one. What's on your mind?"

"A couple of things. First, I'm sorry for the way I acted today. Outside, upstairs, it was like I was a helpless, whimpering little girl. I was no help to you and Celeste. I might've made things worse. I was scared, never been more scared in my life, but that's no excuse."

After a pause, Agnes responded. "I'd be lying if I said I didn't notice. I thought about it while we were all on the couch. I knew that wasn't you. You're not one to curl up in a ball and cry. I figured it was the demon. Somehow, it must have reached us after the investigation at the Millman home. It could be something the demon sent that we both had contact with. I'm wondering if it was that belt buckle. Maybe it was those pictures Father MacLeod emailed us. Whatever it was, it was able to get into our heads and plant seeds. Maybe we were too far away from the demon for it to cause us any real harm, but it must have been powerful enough to influence us. I know it got to me. When we made love last night, I wasn't myself. I knew I was too aggressive, but I was unable to stop myself. To tell you the truth, I didn't want to. When I woke up this morning, I reflected on what I'd done to you. There was no shame. I couldn't wait to do it again."

"I kind of liked it."

Agnes chortled. "Now that's the Nora I know and love."

Nora laughed, but it dissolved into a mild cough.

Worried, Agnes stared hard at her. Would this be the last long talk they would ever share? "What're the other things you want to talk about?"

"Confession," Nora answered. "I hear it's good for the soul."

"Forget it. This is not the time for us to be telling each other all the terrible things we've done. I'll make you a promise: if we somehow get out of here, then we'll discuss our shortcomings. But not now. Anything else?"

"Yeah, one more thing. Do you believe that suicides go to hell?"

Agnes' head dropped. The pain in her shoulder intensified at the action. She raised her chin so quickly the base of her neck ached. Grimacing at both the pain and the question, she replied, "I'm afraid to ask why you want to know."

Nora's breathing was labored. Her answer came hesitantly, with small pauses between words. "The demon's existence proves hell is real. If it gets us, I could be dragged to hell for my sins. Believe me, Agnes, I'd be on the fast track. But, if there's a chance God does forgive those who have sinned grievously and are repentant, I'm thinking He might issue me a *get out of hell free card*. And, Agnes...I can't tell you how sorry I am for my past actions. The only solace I take from my sins is that they led me to you. I've made my case to God. I've prayed and begged Him for forgiveness. I've since led a life I thought He would approve of. If I did make amends in His eyes, would God understand if I took my own life? Would it be wrong to avert suffering at the demon's hands that way? Does the demon have the power to send me to hell despite my penance?"

Agnes couldn't hide the sorrow in her eyes. Tears flowed as she answered. "I don't know, Nora. I could quote scripture, but you already know what the bible says about suicide." A vision of Linda swinging at the end of a rope flashed through her mind. "You know, I believed in God before I was acquainted with the Devil. The only thing that's changed about my way of thinking is that after meeting this demon, I believe God doesn't have a clue about us. He doesn't know who we are or what we've done in our lives. Until we die, that is. Then, *that's* when it's all laid out before Him. The good and the bad. Who or what we were *when* we died decides our fate. What I'm trying to say is, I think God judges us in totality. That ascension into heaven or an eternity in hell is decided by all our life's actions, not by a single or even a series of sins. With that in mind, I would say God would take any suicide in context."

Nora stared at Agnes. "Sounds like something a woman with a past would say." A smile crept onto her lips.

Agnes returned the smile. "Yeah, I guess it does."

They held their gazes on each other for a few seconds.

Nora lifted her right hand. It held a shard of glass, which she positioned just below her throat.

"No," Agnes pleaded, "Don't."

"Yessss." The voice came from above.

Agnes looked up through the hole in the living room floor to see the body of Officer Jones peering down at her. Next to it was Celeste, sobbing, shaking her head.

"Though I'll miss your suffering here, I'll make up for it when we next meet, in hell," the demon continued.

Nora dropped the fragment of glass and leaned her head back against the wall. She whispered a plea for God to help her.

Thud. Agnes heard the sound a fraction of a second before the house shook. *Thud.* Debris fell through the hole. Celeste and the demon had turned away from them, toward the front of the house. Celeste's eyes were frightened and wide as she stepped out of Agnes' view.

    Now what? Agnes wondered.

CHAPTER 25

Father MacLeod had had enough. Ten minutes had elapsed and the mystery man was nowhere in sight. He said to the pawnshop owner, "Okay, we've waited long enough for your assistant. It's time. I don't know if they're still alive in there, but if they are, they need our help. No more waiting."

"I agree—what's the plan?"

"For one," he pointed to Mr. Lewis, "You stay here. You'd only be in the way." He saw relief cross the old man's features. Turning back to the pawnshop owner, he said, "It's up to you if you want to come in. I'll tell you straight up your life will be in danger, not to mention your soul. Think of all the scary stories you've read about demonic possession. Remember all the horrible scenes you've seen in horror movies. This will be worse. This demon we're trying to exorcise is ancient and powerful. It will use every deceitful trick it has to drive you mad, torture you, and possess you. And all you have is *that*," he pointed to the bowl, "To protect you."

The man nodded. "You got anything on you I can use to keep that...*thing* away?"

Father MacLeod produced three crucifixes and a glass vial filled with clear liquid. Not attached to rosary beads but a simple loop of string, the crucifixes fit easily in the palm of his hand. He opened the vial and sprinkled them with the holy water. In a low tone, he recited words in Latin. He sealed the vial and returned it to his pocket.

"Put this around your neck. I don't have a hope in hell it will protect you, but you never know. It could be untrue, of course, but the holy water I doused these in is said to originate in Lourdes, and blessed by each successive pope since the miracle.

"Miracle? Lourdes?" Asked the pawnshop owner. "I hope you know what you're doing." He placed the crucifix around his neck and placed the other two in his pocket.

The priest sighed. "As I said, this demon has been around for thousands of years, it's adept at getting around our defenses and offenses. I brought three crucifixes, one for each of the women. If they're alive, I expect you to give one to each, or place one around each of their necks yourself if they can't. Including the one you just put on. I suspect I won't have time to do it myself."

The man nodded, tucking the crucifix under his shirt. "What makes you think you can exorcise the demon if it's that powerful?"

"The exorcism rites have evolved over the life of the Church. They're much more effective since the time this one was banished. And I possess something the demon isn't expecting me to have."

"Its name?"

Father MacLeod nodded. "Yeah."

The pawnshop owner exhaled. "Okay, let's do this."

Mr. Lewis stopped them. "Wait—take the flashlights. Is there anything I can do?"

Father MacLeod and the proprietor each took a flashlight, turning them on. "Have your cell phone ready. We may need ambulances," the priest answered while walking to the front door of the Moore house.

The old man said nothing.

The pawnshop owner and the priest climbed the steps to the front of the house and paused before the door. Father MacLeod removed the vial from his pocket, splashed a few drops of holy water onto the door, and then slid it back into his pocket. He lowered his head and recited a prayer. The proprietor attempted to listen to the words, but the priest's voice was too low. What he did hear sounded like gibberish. The prayer ended, and the priest faced him and asked, "Ready?"

After glancing around to see if his assistant had arrived, the pawnshop owner held tightly to the bag in one hand, the flashlight in the other. At the door, Father MacLeod turned the knob. It rotated and kept on rotating. The latch stayed engaged. The priest rammed his shoulder into the door. For his effort, all he got was pain.

"Shit. Now what do we do?" Father MacLeod asked.

A weight on the pawnshop owner's shoulder nearly made his knees buckle. He ducked and turned to look behind him. He grinned, tapped the priest on the back, and said, "The key to the door just arrived."

The proprietor saw Father MacLeod's jaw drop. The priest was looking at a freak of nature. Rex was over seven feet tall and was wider than the pawnshop owner and the priest put together. The giant had to weigh over five hundred pounds, possessing massive arms and legs that strained the fabric of his shirt and khaki pants. Barrel-chested, the brute was all muscle. The giant's ears folded out ninety degrees, exposing every crease and ragged scar inside those mountainous cups of flesh. Though it was dusk, a sweaty sheen reflected off the giant's bald head. Beady eyes, a ruddy pug nose, and lips as fat as sausages completed the visage of a human killing machine.

Father MacLeod stepped back, bumping into the door "Is—is that your assistant?"

"Yeah, give me a moment with him."

The proprietor motioned for the giant to meet with him at the bottom of the stairs. As they descended, his admiration of Rex grew— the guy was huge but had still managed to get behind both him and the priest without a sound. It was no wonder he'd had success as an assassin. When they both set foot on solid ground, he looked up to his assistant and froze—he felt like he was gazing into the face of madness.

His assistant's eyes darted from left to right at an incredible speed. Though the giant grimaced, his lips trembled, and the pawnshop owner could hear teeth grinding. Every few seconds his assistant's head shook, and a moan slipped out from the huge man's mouth.

"Rex, are you with me?"

The giant lowered his gaze and stared at the man for a few moments before nodding. Though Rex's eyes were now half closed, the pawnshop owner could almost feel them burning holes into him. The big man's bulky cheeks drooped, as did the corners of his mouth.

"Rex, this is important. Do you remember what we discussed on the phone earlier, about this house and the situation here?"

Once again there was a stare, only this time the giant shook his head.

The proprietor sighed. "Okay, listen. There's a demon in that house. It has three women imprisoned in there. It's *torturing* them, Rex."

The giant's eyes opened fully. There had been rumors of Rex's encounters with two separate men who had set off his trigger points. One man had been almost decapitated from a chain wrapped around his neck—he was found hanging from a tree over the doghouse of a Rottweiler. Another man, left to bleed out and die on a young girl's bed, had his penis ripped off and shoved down his throat.

The pawnshop owner hoped that, despite Rex's state, he continued to harbor these feelings of disgust at the suffering of innocent women. In fact, he hoped for more—maybe Rex's madness would feed his aggression, and possibly protect him and the rest of them from the demon.

"Rex, we need to get in there and save those women if they're alive. If they are, your task is to remove them from the house, to bring them out here. One of those women is named Celeste. She's the youngest of the three, and she is special to me. She has something of mine that I'd like to have back, so please, be extra careful with her. Once we're inside, the priest is going to try and perform an exorcism. I'll be by his side, but if things get bad, if possible, I want you to extricate me from the house, too. Saving the priest is the last priority. Do you understand?"

The giant nodded.

The pawnshop owner studied the big man for a moment, coming to a decision. He reached out and tucked an object into the giant's rear pants pocket. He did not comment on what it was, and Rex didn't ask.

What happened next occurred so fast the scene was a blur. The door opened wide with a resounding *clunk* and before there was time for either of them to react, the Moore House claimed Father MacLeod. There had been no scream from the priest; he was gone in an instant, the door slamming shut after him. Where he'd stood, only the flashlight remained, still spinning on the ground.

The pawnshop owner and the giant faced each other. The smaller man went to the door and turned the knob, which moved, but the door wouldn't open.

"Rex, can you get us in there?"

For the first time since he'd arrived, the giant grinned.

There was tremendous pressure around his waist, then Father MacLeod's was in motion. His head snapped back as his feet left the ground, pulled through the air with no time to register as to how. The pressure vanished, and he fell, his body hitting a hard surface.

He managed to lift himself to his hands and knees, shaking the confusion from his mind. When he was able to focus, he took in his surroundings and knew he was in the living room of the Moore house. An odd yellow hue infused the room. Celeste and Officer Jones stood several feet in front of him, alongside a large gaping hole in the floor. He saw no trace of the pawnshop owner or his assistant.

"Hello, Father MacLeod. Welcome to the party," greeted Officer Jones.

The priest studied the man. His suspicion was confirmed, Officer Jones was dead, his body possessed. As bad as he appeared with his neck bent the way it was, the black eyes were more convincing.

Father MacLeod stood and warily faced the abomination. "I'm here to send you back to hell," he said, his words soaked with courage he didn't feel.

What passed for a grin appeared on the demon's face. "Give it your best, priest. But the moment you open your mouth to banish me, you'll regret your action."

"I'll take that chance."

The demon gestured toward the hole. "Before you attempt it, take a look what lies below. I give you my word, I won't hurt you."

"Your word is worthless."

Celeste whimpered. "Nora and Agnes are down there."

The priest swallowed hard; he reached for a crucifix and held it out in front of him. Steering wide of the demon, he approached the hole. Though the basement was dark, the yellow light penetrated the hole enough for him to see two pairs of legs on a concrete floor protruding from the darkness.

"Nora! Agnes! Are you okay?"

Two distinct voices cried out. Both were weak but betrayed the pain they suffered.

"I'm going to get you out of here." He had no idea if it was possible to save them, but he wouldn't deny them hope. The priest backed away from the hole, faced the demon, and commenced the ritual. "Heavenly Father, I call—"

"I warned you, priest. Now, they die."

An impact shook the house. Celeste screamed, fighting for balance as she backed away from the hole. Undeterred, Father MacLeod raised his voice and held the crucifix high. "I call—"

Another concussion boomed throughout the house. Wood fragments danced on the floor and a section of ceiling fell.

It's not going to let me do this, Father MacLeod thought, but he saw the demon's eyes were no longer focused on him but at the front door. Something was off. The priest followed the demon's gaze.

The door burst open and the giant's body filled the doorway. His shoulders lowered until his head came into view. He entered the living room, followed by the pawnshop owner.

Father MacLeod stepped back. As did the demon.

☩

The pawnshop owner's gaze landed on Celeste.
She's alive!

Though he'd wanted the necklace returned, he was equally relieved that she appeared to be okay.

"Celeste, are you all right?" There was a possibility she was possessed, but from the expression on her face, he didn't think so.

The woman nodded. "Yes, yes I am. Because of you."

He smiled. "Well, that puts one issue to rest." He held up the bag, "I've got one more that needs proving out." He pointed to her. "Rex, would you please remove Celeste from this house."

"No! Agnes and Nora are down there," Celeste shouted before the giant could move. She pointed to the hole. "I'm not leaving until they're safe."

The demon took a step toward Rex. "No! They stay. They're mine."

Rex stood rigid, his face tight. The two didn't take their eyes off each other for several moments.

The demon went to speak as his gaze went to the hole.

The giant pounced before the demon could get a word out.

With his fingers curled inward, forming a fist, Rex's arm propelled from his side with the force of a launched rocket. His blow hit the dead officer's chest, and the sound of the dead man's ribs shattering was loud enough to hear. Jones' body went limp and fell to the floor. The giant picked it up with one hand and threw it against the far wall, coming within inches of Celeste as it flew past her. Sheetrock crumbled, and the possessed man lay still on the hardwood. The pawnshop owner waited for it to move. Seconds passed, but the body did not reanimate.

Celeste pointed to the hallway that led to the kitchen. "The door to the basement is in there."

The proprietor ordered Rex to retrieve the two women. The giant headed for the hallway as Father MacLeod approach the fallen demon.

"What now?" asked the pawnshop owner.

The priest shook his head. "I'm going to perform an exorcism, but something's not right here. Maybe the demon is trapped inside the officer's body, but I don't know. This feels too easy."

"Well, don't waste time. Get on with it. I'll stay with you until it's finished." He then said to Celeste. "You should leave now in case this isn't over."

"I'm not leaving until Agnes and Nora are safely outside." She reached out to him. "And I'm not going without you."

Unsure how to respond, he nodded.

Father MacLeod stood near the body and once again began reciting the rites of exorcism. While the priest went through the ritual, Rex retrieved the two women from the basement. Both were unconscious, nestled in the giant's arms. The pawnshop owner removed his crucifix and placed it over Nora's head. He fished a second out of his pocket and fastened the loop of string around Agnes' neck. Celeste had all the protection she needed with the necklace.

"They're hurt bad," Celeste said, forlorn.

"Mr. Lewis is outside waiting. He'll call an ambulance."

As Rex walked out the door, Celeste focused her attention on the priest and listened to him chant in a mixture of English and Latin. Rex came back into the house and stood in the doorway behind them.

Celeste understood rudimentary Latin, but many of the words the priest uttered, escaped her.

Though she'd never been to an exorcism, she had either been taught during her discernment or learned through second-hand recounting about many of the cases. Recalling the instances, she hadn't heard of an exorcism that was effective on the first try. It usually took several days, at least, for the ritual to prove successful. In other cases, like Catherine White, it could take months. She also knew of a few instances where the ritual had failed completely. But the effectiveness of this exorcism wasn't the only issue bothering her.

What happened to the demon? Why isn't it fighting back?

She shifted her gaze to Officer Jones' body. There was no movement, no voice, and the demon didn't appear to be reaching into any of their heads. The pawnshop owner's assistant had removed Agnes and Nora with no trouble. The priest had a point—this was too easy.

"Hey, something doesn't feel right," Celeste whispered to the pawnshop owner. "Exorcisms usually take time—I'm talking days. Why does he think he can banish the demon so quickly?"

The man kept his voice low. "The priest has its name. From the books I have, they say names have power, and I'm guessing inserting its name into the ritual should be enough to send the damn thing back where it belongs."

"Father MacLeod knows the demon's name?"

"Yes."

"How'd he find that out?"

"From what I understand, he got it from another demon, one who has possessed a woman."

Catherine White! It made sense. But how was he able to get Catherine's demon to give him the name of this one? That also seemed too easy, and it was making Celeste uneasy.

Officer Jones' body rose inches off the floor and fell back. The stench of feces filled the room. "What the hell is that all about?" asked Celeste.

"I don't know. Maybe it's the result of the exorcism."

"Ugh."

"Look," the proprietor pointed, "It sounds like the priest is coming to the end of the ritual."

Father MacLeod switched entirely to English, his voice rising to the point of shouting. He sprinkled holy water on Officer Jones' body and placed his crucifix against the dead officer's hand. "God demands you leave this man's body. God demands you leave this house. God demands you abandon this earthly plain and return to the hell that has spawned you. Ancient demon, tormentor of Christ and his apostles, inflictor of suffering onto Mary Magdalene—"

Wait. What's he talking about? This demon didn't exist during the time of Christ and Mary Magdalene. It isn't ancient. It told me it was of our time. Its story rang true, I believed it. Who does Father MacLeod think he's exorcising? "Something's wrong here," she said to the pawnshop owner.

The priest's eyes were shut, his face strained. "Now, ancient hellspawn, the power of God demands, you, BELPHEGOR, to return to the pits of hell!"

Ancient hellspawn? Belphegor? What the...? Oh, no!

The house went completely silent. The floorboards didn't creak or moan when she took a step. The pawnshop owner's lips moved, but he appeared puzzled when no sound came out. *Were they both struck deaf?* She pointed to her ears while shaking her head; he nodded and pointed with an index finger to his own ear. They both looked to Father MacLeod whose head was cocked to one side, his eyebrows arched, his lips pursed tight. He was as confused as they were.

A chilled formed on the back of Celeste's neck. The hair on her head lifted and stretched out in front of her, the ends dancing before her eyes. A force pushed her backward, and the chill spread down her back. She looked to her right where the pawnshop owner was bent over, grimacing, struggling to stay upright.

The floor shuddered. Celeste looked to the living room. The debris had taken on life, bouncing across the floor and falling through the holes and into the basement. Paper and dust floated in the air, drifting toward and around them as if propelled by a silent wind.

Celeste was lifted from the floor. Instinctively she crossed her arms in front of her chest. When she hit the wall, they took the brunt of the impact, but her forehead slammed against the sheetrock. She slid to the floor, grunting. After taking a moment to deal with the pain, she flipped around to face the living room. The wind continued its assault, forcing her to squint, yet she still saw little black stars floating in front of her. Her forehead was sore to the touch and she felt a lump forming.

Scanning the room, she saw Father MacLeod and the pawnshop owner on the floor on either side of her. Both were moving—hopefully not hurt. The position of Officer Jones' body hadn't changed.

A new shudder from the floor, much larger than the previous one, grew in intensity until the entire house was shaking. More of the ceiling dropped, exposing nearly all the rafters and plywood. The chair Officer Jones had been sitting in earlier slid across the room, lodging at a corner of the wall.

A yank on her arm forced a gasp; the pawnshop owner had gripped her. She put her hand over his. Pinned against the wall, she could do little as the wind pressed against them.

A huge figure appeared near the front door.

Rex. She had forgotten about him removing Agnes and Nora outdoors. He stood still, the wind having no effect on his bulk.

The pressure that had been holding her and the others against the wall vanished. She had battled it for so long her body jolted forward. Heavy breathing from her left and a sigh from her right caused her head to lift.

I can hear again.

The pawnshop owner and Father MacLeod jumped to their feet; she followed their lead. "What was that?" she asked.

"I don't know, but do you smell that?" The pawnshop owner asked.

Celeste sniffed the air. "Yeah. It smells like sulfur."

The priest sniffed, and dread filled his eyes. "Oh no."

A column of flame, roaring, erupted from the hole in the center of the floor. Celeste backed up tight against the wall. She thought the heat would suffocate them all.

"What the hell is that?" she screamed.

Father MacLeod answered. As loud as the flames were, she had no problem hearing his reply.

"Belphegor."

CHAPTER 26

Rex carried the two bodies out of the Moore house, one cradled in each massive arm. He approached Mr. Lewis and placed them gently on the ground at the old man's feet. He tore a section from his blood-soaked T-shirt and bound it around Nora's leg. The woman's eyes were closed and she made no sound during the ministrations.

Mr. Lewis stared at the women at his feet. "Thank God, they're alive."

The giant nodded.

"Okay, I know what to do," the old man said. "How are the others? Are they all right?"

Rex shot a penetrating glare at Mr. Lewis. After a few moments, the giant shrugged.

Mr. Lewis returned the stare, using the time to study the assistant. His eyes were wild. They'd been focused on him, but the old man noticed they weren't still—they oscillated like angry flies caught in a jar. He thought the man insane, and he could only imagine what was going through the giant's mind.

"You don't talk much, do you, Rex?"

There was no reply.

Rex stepped back from Mr. Lewis and walked toward the house. He paused halfway to the door and spun around. The giant was having another look at the old man.

"Why do you keep staring at me?" Mr. Lewis held up his cell phone. "I'm calling for help—please, get back in there and get the rest of them!"

Rex didn't move. He kept his gaze on Mr. Lewis. He must've come to some conclusion. He shook his head, turned, and continued back to the Moore house.

Once the giant passed through the front door, the old man tried to dial 9-1-1. His arm shook as if someone were pulling at it, preventing him from doing so. The tug of war lasted a few seconds. Instead of making the call, Mr. Lewis threw the phone to the ground. It landed next to his discarded flashlight.

The demon thought Mr. Lewis had more fight in him than that. Fleeing the house had taken more of a toll on it than it had anticipated. After leaving Belphegor's summoning token of shit, it was glad to be out of the policeman's body. While the old man wasn't as physically agile as the cop, it was easier to manipulate a live person than a dead body reduced close to pulp.

It made its way past the women on the ground and trekked to the Moore house. When it arrived at the front door, Rex stood in the doorway. The demon took a position behind the giant.

CHAPTER 27

Father MacLeod was fixated on the column of fire. The flame erupting from the hole was a cylindrical column around three feet wide. It shot up to the ceiling but ended inches from it, avoiding contact. The exposed wood above exhibited no signs of scorching. The top of the column appeared flat, as if neatly trimmed by a pair of shears. Its roar rivaled that of a tornado.

The priest lowered his sights to the floor, which had not ignited; neither had any of the debris surrounding it. *It doesn't want to burn the house down.* The heat was intense, but not enough to hinder his breathing or cause his clothes to smolder. He also noted a lack of smoke. There was a tug on his shoulder.

The pawnshop owner was shaking him. The man raised his voice above the roar of the fire. "What the hell did you do, priest? I thought you were exorcising the demon. It looks like all you did was piss him off!"

"I don't know. This wasn't supposed to happen."

"I think I know," Celeste interrupted, raising her voice. "I think I know what happened."

In the middle of her sentence, the room went quiet and her last two words were loud enough to cause Father MacLeod to flinch. The silence afterward left a high-pitched ringing in his ears.

The priest snapped his attention back to the column of fire. The flames burned as brightly and feverishly as they had moments ago, but the flames were now coalescing, taking shape. Transfixed, the priest stared as fire molded into the distorted figure of an obese man. Arms with hands sprouting elongated fingers appeared, as did legs with cloven hooves. Below its massive torso, an erect penis sprouted. The flaming and flickering yellow, orange, and red physique continued to morph. What the priest took for fat kneaded and compacted into muscle, and a comparison to Rex entered Father MacLeod's mind. It was short-lived. A head appeared. Horns, as black as coal and as pitted as corral, jut from the burning skull. Curved, the horns came to points reminiscent of a bull. A jaw formed. Below swollen lips stretched wide, an elongated chin concluded in a point as prominent as the horns. As fat as a sausage and as crooked as a bent spike, a nose formed. Above it, two ovals pressed out from the skull—eyes, so full of hate they burned a brighter red than the flames.

Father MacLeod had seen demons like this before in ancient texts and in paintings that hung in the bowels of the Vatican. They were one-dimensional, banal compared to what he was witnessing. None of his teachings—nothing he had ever experienced—prepared him for the atrocity born from this fire.

As the demon hovered, the flames all but extinguished. Smoke curled up from the body and vanished before it could hit the ceiling. Father MacLeod noted the skin covering the shape—it was as black as the dead officer's eyes and crazed as well-used leather. The demon remained suspended over the hole, its bulk stretching from the floor to a few inches below the ceiling. Its eyes held the vestige of the flames: they focused on Celeste.

"Rex," the pawnshop owner called, "I think we're going to need you."

Blocked from his view, Father MacLeod had forgotten about the proprietor's assistant.

Behind the giant, a voice rose. "Rex, remain where you are. I'll tell you when to move."

The pawnshop owner's eyes went wide. "Who the hell?"

Father MacLeod recognized the voice right away. "Mr. Lewis."

The old man stepped from behind Rex, moving close to the hovering demon. "Well, yes and no," he replied.

The pawnshop owner glared at Father MacLeod. "Did this just get worse?"

"Yeah," said the priest, lowering his head.

Mr. Lewis laughed. "I disagree, priest. It seems to have worked out exceedingly well."

"Okay. I'm guessing Father MacLeod screwed up. Instead of exorcising Bel—", the pawnshop owner caught himself before speaking the name. He pointed to the beast hovering over the hole, "— Exorcising *it*, he actually summoned the damn thing." He faced Father MacLeod. "You're a damn priest! How the hell does that happen?"

"I—I don't know."

"Could it have made you recite the wrong words?"

Mr. Lewis chuckled. "Correct, pawnshop owner, or should I call you, Smith? MacLeod isn't as protected as he thinks he is."

"You know who I am?"

The demon possessing Mr. Lewis nodded. "This vessel does, though it does not seem to be sure of your name. I look forward to seeing what's inside your head. From what I gather, you might possess some objects in your shop that could assist me during my return—or at the very least, amuse me."

The priest's gaze swept toward the fiery demon. "Fuck all this talk. What the hell is this all about?" His focus then went to Mr. Lewis, "And who the fuck *are* you?"

The old man's legs rose from the floor, his body rising until the top of his head was even with Belphegor's. Mr. Lewis ignored the priest and spoke to the ancient demon. "Be patient a few more moments, my brother. You will have the woman, the pawnshop owner, and his assistant, to do with what you will. I'll take the priest, but not right away. I want him to watch what you do to the woman."

Belphegor nodded, a heinous and eager smile transforming its face. Celeste sobbed as the pawnshop owner held her in his arms, but it did little to stop her shaking.

"What's this all about?" Mr. Lewis said, finally acknowledging the priest's question. "It's about *you*. You abused your authority, my trust. I brought my daughter to you for help; instead, you fucked my wife."

The pawnshop owner shot the priest a look. "I know it's a demon and all that, but how come I don't have a hard time believing what he just said?"

The priest ignored the comment. He wracked his brain, searching for a memory of who the demon could be referring to. His eyes widened with the memory as it came to him. "You're Melanie's husband? James Moore?"

"I was."

"So, you planned all of this to seek revenge on me?"

"I did," said the demon. "I needed one of your empaths to host a demon-brother, and Catherine White worked perfectly. When you visited her, you thought my brother was going to give you my name, but instead, he gave you my mentor's, Belphegor. Belphegor taught me everything I've learned in hell, priest. I not only caught on quickly, but the pupil soon turned into the master. In return for mentoring me in the dark arts, I pledged to end his banishment if he would follow me upon my return. A deal was struck."

The priest lowered his head. He was the cause of all of this: Catherine's possession, Nora and Agnes teetering on the edge of death, Celeste possibly being raped by this new demon he called forth. This, in addition to the other people the demon had claimed over the last six months. He needed to do something, but what?

"Hey, priest." It was the pawnshop owner. "You brought us here to die. Couldn't you have brought something with you other than your useless exorcism babble that would've protected us?"

Father MacLeod wondered what the man was talking about. They had discussed the perils of battling the demon and the man had agreed to come of his own volition. The pawnshop owner researched the demon on his own. He didn't have to...*wait*. The bag. He caught sight of it on the floor. Inside, the bowl that might have belonged to Mary Magdalene. It was near the proprietor's feet, close enough for the man to reach down and grab.

The priest made eye contact with the pawnshop owner, then directed his gaze to the bag and then back to the man's eyes. The shop owner pursed his lips and blinked in return.

Nerves raw, Celeste flinched when the pawnshop owner turned his back to both demons and whispered to her, "You need to trust me."

His hand shot out. He gripped her by the neck and spun her away from the wall. Though his hold on her was enough to get her moving, it was not so tight as to cut off her breathing. She had a sense of relief when he released the hold, but it was brief. He gathered her hair in his hand and yanked hard. Her head snapped back, and his other hand pressed against her shoulder. He pushed her toward Mr. Lewis.

A moment earlier, she'd acknowledged her trust in him, but now she wasn't so sure. *What is he doing?*

The pawnshop owner addressed the old man. "Mr. Lewis—or whatever you are—I need to talk to you."

"Stay where you are."

The man complied.

"What do you want?" the old man asked.

"I'm a bystander in this affair. I have little to do with this woman or your revenge on the priest. Let me go."

The demon stared at him. "You are merely one more soul for Satan—he doesn't care how innocent you are in this matter."

"I understand, but what if I made a deal with you? Give you something, and in return, you let me leave here intact?"

"What can you possibly give me that I can't take?"

He pushed Celeste closer to the demon. "Her."

Celeste stiffened. She twisted to escape his grip, a painful decision, as he turned his wrist to wrap her hair tighter around it. Her back arched, she gritted her teeth and grunted as she tried to balance herself.

"What are you doing?" she shouted.

The demon was thoughtful for a moment. "Go on."

"The reason you can't possess her is she's wearing something that prevents you from doing so. I will remove the item and place it on me. She'll be yours to do with whatever you will, and I'll walk out of here unharmed."

Celeste gasped. *He's betraying me to save his own skin.*

"I see," the demon replied. "So, that's what prevents me from getting into her mind. If this vessel I occupy knew of the object, I'm impressed he was able to hide it from me. You have a deal. Take the item and leave. Though be aware we will meet again."

The pawnshop owner pulled Celeste to within three feet of Mr. Lewis. He reached out with his free arm, snaked his hand down inside her blouse, spread his fingers and searched until he found the cross.

Celeste didn't fight him, her only hope being that this was part of a plan, though she couldn't imagine what it was.

He grasped the cross, lifted it out from beneath her blouse and displayed it to the demon. When the demon nodded, the pawnshop owner released his hold on Celeste and pulled the necklace up over her head.

Celeste pushed back from him, shaking. "I trusted you."

"That's your mistake, Celeste," the pawnshop owner responded. He faced the demon and lifted the necklace above his own head.

When the demon inside Lewis faced Celeste and grinned, the pawnshop owner sprang forward with the necklace held high before him.

There was enough time for the old man's eyes to widen, but nothing more. The pawnshop owner quickly slipped the necklace over Mr. Lewis' head and tackled the old man to the floor.

"Rex, help me hold him down," the shop owner pleaded.

The giant stared at the two men on the floor. His eyelids drooped, as did the corners of his mouth.

"Rex," the pawnshop owner cried out again. "Please, help me!"

"No," Mr. Lewis calmly stated. "Rex, take this fool off of me and hold him. I'm going to delight in his agony."

The giant remained unmoving.

"Rex," demanded the demon. "You belong to me! I order you to take this man off of me!"

The giant's eyes widened, but his frown deepened. He lumbered over to the two men on the floor and knocked the pawnshop owner off the demon with a mere wave. He took a heavy breath and placed one of his huge hands on the demon's chest, covering the cross with his fingers. Lowering his head, he brought his face within inches of the demons. "I belong to nobody," he hissed.

"Rex," the pawnshop owner said, "The demon is trapped inside Mr. Lewis. We don't want to hurt the old man unless we have to. Hold him for now—don't let him remove the necklace. And cover his mouth."

"Belphegor, kill them all, now—" The demon in Mr. Lewis demanded, but it never finished getting the words out.

The pawnshop owner turned to the priest. "The bag, hurry!"

The hovering, ancient demon let out a roar. A gust of wind carrying the scent of sulfur swept Celeste to the floor. She pushed herself up to see the demon, its eyes ablaze, trained on hers. Both hands gripping its erection, it bent forward at the waist, its head snaking toward her. As it moved closer, its lower body pivoted up until it was horizontal to the floor. It floated, hovering over her like a wolf with prey. She instinctively curled into a ball, protecting her crotch with her hands. She turned her head to gaze up at the demon, its face inches from hers.

She screamed, but only once. A nearby voice cut her off. It was loud but calm. And familiar. "Belphegor," Father MacLeod said.

The ancient demon cocked its head to the priest, who was standing close enough to touch it.

Celeste wondered what Father MacLeod was holding.

Was that a bowl?

The wood was thin, greasy to the touch. It had a slight film of dirt and the priest's fingers slipped over its surface. Clutching the bowl tightly, he hurried to Belphegor. It was levitating horizontally, leering at Celeste. The demon's hands clutching at its groin made its intentions obvious.

The priest held the bowl with the inside facing the beast.

What the hell am I supposed to do with this? Macleod wondered.

His hands shook. He thought back to his teachings and readings on Mary Magdalene. He could recall no mention of a bowl, or of how the woman's demons had been vanquished. A hollowness spread through him. He was a helpless man whose bravado and self-assuredness had deserted him.

As loathe as he was to do it, Father MacLeod closed his eyes and prayed. *God, I need some help here. I'm not asking for myself, but for Celeste and the others. Please, God, do with me whatever the hell you want, but help me save them.*

The priest opened his eyes. Not that he'd expected otherwise, but nothing had changed. He sighed. He had an idea, nothing grand or complicated, but it was the best he could come up with at the moment. He spoke the demon's name again. "Belphegor."

Belphegor's gaze went from the priest to the bowl.

Father MacLeod stepped closer and slammed the bowl down over one of the demon's horns.

Shit, nothing's happening.

Belphegor stared at the priest for several seconds and then swung its arm, batting Father MacLeod away as if he were an annoying fly.

The priest hit the wall hard enough to leave an imprint and then slid to the floor in a tangle of arms and legs. His vision blurred as he struggled to remain conscious. When he focused on Belphegor, he tried to make sense of what he was seeing.

Belphegor had both hands on the bowl, pulling and pushing, struggling to remove it. It bellowed in frustration, then the rest of its body went into motion. Its legs swung outward, Belphegor dropped to the floor, and then stood upright. Its bulk wavered as it worked to pry the bowl off its head.

The demon is shrinking.

No, I'm wrong. It isn't shrinking; the bowl's descending.

The priest shook his head in disbelief. *Holy shit, it's working.*

Belphegor's grunts of frustration turned into howls of panic. The bowl inched its way down, and the ancient demon's screams brought the priest's hands to his ears. Like pulled taffy, Belphegor's eyes elongated and thinned as the bowl covered them. Father MacLeod blinked when he realized that the wooden vessel was not so much pressing down onto the demon as it was sucking the creature up. A tearing noise, louder than the beast's howls, sifted through the priest's hands and into his ears. Belphegor's nose lifted and disappeared into the bowl. Like melting plastic, the flesh on the ancient demon's cheeks twisted and knotted as the wooden vessel funneled them up. The howling ceased when its mouth vanished. As the bowl continued to descend, the demon's body stilled. Its bulk impeded the progress but did not stop it from completing its task. The priest lowered his hands and stared as Mary Magdalene's bowl sucked up what was left of the demon. Neither blood nor bones littered the floor, and the sulfuric stink of the beast lessened. Minutes later, Father MacLeod heard a muffled clunk as the bowl contacted the floor.

Belphegor was gone.

The priest looked up to see Celeste and the pawnshop owner staring back at him.

The pawnshop owner said in a low disbelieving voice, "It—it worked!"

The priest let out a breath. "No shit. But we're not done yet. Don't touch it."

Father MacLeod picked himself up, removed the vial of holy water from his pocket, and splashed the bowl. He dug his crucifix out, turned the bowl over, and placed the cross inside. "Now I've got to figure out what to do with this thing."

"I'll take it," the shop owner said. "I have something in my shop— it's called the Prexy Box—that should hold Bel...it. The demon will be in good company."

The priest's expression tightened. "What the hell kind of pawnshop are you running?"

"Exotic items."

"Hey, guys!" Celeste's voice cut off their conversation. Pointing, she added, "We've got another problem here, and it's getting worse."

Both men turned to see Mr. Lewis and Rex. When the giant screamed, they both took a step back.

✝

It wasn't the old man's body Rex struggled against. Mr. Lewis was fragile, and he couldn't have topped 140 pounds with his clothes on— it was the demon, trapped in the old man's body, trying to get into the giant's mind. The visions, creeping in and out of Rex's consciousness, some flickering like an old movie reel sticking to the gears, had him shaking his head violently to dislodge them. Images of his past—the killings, the tortures, the women who had betrayed him floated in front of his eyes, and then vanished when he refused to emotionally react to them.

The demon was rooting around in his subconscious, plucking out various memories with which to tempt or taunt him. What the demon didn't understand was that Rex had not only come to terms with what he was, he reveled in it. But that wasn't to say the probing didn't have an effect.

Rex was insane. He was functional to a high degree, but on occasion, the chaos in his head was too much to handle. During those moments of high tension and confusion, he'd seek out the pawnshop owner, who knew how to deal with him. Most of the time, the man locked him in the back room of the shop until the episode passed. If there wasn't an opportunity to seek out the owner, his madness reigned—resulting in death and destruction.

218

The urge to kill was building inside Rex. The demon had hit pay dirt.

Like a sheet of paper pushed under a door, images of women forced into degrading acts slipped into the giant's mind. Depictions of animal cruelty followed. When the demon saw it was getting a reaction, it combined the two. Rex grimaced as he fought the demon's influence. His eyeballs rose high into his lids. He strained to concentrate. A moving image of his mother, beaten to death by his father, nearly broke the giant. He screamed his rage, but the movie persisted. Rex had reached his breaking point. He released his hand from the old man's mouth.

"Rex, no!" the pawnshop owner shouted.

The giant's hand shook as he lowered it back over Mr. Lewis' mouth.

"It's the demon," Father MacLeod said. "It looks like your assistant is losing the battle."

"Can you do an exorcism rite?"

The priest exhaled loudly. "I can try, but I doubt there's enough time."

"If Rex loses it, he'll kill the three of us."

Celeste broke into the conversation. "Can you delay it? Hold him off for another minute, maybe two?"

The pawnshop owner frowned. "I can try. Why?"

Celeste pointed to the necklace around Mr. Lewis' neck. A tear slipped from her left eye. "When Father MacLeod tells you to, remove the necklace, put it on Rex's head, and stand far back. Then, only when told, remove it from Rex, and then place it back over my head."

The pawnshop owner squinted. "I don't understand—you want to let the demon out of Mr. Lewis while protecting Rex?" He glanced at the priest, hoping the man could clarify what she wanted him to do.

Father MacLeod appeared to be just as confused. Then his eyes widened.

"Celeste!" The priest's voice was loud, urgent. "No!"

"I have no choice, Father. I'll be counting on you later on."

The pawnshop owner shook his head. "I don't understand what's happening here."

"There's no time to explain. I want to thank you. You saved my life." More tears. "Come on, let's do this now before it's too late."

She led the pawnshop owner to Rex and Mr. Lewis. "Try to keep Rex calm; I don't need much time. Remember, stand way back after you place the necklace on Rex."

"But ..."

Celeste glared at the pawnshop owner. *"Just do it!"*

The man nodded and leaned toward his assistant. "Rex, it's me. You have to hold on for another minute. Can you do it?"

The giant ceased his thrashing. He stared at the pawnshop owner with eyes that blinked white, then black. His upper body vibrated as he struggled for control. "It—it's showing me things..."

"I know, but we may be able to stop it." The owner turned to watch the ex-nun.

Celeste stood stock-still, her eyes closed, hands hanging limply at her sides.

"Get ready," directed Father MacLeod.

"But—"

"Look," the priest retorted, "I don't like this any better than you do. But it's our only chance." He paused for a moment. "I'm waiting for a sign. When I get it, I'll let you know."

The proprietor swallowed hard. He nodded and faced the giant.

Celeste walked up to Mr. Lewis, kneeled, and placed a hand on the old man's hip. The pawnshop owner waited for the prompt. It came, not as a shout, but with a barely spoken whisper when MacLeod said, "Now."

The pawnshop owner leaned over, and despite the old man's attempts to break free of Rex, he removed the necklace from Mr. Lewis with little trouble. He placed it over the giant's head. With a quick gaze behind him to avoid any holes in the floor, he stepped away from Rex and the demon. He turned his attention to the priest, whose eyes were locked on Celeste.

☩

Celeste closed her eyes.

She focused, pushing deep into her mind.

She was floating.

Darkness surrounded her. It was absolute—until it wasn't. The tiny pinpricks of light she had equated to stars blinked into existence, filling the distant void. Though she was once again in what she thought of as God's universe, her emotions were anything but blissful.

There was a pull; her unearthly body flinched.

Someone was calling to her. The voice wasn't comforting.

She held back. It was too soon.

Celeste prayed. She waited.

But not for long.

The demon slammed through her mind. Snapshots of her past sins crowded her thoughts. Scenes, one after another flashed before her of Father Montclair, standing in the shadows at the back of the room as Mother Superior forced Celeste to strip naked. Then, a view of the switch held in the old woman's hands as she struck it against

Celeste's buttocks, the scene morphing to wet, angry welts. Celeste saw herself wincing in pain at the start of the beatings, until her face twisted with pleasure. She heard herself moaning as the Mother Superior massaged the bruises, and then slip her wrinkled hand down, between Celeste's thighs. The sounds of Father Montclair masturbating filled her ears. The images were momentary, but each spiked a visceral reaction. After leaving the convent, she battled the dead feelings inside her soul from her participation in those perverted acts. She had betrayed God's faith, and the guilt proved to be overwhelming. Leaving the Sisterhood, she sought therapy, both spiritual and psychological. Over time, the counseling succeeded, and she had come to terms with her actions. Making peace with herself allowed her to function, to continue to do God's work, culminating with her acceptance into Father MacLeod's team. Seeing these scenes of her past not only rekindled her guilt, but also those suppressed urges for forbidden pleasure. She fought back by concentrating on God's immense love and authority. The images abated as wisps of ebony smoke materialized in front of her.

James Moore appeared before her as he must have in life. He was stout. He wore a crooked grin, framed by a neatly trimmed beard. His eyes were black; within them, darker swirls spiraled to a vanishing point.

"Hello, Celeste. I've been waiting for you." The demon said and laughed, its timbre carrying loud and deep into the void.

She reached out and embraced the demon.

Contact was made, and their consciousness melded.

Celeste gathered her last bit of mental strength as the possession commenced. She channeled it into her physical body, hoping it would be enough.

Celeste's body in the Moore house stiffened, and her head nodded.

Seconds later, as she floated in the void, coldness spread through her. The connection to her physical body was severed. The pawnshop owner had fulfilled her request.

"*No!*" The demon pushed at every corner of her mind. It thrashed in fury, seeking release.

Celeste singled out one of the pinpricks of light in the distance. She flew toward it, the lights blurring as she picked up speed. *Will I reach it?*

Trapped in her mind, the demon screamed.

Welcoming her, the void expanded. She imagined herself soaring, hair whipping behind her as she held out her arms Christ-like, waiting to embrace God. She pushed the screaming demon in her mind as far back as she could, in the hopes that she would hear her savior's greeting.

The streaks of lights she thought of as stars were gone now, only darkness surrounded her. She had no way to gauge if she was moving or floating aimlessly.

God, please, end this. Welcome me to heaven.

A flare exploded in the distance. The size of the fireball increased, growing at a phenomenal rate until it encompassed all she could see. The center of the fireball burst, spewing out a blaze of red tentacles that blossomed into a yellow brilliance that would have been blinding if she were earthbound. A stream of white light emerged from the yellow. It grew larger and Celeste thought it the most beautiful sight she had ever seen. The shadows of people appeared in the center, and as the light approached her, they came into focus. She recognized them, all of them as family members and friends who had passed.

I'm ready, God. Focusing on the light, she opened herself up.

"*Not so fast, Celeste.*"

The demon. It was her last untainted thought.

CHAPTER 28

Father MacLeod focused his attention on Celeste. He refused to allow his emotions to intrude, to keep him from doing his job. There was no time for alternate scenarios, second-guessing, or heartbreak. If Celeste's actions succeeded, the future would provide an opportunity for reflection. He waited for the sign.

When it came, a leak sprang in his resistance.

Celeste nodded.

He turned to the pawnshop owner, battling the urge to weep. "Now," he said.

The man rushed to the giant. Rex's body shook as he pinned the old man to the floor. Sweat soaked the big man's face as he struggled against the demon's mental assault. The giant's grunts were low, but Father MacLeod had no doubt as to the pain Rex suffered. The pawnshop owner removed the necklace from Mr. Lewis and slid it over Celeste's head.

The priest sighed. *He doesn't understand what he just did.*

The proprietor backed away from Celeste to stand near the priest. Seconds later, she collapsed to the floor.

"*Celeste!*" The pawnshop owner rushed to her and then looked at the priest. "What can we do?"

"Nothing now," Father MacLeod replied.

"Should I take the necklace off her?"

"I'm not sure. From what Celeste has told me of her abilities, she's removed the demon to a realm far from here, so it might not matter. I wouldn't test that theory by removing the necklace, though. It's keeping the demon trapped inside, for now."

The priest didn't know much about the man, but from their limited interaction, he thought him pragmatic. If he removed the necklace and Celeste hadn't yet banished the demon to her enigmatic void, they'd all be right back where they started.

"She must be going through hell. Can you exorcise it out of her?" asked the proprietor.

"This demon is smarter and more powerful than any other I've encountered. It has the ability to plan, and more troubling, it can jump from one person to another with relative ease. A lot will depend on how strong Celeste is, and where she was when the demon took her."

"What do you mean, where she was?"

"Celeste's abilities are unique. She's an empath, but her methods differ from Agnes' and Nora's. I can only tell you what she once related to me, and even then, she didn't understand it all that well. Celeste's consciousness can travel to another realm. She didn't know where or what this realm was, but she called it God's universe. I believe Celeste has taken the demon to this universe."

The pawnshop owner straightened and the priest's hand fell from his shoulder. "How did she know it would possess her? Not you or I?"

"I'm thinking proximity. She told you to stand back, and I was already a distance away. She was the closest, and she had placed a hand on the old man. I think when it fled Mr. Lewis, it took the path of least resistance. Don't forget, I also gave you a crucifix, affording you some protection, though she didn't know that."

The proprietor shook his head. "I slipped the one you gave me into Rex's pocket."

The priest was silent for a few seconds. "That explains how Rex was able to fight off the demon for as long as he did."

"Maybe. Rex has strength and abilities of his own. I wouldn't discount them."

"Yeah, I bet he does. No matter. The demon possessed Celeste as she expected it to, saving all our lives in the process."

The owner released a heavy breath. "What now?"

"I'll take her to my office in Haverhill. We'll do our best to bring her back."

A grunt off to their side caused both men to turn.

"If you two are done chatting, could you please order your brute off me?" The voice belonged to Mr. Lewis.

"Rex, are you okay?" asked the pawnshop owner.

The giant nodded.

"Right. Would you please pick up Mr. Lewis and place him outside alongside Agnes and Nora?"

The giant slid to his feet, slipped an arm around Mr. Lewis' waist and carried him to the front door and out of the Moore house. He returned minutes later for Celeste.

Father MacLeod and the proprietor followed Rex as he carried her outside. "You know," said the priest, "I can't give you that necklace back. The Vatican will want to study it if there comes a time we can remove it."

"Yeah, I figured that."

Once the four of them were outdoors, Rex placed Celeste next to Agnes and Nora.

Mr. Lewis pointed to a spot on the ground beside Agnes. "The cell phone—it's over there—can you please hand it to me? I'll get ambulances here right away."

The priest found the phone and handed it to the old man. "What are you going to tell them?"

"I'll have a private conversation with Lieutenant Rivera. I'll tell him enough to give him an idea of how to handle the situation, but not everything. The force lost two men here—there'll be an investigation from the New Hampshire Attorney General's office."

He addressed the pawnshop owner. "I'll keep you and Rex out of this; at least, I'll try. As for your involvement, Father, I won't be able to keep that hidden, given the circumstances."

Father MacLeod nodded his understanding.

The pawnshop owner thanked Mr. Lewis. "Rex and I will be leaving now. Father, I'm counting on you to keep me informed of Celeste's condition. If you would do so through Mr. Lewis, I'd be grateful."

Once more, the priest nodded.

"One thing, Mr. Lewis," the priest said. "I need to speak to someone before you call for the ambulances. I know it's a lot to ask at this point, but I need you to wait another five to ten minutes before you make that call. I believe the ladies can handle the wait."

Lewis offered Father MacLeod the cell phone. After less than a minute, the priest clicked off and handed the device back

Eight minutes later, Mr. Lewis called for assistance.

CHAPTER 29

Three Months Later

Wearing his street attire—a white shirt and black pants—Father MacLeod relaxed on the sofa in Agnes' living room, one ankle resting on the opposite knee. A manila folder covered his lap.

Facing him, Agnes leaned back on an oversized stuffed chair, her arm nestled in a frayed sling emblazoned with colorful patches. He couldn't help smiling. She'd pulled through the ordeal at the Moore house with little to show for it, except a few broken bones. She returned the smile, but her eyes spoke of her true condition. Bags and heavy lids betrayed her weariness.

Alongside Agnes, Nora's bulk rested in a wheelchair, her injured leg wrapped in a brilliant white cast. The priest couldn't determine if it was new or if she and Agnes had spent an inordinate amount of time scrubbing it for this meeting. Nora had gained considerable weight since the incident at the Moore house, though she didn't appear to display any discomfort from it. He had received reports on her progress from the Church psychologist. For the past few months, she'd been wrestling with her actions and mental state from her time in Goffstown. Counseling and consoling from the psychologist, Agnes and himself had gone a long way to convince her it was the demon's influence that caused her breakdown at the Moore house.

Nora had thought herself a coward, her contribution to their effort slight, even dangerous. It was only this past month she'd appeared to have accepted their explanation for her actions and come to terms with them. Father MacLeod imagined her insecurities ran deep, and he questioned if she'd ever return to her former self-assured, cocky self.

Mr. Lewis balanced himself on the edge of a cushion on the other end of the sofa, holding his cane with both hands to provide the support needed to remain comfortably seated. His frailty was apparent, as he seemed to have difficulty keeping his chin from dipping onto his chest. The old man shouldn't have come in his condition. He'd been offered a briefing of the meeting but insisted on attending. The priest couldn't decide if Mr. Lewis was here out of a sense of guilt or if he simply wanted closure. Either was good enough reason, in Father MacLeod's estimation.

"Anyone want a drink while I'm up?" came a voice from the kitchen.

"Yes, please. I'll take a Glenfiddich, one ice cube, please," responded Father MacLeod. "Thank you, Catherine," he added.

"Anyone else?" When no one replied, she stepped to a cabinet for the scotch.

The priest closed his eyes in satisfaction and inhaled heavily. Catherine exhibited no ill effects from her possession. The Church had been astounded by her recovery. The Vatican exorcists took credit for it, and Father MacLeod was more than happy to let them. His part in her recovery was between him and Catherine, with the mutual understanding they'd keep the details to themselves. He'd approached her last week to ask if she wanted to discuss her possession, but she put him off, assuring him they'd get a chance to talk about it in the future. Though Catherine's breakthrough had occurred the same day Celeste had been admitted, not one of the exorcists questioned the timing.

Sister Bernice was another matter. Her stares and angry eyes followed him whenever he visited Celeste's room. After a month of this, his patience had worn thin, and he took the nun aside. His intent had been to admonish her, to explain the affairs of God were not hers to question, but his resolve crumbled. She'd assisted him in his time of need and considered that her motivation for dogging him. Her accusatory facial expressions might've been her attempt to assuage her guilt. After he'd recounted Celeste's involvement and sacrifice at the Moore house to Sister Bernice, her staring recriminations were replaced with sorrowful side glances. He didn't know which of the two bothered him more.

His thoughts of Sister Bernice were interrupted when Catherine tapped him on the shoulder, handing him his drink. She sat in a chair to Agnes' right. As he gazed at the three of them, he thought, *Worse for wear, we're all together again.*

Absent from the meeting were the pawnshop owner and his assistant, Rex. Father MacLeod had asked Mr. Lewis to convey the intent and the time of the meeting to the pawnshop owner. The old man replied that he doubted either of them would attend, and his prediction proved correct. The priest wasn't disappointed by the refusal.

"Ahem."

Chief Rivera, the officer who'd replaced Dodd, stood in the center of the living room. All eyes focused on him.

"At the request of Mr. Lewis, I'll update all of you on the preliminary findings from the investigation of the Moore house. Before I start, let me say the case isn't closed. The state attorney general's office has jurisdiction, and I assure you they will keep it open for years to come.

"I won't bore you with the transcripts—the report is over a hundred pages, and it's long on supposition and short on conclusions. I'll give you the salient points if that's okay."

Mr. Lewis nodded.

"Initial evidence points to a serial killer. The suspect used the

Moore house as his base of operations and the attorney general's office believes he's responsible for seven unsolved homicides in the greater Goffstown area. They also believe he was responsible for the death of Officer Jones.

"At the behest of Mr. Lewis, the Catholic Church was requested to perform a blessing on the Moore house for the benefit of Mr. Lewis' granddaughter, her last known location. The suspect was in the house at the time of the blessing and attacked two representatives of the Church, Agnes Levesque and Nora Fournier, who preceded Father MacLeod's arrival. When Officer Jones, who happened to be passing by, stopped at the residence and attempted to assist those representatives, he was assaulted, tortured, and killed.

"The whereabouts of Chief Dodd are unknown. He is presumed to be deceased. His DNA was discovered on one of the walls in the living room of the Moore house, so it's known he entered the house at some point. There is speculation that the suspect abducted the chief and disposed of the remains elsewhere.

"When Father MacLeod arrived at the home to conduct the blessing, it's believed the suspect fled. The priest's arrival prevented the suspect from killing the two representatives from the Church. Father MacLeod administered first aid to both women. Mr. Lewis arrived shortly thereafter and called 9-1-1 to report the incidents."

Father MacLeod noted that in the chief's summary, the officer mentioned only two representatives from the church. There was no mention of Celeste.

After his last visit with Catherine in the bowels of his office in Haverhill, he'd phoned Mr. Lewis with the name of the demon. When that call was over, he made one more. He'd called the local parish, alerting Father Brickley to stand by with a vehicle in case it was needed. Father Brickley was summoned before Mr. Lewis called 9-1-1, and together, they removed Celeste and arrangements were made to transport her to his Haverhill office.

Chief Rivera continued. "A thorough search of the Moore house was conducted the following day. A forensic team was brought in to collect evidence. The investigation soon focused on the basement. Two bodies were discovered. The first was Mr. Lewis' granddaughter, Gam Lewis. Forensics concluded that she was recently deceased, death occurring approximately two days prior to the discovery of her body. She was found in a crawlspace dug into the cellar floor. The crawlspace was concealed, but strangely, not well enough to avoid detection. Investigators are perplexed as to how it was not discovered during the many searches conducted on the property."

Now, Father MacLeod had an answer to something that had bothered him since the Moore house incident. Demons fed on innocence, taking strength from it. Gam may have been a drug addict, but she must have been otherwise moral. The demon used her innocence to sustain itself, then when the team showed up, it either let her die or it killed her. As to not discovering the crawlspace, keeping that hidden would have been child's play for the demon.

"The other body was a Ms. Melanie Moore. Ms. Moore was the former wife of James A. Moore, listed as the prior owner of the property. She disappeared several years ago, along with her daughter."

Nora spoke up. "Her daughter's body wasn't found?"

"No. We have a nationwide missing person's bulletin issued on her, but there's been no response."

He continued. "Further evidence taken from the scene turned up the DNA of James A. Moore. The amount of blood indicates he suffered mortal injuries, but as I mentioned, his body wasn't at the scene. Farther into the basement, we found numerous occult markings on the floor and walls. A large pentagram had been painted on the floor in Mr.

Moore's blood, and all four walls contained scribbling using various blood types. The DNA results from the walls revealed the blood used was a combination of the seven homicide victims, Mr. Moore's, unidentified human sources, and an unidentified animal. Again, investigators are confounded that the markings and blood stains were not mentioned in earlier police visits."

Father MacLeod opened the manila envelope on his lap, jotting down notes onto a sheet of paper. It would be inserted later into his personal file on the Moore House. He also made a note to ask Mr. Lewis for a copy of the official report, *if* the man could use his leverage to obtain it.

"To finish this up, interviews with all parties involved at the Moore house have been non-productive. The two female representatives from the Church claim they cannot recall the events that occurred after they entered the house. In addition, Father MacLeod and Mr. Lewis both claim not to have witnessed the suspect flee the premises. The AG's office does not believe those claims, and they'll continue to question the parties involved. Due to the occult markings in the basement, the condition of Officer Jones' body, and the presence of the three individuals representing the Catholic Church, they believe a religious ritual was in progress. The report hypothesizes it was an exorcism."

The priest turned his gaze to Agnes and Nora. He wasn't surprised to see they were staring at him.

"This leaves the State of New Hampshire on the hunt for an unknown serial killer with little to go on. Though the evidence suggests he's dead, an ABP has been issued for James A. Moore."

The room went silent. Father MacLeod assumed they were all lost in thought.

Mr. Lewis broke the silence. "Thank you, Chief—you may go now."

The officer's mouth dropped. "But, wait, I have my own questions—"

"—and I will answer them to the best of my ability in a few more days. Off the record, of course."

The chief sighed. "Of course, off the record."

"Again, thank you. Now please, see yourself out."

Chief Rivera complied.

Father MacLeod addressed Mr. Lewis. "How did you do that?"

"Do what?"

"Dismiss that officer so easily? He's not much of a cop that I can see."

Mr. Lewis smiled. "Father, I think I had mentioned to you at our initial meeting that I am a large benefactor to the police force. I am very influential with the department when it comes matters that concern me. I will also point out, that man you proclaimed not much of a cop is my wife's nephew."

The priest grinned. "Ahh. How much does he know?"

The old man shook his head. "Not much. I'll give him a few facts, make him feel he's important, but nothing that'll contradict our story. I have no pull, however, with the attorney general's office—we're on our own where they're concerned."

Agnes asked, "How about the Church? Will they intercede if the Attorney General pushes too hard?"

The priest nodded. "Yeah, they will. Let's wait and see if it's needed."

"I have one last thing," said Mr. Lewis. "The pawnshop owner asked about Celeste. He would like an update on her condition."

Father MacLeod stood from the couch, stepping into the middle of the room. His left hand went to his chest, and he opened his fingers wide and placed them over his heart. "Celeste is still, for want of a

234

better phrase, in a coma. She hasn't moved on her own or spoken since she was brought to Haverhill. I'm doing everything I can for her. I perform the exorcism ritual daily, but there's been no response. We keep her alive, and we pray. There is always hope. Before she absorbed the demon and took it to God-knows-where, she said it was up to me to bring her back. She believed there was a way for her return through the Church, through God, and through me. I won't give up on her."

The priest heard Nora restrain a sorrowful moan. Tears followed. Agnes had lowered her head but didn't cry.

Catherine nodded, adding, "I'm proof it can be done."

"Yes, it can be. To change this up, as you three ladies know, the Church will continue to employ you. As charitable as they project themselves to be, I would expect it to be indefinite. They want me to keep going with my work, no doubt *because* of the incident at the Moore house. You were my team, and I hope you'll continue to be. What do you say? I don't expect an answer right away. Take a few weeks to think about it."

Agnes snickered. "A few weeks? That's all?"

"I'm not asking you to come back to work in a few weeks; I only want your answer by then. If it's yes, I see us working together once your injuries are healed—hopefully, in a couple of months."

Nora shook her head. "No way. No way I'm going through that again."

The priest nodded. "I understand, but please wait a couple weeks before giving me your answer."

Catherine locked eyes with Agnes and Nora. A moment later she said, "Yes, give us a couple weeks. We need to discuss this."

Father MacLeod grinned. "Okay then. I'd love to visit with you more, but I have an appointment back in the office. Thank you, Mr. Lewis, for calling this meeting, I'm grateful to be up to speed."

"Ladies," the priest continued, "I'll be back in a few weeks to pick up where we left off."

The three of them were silent.

Father MacLeod saw himself to the door. He was almost through when he stopped and poked his head back into the room. "Oh, and thanks for the scotch." With a smile, he stepped through the door and closed it behind him.

He'd made this trip many times before. On the last, his mood had been jubilant. His team had just confirmed the Moore house wasn't possessed, and he couldn't contain his joy. Of course, the opposite had been true, but at the time he was blissfully unaware of it. He was as excited now as he'd been then. Pulling into the parking lot adjoining the old factory, the size of his grin was huge.

Father MacLeod smiled for the camera. The buzz sounded, and he slipped past the door into the waiting room.

The madame greeted him. "Hello, John! This is fortunate."

He tilted his head. "What do you mean?"

The woman laughed. "I have a new girl for you. One I think you're really going to like."

"Oh?"

"Yes, John. She signed on with us two days ago. Her physical and blood work came back fine, and today's her first day with us. In fact, if she's to your liking, you'll be her first customer."

"Well, it doesn't cost me anything to look, does it?"

The madame shook her head. "No, dear, looking is for free. Shall I bring her down?"

The priest nodded.

A few minutes passed before the madame stepped down the spiral staircase with her newest employee. On her heels was a woman: a familiar one, and he was momentarily taken aback. When they reached the bottom, the madame stepped aside and her employee posed for him. He knew the woman to be in her thirties but, almost naked as she was, he would've guessed she was ten years older. She was busty but plain-looking, average at best, and he thought if she were a wife, a man would be comfortable enough with her. His mind changed when she approached and they stood nose-to-nose. Her lips were curled into a cruel grin. Her pupils were enormous and black. They were cold, and her stare chilled him. No man could survive being married to her.

"Hello, Celeste." He paused, then added, "Or whoever the hell you are. I will say I expected something, but not this."

"Hello, Father MacLeod. You've broken some promises. You're indebted. I hope you're ready to pay."

The priest took a step back. His eyes went wide, but then he returned her grin. He pulled his shirt collar to the side and slipped his hand down the front of his shirt. He removed it, clutching the necklace the pawnshop owner had loaned to Celeste.

"Actually, I *am* ready. And, I'm delighted you were the one sent. As for our bargain, Asmodeus is just going to have to wait a while longer."

His free hand snaked out and he wrapped his fingers around the demon's wrist. He let go of the necklace, letting it dangle from his neck. Digging into his back pocket, he removed his wallet and tossed it to the madame. "I don't know how much time this will take. I'll settle the bill when I'm done."

A confused look on her face, the madame caught the wallet. "I'm not sure I understand what you two are talking about. Do you know each other?"

"Not intimately, no. But that's going to change. I'm sorry to say, I am going to ruin her for anyone else."

After a hesitant laugh, the madame replied, "Enjoy yourself, John."

"Oh, I plan on it."

He stood in one of the rooms in the bowels of his Haverhill office building. Having spent several hours at the brothel in Nashua, he was exhausted. Despite having trouble keeping his eyes open, he gazed down at the prone form of the woman tied to the bed. The restraints hadn't been needed since she arrived, but he thought them prudent. She was so thin he worried her bones might break when and if she did come back.

A noise behind him jerked him to attention.

He turned to see Sister Bernice entering the room.

"There's been no change from this morning, Father. I did my best to make her comfortable. After you performed the rite again, I had prayed we'd see some change."

He sighed. "I know, Sister. Were you by her side all day? Until this moment?

"Yes. I had my food brought down and made sure someone was present when I had to use the bathroom. I wasn't out of the room more than three or four minutes, and that was in the early afternoon."

He managed a weak smile. "Thank you, Sister—you can leave now."

"Will you perform the exorcism ritual again tomorrow?"

The priest nodded. "Yes, of course."

"Bless you, Father. You, know, we will get her back."

He lowered his head, watching Celeste through half-open eyes. "I hope so.

BONUS STORY
THE REVEREND'S WIFE

A SHORT INTRODUCTION BY THE AUTHOR

Thank you for purchasing a print edition of **The Moore House**. In gratitude to those who have made this commitment, we have included a bonus story not available in the e-book version of the novel. John McIlveen (the publisher) and I discussed which bonus story we felt would be appropriate to follow **The Moore House** and concluded *The Reverend's Wife* would be the best fit. However, the decision was not as easy as it sounds.

The Reverend's Wife is a tale with graphic and extreme content that might not resonate with all the readers of **The Moore House**. The story contains sexual representations that are violent and unsettling, not to mention more than a few swears. If you are offended with this type of storyline, please consider this introduction as a warning. Proceed with caution or close the book now and keep your perception and opinion of **The Moore House** novel (good or bad) intact as they are. With that said, let me tell you about, The Reverend's Wife.

In, The Moore House, it's mentioned that the character named Rex was driven close to insanity after his involvement with a nightclub called *Painfreak*. Rex's exploits that fateful evening are vividly detailed in *The Reverend's Wife*.

In the late 1990's, Gerard Houarner authored a horror novella about a nightclub called Painfreak. As Gerard put it, the story didn't suck, and he built upon the framework of that original Painfreak tale to create a mythos that found its way into his *Max the Assassin* series of books. At the time, I reached out to Gerard on the old Horror World chat room site to let him know how much I loved his Max books, and a friendship was born.

Jump ahead to the summer of 2016. I received an email from Gerard asking me if I would like to contribute to an anthology he was putting together. Its central theme—his Painfreak mythos. I emailed him back asking if he had the wrong Tony Tremblay. The Painfreak mythos is one of extreme violence and explicit sexual encounters. I, on the other hand, wrote horror stories that were considered mainstream, i.e., more accessible to the reading public.

As I read Gerard's response, I could picture his smile. "No", he replied, "I did not make a mistake." He had read my debut collection of stories in The Seeds of Nightmares and thought I had the chops to take on a Painfreak tale. As for my writing an extreme horror story, he said as a writer, I should look at it as a challenge. He told me an author should always be looking to grow, to try something new, and to expand his readership. His words had an effect on me, and I agreed to write the story for him.

The Reverend's Wife came swiftly for me. For the protagonist, I used a secondary character named Rex who played a role in my story entitled *The Pawnshop*. Inspired by a combination of Rex Miller's character *Chaingang,* introduced in his novel **Slob,** and Gerard's Max character, Rex seemed like a natural choice to plunge into the debauchery required for the tale. It took me a month to write, the quickest I have ever written a story. I sent it to Gerard and waited for him to let me down gently.

His reply was short: "Tony, your fans are going to hate me."

I do have two fond memories of the story. The first is when I shared it with John McIlveen long before he took on, The Moore House. His reply was short and positive, and it ended with something like, "I hope the big galoot is yours and you own the character." The other memory that makes me grin is when I posted the cover on Facebook and Bracken MacLeod commented, "Holy Fuck!" Any doubts about my writing the story vanished when I saw Bracken's post.

The reviews that mentioned The Reverend's Wife have been positive, and, as of yet, I have not received any hate mail about the story. If you read it, I hope you enjoy it. If you don't, you can't say I didn't warn you.

Tony Tremblay
5/16/18

THE REVEREND'S WIFE

The Reverend Jones touched his index finger to his forehead. He then slipped it to his chest. After a quick tap, he moved it to the left but stopped midway. For the first time in his life, he was unable to complete the ritual. *Please God, forgive me.*

He stood before a door that was insanely large for a residence. It was made of steel—the metal tarnished and creased in places. Small, round dents pockmarked the surface. Locks, both keyed and numerical, lined the left side. In the center was a knocker—a simple cast iron ring—flaked with rust.

Jones beseeched God once more, lifted the knocker, and let it fall. Seconds later he heard the sound of a bolt sliding. The sound repeated twice more, followed by the *clicks* of locks disengaging. When the door opened, Jones gasped and took a step back. An abomination of a man stood before him.

The largest person he had ever seen took up the width of the doorway. He had to weigh at least 500 pounds. He stood over seven feet tall with scars crisscrossing his face. Bald, his pate reflected the sunlight. He had small black eyes, a flat nose, and his ears stuck out at 45-degree angles.

"You Jones?" The giant asked in a guttural voice that was as ugly as his features.

"Y—yes."

"Come."

When the giant man stepped aside, Jones crossed the threshold. As the Reverend walked into a living room the sounds of bolts sliding and locks engaging echoed in his ears. When the giant had finished securing the entrance, he followed Jones in.

"Sit," the giant grumbled. Jones did as he was told. The giant sat in a love seat opposite him. Jones marveled at the strength of the springs.

"Start talking," the giant commanded.

"It's—it's my wife. She's been missing for two days." Jones expected a reaction, but the giant stared at him without speaking. He swallowed and continued. "She was walking home Tuesday afternoon after getting her hair done when she disappeared. We live in a small apartment behind the Unitarian Church—it's only a fifteen-minute walk from the hairdresser's." He struggled to control his voice from cracking. "I went to the police early Tuesday evening when she didn't arrive. They said it was too soon to file a missing persons report so I came back early the next morning. I walked the route with Officer Linson, he's is a member of our church and our friend, to see if we could find anyone who might have seen her. Officer Linson spied a surveillance camera hanging from the Goffstown Pawn Shop, so we went in to see if we could view the footage from the day before. The owner of the shop obliged. When we played the recordings, all three of us saw what happened to my wife." Jones stifled a sob.

The giant nodded for Jones to continue.

"A small person, walking with a crooked gait—it could have been a dwarf—went up to my wife as she was walking home. They spoke for as long as ten minutes. At the end of the conversation, the dwarf pulled out an object. We couldn't tell what it was from the recording. My wife backed away but he grabbed her hand. He opened it and forced her palm down. He placed the object on top of her hand. My wife must have been in shock because her whole body shook for around five seconds. Then, he led her by the hand to the entrance of the brick building in front of them. She didn't resist. They walked in and then...nothing. We sped up the recording. She never walked out of the building." Jones leaned forward and mumbled a short prayer. When finished, he sat upright.

"The three of us left the pawnshop and rushed over to the brick building. There was no entrance, only a solid wall. We pressed against the bricks and searched for any sign of a hidden doorway, but there was none. All the bricks looked equally weathered, and we saw no fresh mortar. There was an entrance on the right side of the building, but it looked nothing like the one on the recording. We hurried back to the pawnshop to re-watch the recording. Clearly, the entrance was there, and it shows her going in. When we fast-forwarded it to our search of the building, we discovered that the camera had stopped functioning when we had left the pawnshop. There was only snow.

"Officer Linson took the video chip and told us he was headed back to the police station. The pawnshop owner and I went back to the wall to search for anything we might have missed. That's when I saw the card."

The giant raised his head.

"It was wedged in a gap between two bricks where the entrance should have been. Neither of us had seen it earlier. I plucked the card from the wall and it had only one word on it. I was puzzled, so I spoke the word out loud. *Painfreak.*"

If the giant recognized the word, he didn't express it.

"The pawnshop owner asked me to repeat it. When I looked at him, his face was drawn. "Your wife is in dire straits," he told me, "and you have little time to get her back."

I questioned him, begged him to tell me more, but he refused. Instead, he advised I come see you. He told me your name is Rex and I should bring money." Tears streamed down Jones' eyes. "Can you tell me what's going on, Rex? Can you help me? I'm...."

⊕

Rex lifted one of his immense hands, raised an index finger and placed it against his lips. If he didn't hush the Reverend, he knew the man would keep jabbering on. He needed a few moments to think.

Painfreak. He'd heard rumors of a nightclub called Painfreak, but he had always dismissed them. The talk was that its patrons were nightmarish—perversions of humanity—and that it was a sadist's paradise. People said it was vast and was located in a time and space different from ours. The entrance to the club was ever changing. Nobody knew when or where it would appear. Part of the mythos was that not everyone who entered Painfreak left Painfreak.

The Reverend's story intrigued Rex. On its surface, it was a far cry from the mundane hit jobs he was usually assigned. As a freelancer, his specialty was government commissions—taking out the scum that the local police or Feds didn't want to bring to trial. He reported to no one, the work paid well, and it provided an opportunity to release his baser instincts without the prospect of incarceration. He loved his work and he was known—and feared—for his unique methods of inflicting pain. Working with the government meant periods of feast or famine. When times were slow, Rex would take on outside jobs. These non-government contracts did not hinder his enthusiasm when it came to inflicting pain.

Despite his appearance and line of work, Rex had his principles, and he strictly adhered to them. He abhorred the mistreatment of women, children, and animals, and he harbored compassion for those he deemed innocent or wronged. The Jones woman met at least two of these criteria.

Rex made up his mind. He would talk with the pawnshop owner.

He was obliged to thank the man for the reference, but more importantly, he would need more information about Painfreak.

"Two thousand dollars up front, and no guarantees," he croaked. "If I bring her back within a week it will cost you another eight grand. If I can't find her within that time...tough shit."

The Reverend reached into his back pocket and removed a billfold. The man opened it up and carefully counted out hundred dollar bills. There was plenty more in the billfold after the Reverend removed twenty of them and handed them over. *I should have asked for more. That's a lot of money for a man of the cloth to possess. Will the heating fund be a little lighter this year, Reverend?*

His hands shaking, the Reverend also removed two photographs and placed them beneath the bills. "These are pictures of my wife, Betty. They're fairly recent. My phone number is on the back of one of them."

Rex reached out, took the money and photos. He glanced at the pictures. Betty was mousey—squat, overweight, with her hair brown and cut short to the shoulder. Her heavy breasts sagged to the bottom of her rib cage. Her face was neither attractive nor ugly, with no distinguishing features. Rex placed the photos and money on a small table next to the love seat. After a brief silence, both men stood. Rex pointed to the front door and the Reverend, with his head lowered, walked toward it. *Feeling guilty about the money?* After he unlocked the door and threw the slide-bolts, he opened it and the Reverend passed through. "I'll be in touch," he grunted.

The Reverend didn't look back.

Sixteen hours had passed since the Reverend had paid him a visit. It was dark enough for Rex to travel. In daylight, it was impossible for him to avoid the stares and horrified reactions of people. He climbed into his Hummer and drove to the pawnshop. The owner must have expected him—he could see bright light streaming from the gap between the front double doors.

Much like Rex, the pawnshop owner was an enigma to the townspeople. The owner was seldom seen in the shops or restaurants, and he never advertised. If someone wandered into the shop in pursuit of second-hand goods, they always left disappointed. The only wares on the shelves were esoteric artworks, foreign language books, and mechanical contraptions that defied simple description. If any would-be customer lingered too long, the owner simply mentioned how costly the items were and that was usually enough to goad most of them to leave. If that didn't work, he had other ways. The word in the street was that the owner was an occult practitioner and Rex knew this to be true. The pawnshop owner had approached him over the years for assistance, and Rex saw firsthand the methods he had used.

Rex parked his Hummer a block away and walked back to the pawnshop. The doors were unlocked, he opened them as wide as they would go. With a little effort, he pushed his girth through. Inside, he ignored the shelves of goods and proceeded to a long counter in front of the left wall. The pawnshop owner stood there with a frown, his arms crossed over his chest.

"Good evening, Rex."

"Evening. Thank you for the reference." His voice sounded like a car driving over gravel.

"You're here, so I assume you took the job. This is going to be a bad one, Rex. No one who goes into Painfreak comes out quite the same—if they come out at all."

Rex cleared his throat and growled, "Can you get me in?"

"I think so. Stand on the sidewalk in front of the brick building across the street."

"Now?"

"You don't have much time—it might already be too late. If I can bring the entrance back, I'm not sure I can hold it here too much longer after you go inside. You get in, Rex, and then you get out as soon as you can."

"What happens if I don't?"

"You might still be able to leave. I just don't know where you'll wind up."

Rex knew this job could be the biggest mistake of his life. But the lure of Painfreak, with its rumors of sexual abandon and unfettered carnage, was too deep to ignore. He had to see this place. "Let's do this."

Every passing car slowed. The occupant's eyes widened and their heart rates accelerated when they caught a glimpse of what stood on the sidewalk across the street from the pawnshop. Their headlights revealed a giant — as big as or bigger than any pro-wrestler or comic book movie character they had ever seen—standing still, his gaze set on the bricks before him. If he turned his head and the angle was right, they could see his face. Engines were gunned, some cars leaving rubber in their wake.

Except for an occasional sweep of his head left or right, Rex stared at the brick wall for maybe an hour. Fatigued, he closed his eyes for a moment. When he reopened them, the entrance to Painfreak filled his vision. He breathed deeply, and before he could step toward it, he felt a pull on his pant leg. He looked down and saw a little man bent at the waist. The Reverend's assumption was correct. It was a dwarf.

"Hey there, big fella," the dwarf squeaked, "you want to go someplace where your wildest sexual fantasies come true?"

Rex raised an eyebrow and stared at the little man.

The dwarf continued in his helium-high voice. "Big guy like you, hell, you would fit right in! We got girls. We got small girls with big tits and big girls with small tits. We got boys, too, if you want. You like boys? We got big boys with small dicks and small boys with big dicks. We got other things, too. Things you never dreamed of… and maybe some you have."

While Rex's mind went to images of things he had dreamed of, the dwarf removed a metallic object from his pant pocket.

"Ahh," squealed the dwarf as he spotted the massive erection forming in Rex's pants. He held up the object. "Your admission. You'll have to bend over a bit and give me your right hand, big fella."

Rex obeyed, and the dwarf pressed the object to the top of Rex's wrist. Electricity flowed through his arm. It dissipated before it reached his elbow. The dwarf pocketed the metal object. "Big guy like you, you hardly felt that, I bet. Let's go," he announced in a voice that brought to Rex's mind fingernails on a chalkboard.

Together, they passed through the doorway, where they were met by a tall thin Asian man. "Your right hand," the Asian demanded. Rex held it out, palm down. The Asian waved a wand over the back of his hand. Rex cocked his head when a symbol resembling a bone came into view. The Asian nodded and then gestured with a sweep of his arm toward a hallway leading into the club.

Rex looked down to his side to see if the dwarf would follow, but he was gone. He eyed the hallway, pitch black and as quiet as a mausoleum. He stepped forward.

"Welcome to Painfreak."

Rex jumped, then crouched at the sound. The dwarf's voice had come from somewhere above him.

☩

After no more than three steps down the hallway, Rex's senses were assaulted. Dance music enveloped him—the vibration digging its way through his pores. He cringed—the pain from the booming audio traveled through his ears and pierced his brain. The downbeat was worse—it pricked at his eyes like needles while the bass jackhammered the top of his skull. Why hadn't he heard it when he was wrist-checked by the Asian?

This is Painfreak? A dance club?

Rex compartmentalized the pain. He concentrated on his surroundings. Hundreds of people were dancing under strobe lights, their bodies vanishing and then reappearing in time with the rhythm. The flashes disoriented him and he fought to maintain focus.

A majority of the dancers were nude or semi-nude. Breasts and penises bounced, the flaccid ones lagging behind the beat. Of those clothed, some were wearing costumes and masks.

The smell of fish and bleach permeated the air.

Rex advanced toward the center of the dance floor and bulldozed anyone in his path to the side. No one seemed to care. Those who fell reached out to him. Their hands snaked up his legs. When they reached for his cock, he ignored them or brushed them aside with his tree-trunk arms. Some of the fallen ones would not be deterred—they clung to his legs. He dragged them along. He stepped on some, others fell off. If they cried out, he didn't hear their wails.

Rex pushed on. His gaze swept over the costumes of the dancers. Both sexes wore bras adorned with metallic accouterments. Woven into the fabric were spikes, fragments of saw blades, and razor wire. The objects glistened with moisture when the strobe lights reflected off them. He had no way of knowing what lay beneath their masks, but a grin formed when he imagined that they might be more hideous than he was. He reached out to pull the mask off the closest dancer but stopped short when there was a tap in the middle of his back. With his arm suspended in air, he turned. When he saw who it was, he took an involuntary step away.

It was Brian Stone. Only, Brian Stone was dead. Rex knew this because he had killed him.

Two years ago Stone bludgeoned his wife with a hammer and then had stuck the handle up her ass. She bled to death. Stone claimed he found her that night when he came home from playing poker with some pals. He told the cops she was cheating on him, and that's who they should be looking for. Everyone knew he did it, but the cops couldn't crack his alibi or get enough evidence. They wanted Stone to disappear. When the detectives showed Rex the pictures of Stone's wife lying on the floor, dead, with the handle sticking out of her, Rex was only too happy to accept the job. He beat Stone to a pulp— repeatedly slamming his fists into the man's face until a portion of the prick's skull broke off. His brains still stained the sidewalk.

Now, Stone showed no sign of the beating.

Rex's chest tightened. Not in fear of the dead man—for Rex feared no one—but because the images of what Stone had done to his wife rushed at him like a chained dog.

Stone must have noted the recognition in Rex's eyes. The dead man smiled and then motioned with a shake of his head for Rex to follow. Rex weighed the invitation. Without waiting, Stone turned and walked off the dance floor. Unlike his own entrance into the club, the crowd parted for Stone. Rex decided to follow. They passed a long bar against a far wall, two people deep with customers ordering drinks. Stone turned at the bar's end and opened an oversized door. Rex entered, and when Stone closed the door behind them, the music cut out.

They were in a small, well-lit room, facing each other with only a few feet separating them. Another oversized door loomed at the opposite end.

Rex grunted, "You're dead."

"Yes, I'm dead. Only, in Painfreak, I'm not dead."

Rex cocked his head to the side. *How can someone be dead but not dead?*

Stone continued. "We know why you are here. She's in a room through that door." Stone lifted a hand and pointed. "Before you open the door, Rex, I'm here to tell you that Painfreak thinks you are making a mistake. She belongs here. And so do you."

Stone's words only fueled Rex's hatred for the man. Nobody tells him what he should or shouldn't do, especially a woman-beating shit-heel like Stone. *What kind of place brings people like Stone back from the dead?* Rex balled his hands into fists. One of the pictures the detectives had shown him flashed in his head. He saw the hammer Stone had used to kill his wife. Clumps of flesh, painted red and brown, clung to the handle.

Rex howled at the image and lifted his arms high. Stone's eyes went wide and he leaned back.

The giant brought his arms down.

Tufts of hair and bone fragments exploded from Stone's head. Rex continued to pummel the once dead man until his neck vertebrae wedged deep in his upper torso. Stone teetered for a moment and then toppled over sideways.

"Fucking stay dead," Rex mumbled.

He turned from Stone's body, walked to the door on the other side of the room, opened it and stepped through.

In the center of the small room hung a naked woman. She was bound with rope and suspended upright. Her stretched arms and legs formed an X. Four men surrounded her. They were thin, bald, with skin as pale as a cancer patient. One was positioned behind her, another faced her so close their noses touched. A third man rubbed against the woman's left thigh. The fourth man stood next to the woman's right thigh with a knife. The man drew the blade across the meatiest portion of the woman's skin. With his fingers, he parted her flesh until the blood flowed freely. Then the man plunged his penis into the wound. Rex squinted and shook his head as he stared at the man.

He swung his gaze to each of the pale men. They all pumped into the woman, their asses in constant, rapid motion. The woman's body had too many cuts for Rex to count, all of them dripping with blood and semen.

Rex lifted his head to see their victim's face. Her eyes were tight, and her mouth was open. Her tongue hung limply over her bottom lip. It was the Reverend's wife. He strained to hear if she was aware of what was happening to her. He heard it—a single, continuous, anguished note coming somewhere from deep inside her.

He walked toward the men fucking her.

Rex couldn't remember a time when he had wept—even as a child he had kept his emotions in check. He took a deep breath, hung his head and closed his eyes. His shoulders sagged as he exhaled. His eyes moistened. Scenes of his mother's torture by her boyfriend seeped into his head. Rex saw himself as a child, forced to witness the depravity. He tensed at the recollection. His hands opened and closed into fists.

Now was not the time to revisit those memories. He blocked out the images, and his mind raced to the present. When he opened his eyes, they burned with fire.

Hands the size of melons gripped the biceps of the pale man closest to him. Rex squeezed. The man's bones crushed under his grip. With little effort, he tore the man's arms out of their sockets.

The man continued to pump into the woman.

Rex blinked and took a step back. *What the fuck?* Rex dropped the man's limbs, reached out, and wrapped his fingers around the man's neck. He pulled. The head separated from the body with a slurp. Blood sprayed, adding another layer of gore to Rex's face and chest. The pale man's body continued thrusting into her.

It wasn't enough. Rex fumed. *Why the fuck won't he die?*

Rex pulled the man out of the woman and onto to the floor. His size twenty-two shoes stomped on the body until it was a bloody sludge. Piles of viscera mixed with bones littered the floor. They did not move. Rex turned to the other three men. They had paid no attention to the death of one of their own. If anything, their assault on the woman grew more fevered. Rex tore into them. One by one, he repeated the stomping tactic on the remaining three. When finished, his pant legs were soaked red to the knees.

Rex surveyed the carnage. What could have passed for a smile stretched across his face.

The woman groaned. It brought Rex back to the reason he was here. Had he had time, he would have bathed in the men's blood and devoured their organs, but he had a job to do and he wasn't sure how much longer he could remain in Painfreak before he was trapped. He searched the floor for the knife the men had used to cut her, but he couldn't see it. Using the toe of his right shoe, he moved the piles of sludge aside for a better view. The knife revealed itself under a mashed organ. As he bent to pick it up, he heard a sound above him. He lifted his head and frowned. There was no ceiling. In its place, a dark void. As he stared, he saw something move within it. Seconds later, an object, attached to a thin white rope, slipped down through the ink. When it touched the floor several feet away, Rex stood upright, the knife clenched in his hand.

It was a woman—naked, tall, hairless, and as pale as the four men he had killed. The thin white rope hung slack as it stretched down from the void and disappeared behind her back. A web of sorts, he mused, no doubt spun from her ass. She stood still for a moment, then stepped forward, closing the distance between them.

"Rex," she spoke, her voice low and thick. "You do not want to take her away."

He took a step back and bumped up against the woman tied in ropes. She groaned, but then went silent.

Rex eyed the pale woman—not so much in fear but out of curiosity. "Why not?"

The woman had come to within inches of Rex. She stopped, raised her arms, and then wrapped them around Rex's head. "Because, Rex…," Her lips didn't move, but he could hear her voice, "…you may leave Painfreak, but Painfreak never leaves you." She raised her head and then pressed her mouth against his. Her lips parted and her tongue probed.

Rex stiffened. His body vibrated as if four hundred and sixty volts of electricity poured through him. Pictures played in his head. They were scenes of exquisite debauchery, and he had the lead role in all of them. Rex could taste blood, and he could smell his victim's shit. He saw himself surrounded by women, all of them offering themselves to him, their sex dripping with anticipation. Above it all, a whisper called to him. It was the pale woman's. Her voice breathy as she implored, "Stay with us."

Stay with us.

Us?

Rex bit down on the woman's tongue. In his head, he heard her shriek and the images of the debauchery vanished. She lowered her hands and pushed off him. Blood bubbled from between her lips. Rex shook off the remnants of her physic hold and spit what was hers back at her. The thin white rope pulled tautly and she was lifted into the darkness. As he watched her rise, he raised his fists to her and growled, "Us? There is no *Us*! Nobody owns me!"

He turned to the trussed woman. Starting with her leg restraints, he cut them and worked up to the ties that bound her arms. He slung her over his shoulder.

"No," she pleaded.

"Shut up," he answered, "I've got you now. I'm taking you home to your husband."

Rex retraced his steps. He waded through the piles of mashed organs on the floor and opened the door. Walking through the room, he glanced at the mess that was Stone. *Still dead.* He exited that room and was back at the bar on the dance floor. The music drove spikes of pain into his head and the strobe lights played havoc with his perspective. He searched for the way he had come in. Taking a few moments to adjust to the lights, he thought he had found it. As before, the crowd clamored for him. They reached out, grabbed at his legs and ran their hands over his body. A few attempted to remove the woman from his shoulder. He answered with a punch that snapped their limbs or stove their skulls. He barreled his way through the dance floor, kicking, pushing, and stepping on anyone in his path. When he made it to the end of the room he saw the dark hallway. He stopped before entering and turned to take one last look at Painfreak. Though the music droned on and the strobe lights flashed, no one in the crowd danced. They were still, and they all faced him. When the strobe lights flashed on, he saw their faces. They grinned. His headed clouded. They were pulling at him. Once more it was the woman on his shoulders who brought him back around.

"Leave me alone," she begged. She was disoriented, her voice weak. Rex ignored her, blinked at the mob, and then he spun around. He walked into the hallway.

The music stopped and the lightning bolt echoes from the strobes disappeared. There were no signs of the Asian man or the dwarf. Rex walked to the door at the end of the hallway, opened it and stepped outside.

It was dark, but the surroundings were familiar. He stood in front of the brick building and could see the pawnshop across the street. Its lights were off. He carried the woman to his Hummer and drove home.

Rex entered the house and carried the woman up to the second floor. He placed her on his bed. She was conscious. Her eyes fixed on his. Neither said a word. His gaze wandered over her body. Her wounds trickled red and white onto his blankets—except between her legs. There, a puddle formed beneath her. A snapshot of the men fucking her flashed before him. He saw her bound, the knife cutting her thigh, their frantic pumping.

Rex envied their single-minded purpose.

"Why did you take me from there?"

He lifted his gaze in response to Betty's question. His hoarse reply came quick. "Your husband. He paid me to bring you back."

Betty arched her back and spread her legs wide. "I don't want to come back."

Rex focused on the gap between her legs. Betty was small, too small. He would rip her apart.

After a moment, he murmured, "There's something I have to do."

Rex pulled Betty's picture out from his pocket. He walked to the phone and dialed the number on the back. After three rings someone answered. Rex spoke.

"Reverend, I've got Betty. Come over in an hour, not before. The front door is unlocked, let yourself in." Rex hung up the phone. He disrobed and approached the bed.

"We are going to have company soon."

Betty grinned. "I can't wait."

TELL THE WORLD THIS BOOK WAS		
GOOD	BAD	SO-SO

Tony Tremblay is the author of *The Seeds of Nightmares*, a collection of his short stories from Crossroad Press that made the Bram Stoker Awards Recommended Reading List. *The Seeds of Nightmares* debuted at number two on the Amazon Hot Horror Chart and made the top twenty in the Amazon Horror sales listing. His horror and noir themed tales have been featured in anthologies, magazines, and websites on both sides of the Atlantic.

Tony is the host of *The Taco Society Presents*, a television show that features New England based horror and genre authors. In addition, he has worked as a reviewer of horror fiction for *Cemetery Dance Magazine*, *Beware The Dark Magazine*, and the *Horror World* Website.

He (along with John McIlveen and Scott Goudsward) founded *NoCon,* a horror convention held every September in Manchester, New Hampshire.

You can visit Tony at www.TonyTremblayAuthor.com and on Facebook under Tony Tremblay.

CPSIA information can be obtained
at www.ICGtesting.com
Printed in the USA
FSHW022214191118
53899FS